Lost in Plain Sight is Stevie's first book. He has had the idea for a good few years but decided to put this on hold to concentrate on raising a family with his wife, Angela.

Unfortunately, their youngest son, Craig, was diagnosed with Duchenne muscular dystrophy and looking after him consumed most of their time. He has now managed, with Craig's encouragement, to find the time to finally get it into print. Hopefully, the reader will find it a gripping tale with an enjoyable storyline that will leave them hungry for more.

I dedicate this book to my two wonderful sons, Scott and Craig Strang. Craig sadly passed away at the tender young age of 28, on 3rd January 2019, without having the opportunity of seeing through to fruition the book he encouraged me to write; especially in the days I doubted myself.

His disability, DMD, did not stop him from leading a very full and productive life. He achieved a degree from Stirling University as well as various other honours from NL College. His inspiration was second to none.

Stevie Strang

LOST IN PLAIN SIGHT

AUSTIN MACAULEY PUBLISHERS™

LONDON · CAMBRIDGE · NEW YORK · SHARJAH

A CIP catalogue record for this title is available from the British Library.

ISBN 9781528938860 (Paperback)
ISBN 9781528938877 (Hardback)
ISBN 9781528969734 (ePub e-book)

www.austinmacauley.com

First Published (2020)
Austin Macauley Publishers Ltd
25 Canada Square
Canary Wharf
London
E14 5LQ

My wife, Angela, and especially my oldest son, Scott, who reminded me of his and Craig's childhood times when I had the ability to pull captivating stories from thin air. Without their support, I'm sure this book would not have been written.

Chapter 1

They arrived at an unassuming two-storey building in Hackney, East London, where the old powerhouse nightspot used to stand. The entry was barred by four, very big doormen, who were all very smartly dressed in suits with ties. They amounted to a seriously big unit between them, no one, uninvited, stood a chance of getting past them. They seemed to know the smaller of the two and let them enter.

Once inside, the sight that awaited them sent a small shiver down the spine of the bigger man. He'd never experienced anything like it before, the noise was deafening. He could just about see a boxing ring through the crowd and it was the ring he was soon to be climbing into and it was starting to hit home now, just how real this had become for him.

A very anxious Doug Clement was soon to fight a maniac of a man, Tam Cranston, he'd never laid eyes on him before, but his reputation was fierce. This was no ordinary boxing match, it was an on the cobbles, illegal underground and unlicensed fight and it had been arranged by moneylender and unscrupulous businessman Big Jim Cassidy. Cranston was a crowd pleaser, and he was expected to make short work of his opponent, but Doug had other ideas.

How in the name of Christ did I end up here? he asked himself. The answer to that question was standing right next to him, his new best friend, Johnny Wilson, a work colleague from his recently acquired job as a building site security guard. Johnny was in debt to Cassidy for a small fortune and Doug had foolishly allowed his new pal to rope him into this fight. All because he'd somehow managed to knock out Cassidy's two main intimidators who were beating up Johnny for not paying an instalment on a loan. Far from being unhappy when he discovered his two goons had been hospitalised by Doug, Cassidy propositioned him to take the place of a fighter that'd been injured and couldn't face Cranston. He'd agreed to take him on primarily to help Johnny pay off some of his debt, and to earn himself some cash into the bargain.

The place was packed, and the crowd was thirsty for blood, it was almost feral. There was a fight already in progress, it looked brutal as there also appeared to be bloodstains on the ring floor. The place stank of stale sweat and urine. Doug also sensed, by their reactions, that the hostile crowd had already picked the winner of the fight that they were watching, and it didn't take Sherlock Holmes to work out that most of them had their money on the smaller of the two fighters. He was a dumpy guy, and he was getting all their cheers every time he landed a blow and he appeared to be winning. Doug's fight was the next one.

Three months earlier

It was on the 28th of June 2012, in Walthamstow, East London England, around the corner from the old closed down bus garage. Doug Clement, was as happy as he'd ever been in his life, 31 years old, married for just over five years to Julie, their first baby on the way due in six weeks' time. He had a great job he loved as an electrician. He and Julie had just moved into a fantastic new house, and all his dreams had come true, or so he thought…

***

Doug was driving home from the gym where he had just finished his Thursday night work out; he did this two night a week, Monday and Thursday. Doug was a keen and very competent amateur boxer; he was a super heavyweight at just over 6'2" and seventeen stones. He'd had 15 fights and won them all, twelve by knock-outs, and the other three going the distance, him winning easily on points. Doug knew he was too old to turn pro, but he enjoyed the fitness aspect of it and the respect he had around his gym.

He was listening to the car radio, *Skyfall* by a young British singer was playing, he couldn't remember her name. Julie would know the singer's name straightaway, she was more up to date than he was with current music. He liked seventies and eighties stuff, the song was the theme song to the new James Bond film of the same name starring Daniel Craig, his new favourite Bond. He liked all the actors that played Bond, but his particular favourites were both Sean Connery, and Roger Moore, but he thought Daniel Craig brought a rougher and more ready aspect to James Bond 007. He liked the way he looked after being involved in the usual scrapes and this made Doug think he was probably more believable.

Doug went to Raynes Park School in Merton, London and the only classes he liked were PE, art and woodwork. He was no academic by any stretch of the imagination, but he somehow managed to leave school with three O levels in, English, maths and Woodwork all by the skin of his teeth. His dad, Robert, had tried to convince him to stay on for another year or go to college but Doug was having none of it. He got a lucky break and started working straight from high School. He got a rare apprenticeship as an Electrician. His dad's best mate, John, had told Robert his dad's firm was looking to hire a young boy to train as an electrician. John's dad owned a small Electrical Contracting Company, Robert asked Doug if he would be interested in becoming an electrician.

"Yes, I would be interested," he had said with much enthusiasm.

"OK, let me speak to John and see if he can arrange an interview with his dad."

John had his own business as an accountant and looked after the books for a good few businesses, including his dads' company. After speaking with Robert, John called his dad and arranged for Doug to go in the next morning at nine o'clock. Doug had always liked tinkering about with things, trying to fix his mums broken hair dryers, curlers and the like. He went along for the interview with Richard Smith the owner of Smith Contractors. *Richard was around sixtyish,* Doug thought, they were based in Wimbledon, not too far from his house.

Richard liked what he saw in young Doug and offered him the job, he would be working with his dad's pal's brother, Ricky, Richard's oldest son. He was the electrician, there were four other employees, Pete and Chas, they were joiners, Gaz and Jamie, were the painters and decorators. Doug seemed to get on well with them all, they mostly worked on the same job, at the same time, usually a renovation of a house or small office. Doug liked the variety of his work. Sometimes, just he and Ricky worked together, rewiring folks' houses, or extensions, but mostly, it was full renovations.

As time passed, Doug became more proficient, he attended college one day a week and five years later, Doug was fully a qualified electrician. Two years after that, Ricky gave up his tools to take the helm of the family business after his dad, Richard, had sadly passed away from cancer.

There was talk of Doug getting a young apprentice of his own to train up, but as work was slow at the moment, Ricky thought it best to wait until business picked up a bit before putting strain on their resources. There was just about enough work to keep them all employed and not much more. It was the same for most other smaller outfits. Some of the larger companies were having to make people redundant, they knew this by the amount of phone calls and CVs they received on a regular basis from tradesmen looking for a new job after being laid off.

Doug and Julie had known each other for just over eight years, they met at a mutual friend's wedding and it was love at first sight for them both. After them going out for three years, they got engaged. They had spoken about having a baby and had been trying ever since. Julie got pregnant, but sadly, very early into the pregnancy, she had a miscarriage. After they got over the pain of the miscarriage, they had decided to get married and went to the Dominican Republic for their honeymoon.

When they returned, they had decided they would keep trying for a baby. Almost four years later, they hadn't been successful. Julie and Doug visited many specialists, but they couldn't discover any reasons why they could not become parents, and they spoke about adopting a baby if Julie could not conceive. They had decided that they should keep trying. They were both young enough, so there was no desperate hurry.

One day, out of the blue, about seven months ago, Julie announced she was pregnant. Doug scooped her up and hugged her for ages. They told their parents and his brother, Andrew. Doug had decided he was going to take up boxing just to keep fit, he wasn't unfit, but he didn't want to be out of breath chasing a little one around. He soon discovered he was good at it.

About six weeks after joining the gym, Rob, the manager, spoke to him about having some amateur fights. Doug wasn't sure at first, but he spoke with Julie, and they agreed he should give it a go as long as he was not going to get hurt. Doug assured her he would be wearing head protection, and there would be a referee in the ring to make sure he didn't get hurt.

Doug laughed, as he said, "Look at the size of me, who's going to hurt me?"

Julie laughed too, but said, "There's always someone bigger than you, watch out so you don't get too cocky or you'll end up on your backside."

Doug trained as hard as he could and had countless rounds of sparring with a few other guys from the club. He was getting more and more comfortable with the idea of having some amateur fights.

The night of his first fight arrived, he was very nervous, but he won in two rounds by Technical Knock Out. The referee had stopped the fight early on as

11

Doug had proved far too strong for his opponent. That also gave Doug the relief that, if he ever got into trouble during a fight, the referee would step in and stop the fight before he got hurt. Doug loved the thrill and excitement of that first fight, he was on a high for a few days afterwards. He'd had a couple more winning fights before he had the confidence to ask Julie to come and watch one of his fights. She agreed, but she was taken aback at the sheer intensity of it all. Her husband was like a different man when he was in the boxing ring. This scared her a little, she could barely believe the difference in him, how ferocious he was. But when the fight was over, he was back to being big, old, softy Doug.

The only blemish on his horizon for Doug was the appalling rain outside lashing against the car. He was mostly a careful driver, but he was even more cautious tonight and slowed to what he thought was a sensible speed for the road conditions. Unfortunately, what he could not do was to legislate for the recklessness of another driver who came speeding out of Farnan Avenue and straight onto Chingford Road, he smashed right into him full side on. The impact forced Doug's car straight into the path of an oncoming number 97 bus. Doug was seriously injured, a passenger on the bus called 999 and an ambulance was dispatched to the scene. The other driver and his mate had managed to scramble out of the now wrecked stolen car, and had disappeared from the crash site by the time the emergency services arrived.

The police arrived first, they called for the fire brigade as they could see the driver was trapped in his vehicle, the ambulance arrived next. Through the crushed metal, they tried, to no avail, to communicate with the driver. They could see he was trapped in the smashed car. The firemen arrived within ten more minutes, they had to cut the roof off the car and free Doug from his mangled car. It took them forty-five minutes of delicate precision cutting and grinding. They finally managed to lift the unconscious Doug out and laid him on a stretcher. They put on a neck brace and strapped him in, he was rushed to the hospital.

The police followed the ambulance to the hospital in the hope of speaking to Doug. When he arrived, one of the nurses found his mobile phone in one of his pockets and gave it to a police officer. She retrieved Julie's number easily as Doug had saved her as 'Wife Julie'.

Officer Angela Kennedy called Julie and informed her that her husband had been in a car accident. Julie gave the police officer her address and the officer then arranged to have Julie collected, and brought straight to the Queen Elizabeth Hospital. She arrived at the hospital around half an hour later. Whilst she was waiting to hear about her husband, she called Doug's dad, Robert and told him exactly what the police officer had told her. She also told his dad which hospital they were in.

Robert asked Julie if there was any news on how Doug was. She told Robert that when she arrived, Doug was in the A&E, a team of doctors and nurses were working on him. After about twenty-five minutes, Robert and Doug's mum, Mary, had still not arrived. Julie was starting to panic, she called Robert again to ask him how much longer they would be. They were on route, he told her, and they would be there in another ten minutes.

Robert had called Andrew, Doug's younger brother, he said he would get there within the hour.

"Have the doctors told you anything yet?" asked Robert when he and Mary arrived at the hospital.

"One of the medical team came out about five minutes ago and said Doug had arrived unconscious, they were assessing his injuries; they suspect he has broken at least one of his legs and probably has a fractured skull," cried Julie.

Mary was comforting her as they were sitting waiting in the waiting area. Andrew arrived, he'd managed to arrive quicker than thought he would. He asked his dad if there was any news on his brother's condition.

"No, not yet," answered Robert. Julie phoned her mum, Dot, who was at work and would get to the hospital as soon as possible. Dot arrived an hour or so later. Robert and Andrew were taking it in turns to get the tea and coffee, it could be a long wait, Julie was heavily pregnant, and this was a trying time for her.

Mary and Dot were doing their best to keep Julie calm. About two and a half hours had passed when a doctor came into the waiting area and informed them that Doug had suffered a severe head impact and was in a coma, but surprisingly, he hadn't broken any bones, but he did have a badly bruised and swollen toe on his left foot. He also had some minor cuts and bruises, his face was also very swollen.

"He's had a few stitches put in an ankle cut, other than that we will have to wait and see," the doctor told them.

"Has my husband suffered any brain damage?" Julie blurted out.

"Unfortunately, we won't know if he's suffered any traumatic brain injury until after he comes out of the coma, but he has had a very serious impact to his head," said the doctor.

"I'm sure our son will be fine, he's got some serious fighting spirit," said Robert.

For the next month and a half, they all took turns to be at Doug's bedside, he was still unconscious.

"Will he ever come out of this coma?" Mary asked one of his doctors.

"Well, Mrs Clement, this type of head trauma is very difficult to predict. There have been cases of patients being in comas for years but these are very rare. Normally, we would expect a patient to come out of their coma within one to three months, we have your son linked up to every kind of brain monitor known to man. There is certainly brain activity but unfortunately, that only tells us there is a good chance he will recover consciousness sooner or later, but it's not an exact science, every patient is different."

Julie was having her doubts, she felt totally helpless seeing Doug lying in the same position day after day. She often wondered if her husband would ever recover, but she kept her fears to herself not wanting to let the others know her feelings of doubt, they were like a tag team.

It was now seven weeks since the accident. Julie had gone into labour three weeks after Doug's accident and had given birth to their daughter, Grace. It was a difficult birth, she was in labour for over eight hours. Dot and Mary were with her throughout the whole time, and kept her spirits up with words of encouragement. She had planned to have Doug at her side, they had been rehearsing this for weeks. Doug had every detail planned out, but alas, it was not to be. She was grateful for her two mums to be with her, but it was not the same as having your husband with you when you are giving birth to your first child.

Doug will be so disappointed he missed this, thought Julie, having Grace now focused her attention. Julie was now tending to Grace's needs, and she was not a good sleeper, therefore Julie didn't have as much time to dwell on Doug's predicament. They had picked the names together, Grace, if they had a girl or Adam if they were blessed with a son. A week and a half later and Julie was now back in the rota at Doug's bedside. During the day, she would bring Grace with her to see her dad.

Julie was constantly speaking to Doug, as were the others. The doctors had said it could help bring Doug out of the coma, they informed the family that Doug's toe was mended as were all his minor cuts and bruises, but they were not sure when he would come out the coma. Julie talked to Doug about their beautiful daughter hoping to see a flicker of life in him.

Chapter 2

Julie worked as a receptionist in the Jubilee Health centre. She'd worked there for seven years after graduating from college. She was a team leader in a team of six. They all got on OK, but there was always one of them bitching over pay. They all went through phases of feeling overworked, underpaid and undervalued. This was typical all throughout the National Health Service, but for the most part, they just got on with it. They all worked in the same big area. There were always four staff on during opening hours, and they rotated shifts.

Julie and Doug had been trying for a baby for ages without any success, and before she fell pregnant, she felt the world was against her. Every so often, she would be booking appointments for young girls with unwanted pregnancies, and here she was, desperate to have a baby. Sometimes, life was cruel, but she couldn't really complain too much though, she had a nice life, and a good job she loved, a husband she loved more than life itself.

Now that she was pregnant, she had everything she had ever dreamed of, she was so happy. The expectant mothers and fathers they met were an eclectic mix, and they all had a story to tell, so work life was anything but boring. Some young girls came in with their mothers as they had no husbands or boyfriends. They had fallen pregnant after one-night stands or their boyfriends had left after finding out about the pregnancy. The result of this was the new-born babies would be put up for adoption, this saddened Julie, as there were so many couples in the same pre-dicament as her and Doug.

Doug's dad, Robert, was 60 years old. He was retired now, he had worked as a tanker driver for a chemical company for over thirty years, but he'd had a very bad accident almost four years ago. He was on top of his tanker putting in one of the hoses to transfer the chemicals he was off loading. It transpired that one of the seals on a valve had perished and there was spillage on the walkway. As it was a clear liquid, Robert hadn't noticed it, he slipped and fell off the top of the tanker, break-ing his hip and snapping his kneecap. He was in the hospital for six weeks, he got a high six-figure insurance payment, and the company gave him early retirement, as well as paying for all his private medical treatment. He now had a permanent limp. Mary, Doug's mum, was a couple of years older than Robert and had retired two years ago. She had worked as an administrator for a glazing company. They were both looking forward to being grandparents, and couldn't wait for Julie to give birth to their first grandchild. Doug's brother, Andrew, was two years younger than him, and he had told the family that he was gay when he was around sixteen years old. They had accepted him for who he was.

About two months after his accident, Doug awoke from his coma. Julie was there when he opened his eyes, he was staring at her; she called out for the doctor and was asked to sit outside, in the waiting room, while the doctors assessed Doug. She called Robert.

"This is fantastic," he said, he shouted to Mary, who was in the kitchen, telling her that Doug was awake. "We'll be there in forty minutes."

"OK see you soon," she said and rang off. She could hardly contain her excitement.

Robert called Andrew, and they were all at the hospital around an hour later. Julie was still sitting in the ward waiting area.

"Have they told you anything yet?" Mary asked her.

"No, nothing yet, they just asked me to wait here."

Another forty minutes passed before a young, Indian doctor, Raj, came out to see them. He said that although Doug was out of the coma and awake, he had no memory of his accident. "He couldn't even tell us his name."

"Oh my goodness," shrieked Julie.

"This is not uncommon for this to happen, sometimes, it's only a short-term memory loss."

"Can we see him now?" asked Robert.

"Yes, but please, don't bombard him with too much information, this can be a scary time for a patient."

They all went in, and went to Doug's bedside, Mary rushed over and hugged and kissed her son. He looked bewildered when she did this.

"How are you feeling, Doug?" asked his dad, "It's good to see you awake."

But he was not the same Doug, he had a lost look in his eyes, he did not recognise any of them.

"I'm your dad, and this is your mum, and to my left here is Andrew, your brother, this is Julie, she's your wife." Doug looked panicked now.

Julie tried showing him his new daughter, Grace, "Look, Doug, this is Grace, our daughter," but Doug didn't show even a glimmer of emotion or recognition to any of his family. Julie burst out crying, just then the head consultant, Mr Robinson come over to them. Mr Robinson had overseen Doug's case, he asked them to follow him out of the room. He took Julie, Andrew, Robert and Mary into a family room. He explained to them that Doug may be suffering from a condition known as a dissociative fugue state, or simply fugue state.

"Have any of you heard of this?" he asked them. No, none of them had.

"Dr Raj told us that Doug has lost his memory," said Andrew.

Mr Robinson informed them that some patients can forget everything about their lives, family, friends and sometimes their own name, yes.

"But the accident was a few months ago," replied Andrew, "shouldn't Doug, be remembering something by now?"

"Unfortunately, the fugue state manifests itself sometime after the actual traumatic brain injury. It can occur a few months after, as you all know, Doug suffered a very bad head injury, but we aren't overly concerned that Doug has no memory of the accident or that he doesn't recognise his family just now. In most cases, the patient's memory will return, and it's not clearly understood why. Later, their recollections of the time when their memory was absent might remain hazy." But he reiterated to them not to worry too much at present. "Doug is in the best place for a full recovery," he reassured them.

16

It was very disconcerting for Julie that her husband was confused and disorientated, and that he never seemed to look at their new baby daughter at all. Julie hoped that the consultant was right, and that in a short time, they would see a great improvement in his condition.

"What you can, maybe, do to help him, remember, is just to try and interact with him normally," said the doctor.

For the next few weeks, they all visited him as they did before. Andrew was telling his brother a bit about their childhood, growing up together, he told his big brother that he was a member of a gym, and that that he was a fantastic boxer. He told him they were all proud of him, and that he and Julie had both been to see him win a few amateur boxing matches. Andrew told Doug that he worked as an electrician, he also told Doug that he was gay and that his partner, Jason, had also been into see him, whilst he was in his coma.

Doug seemed less than interested and emotionally unavailable, Andrew got a horrible feeling that his brother disapproved of his sexuality which was very chilling as Doug was the first person he'd come out to as gay, even before their parents. In fact, he couldn't have been more supportive, or happier for him when he'd introduced him to Jason a few years ago, Doug liked him, and was always very friendly toward him. Jason even looked on Doug as the big brother he never had.

When it came time for Andrew to leave, he offered his brother his hand to shake, but Doug never took it, he never even said goodbye. Andrew told Doug that Julie would be in to see him shortly, Doug looked even more disgruntled than before. This was going to be a trying time for the family. Andrew was upset by this but tried to hide his emotions.

Andrew called his dad, and told him about the visit.

"Are you OK, Son?"

"Yes, Dad, I'm just a little shook up, I never expected that, please don't tell Mum or Julie, it will only upset them more."

"OK, I won't say anything to them, let's hope he gets his memory back soon."

When Julie arrived to visit Doug next, he was sitting in the chair at his bedside. He never got up when he saw her, this sent a chill through her, her husband was the most gentlemanly man she had ever met. He would always get up and greet her, usually with a big hug, and a kiss. Although this shook her, she took it in her stride, remembering what the doctor had said, it could take a couple of weeks. She had already waited long enough, another two or three weeks, she could probably handle.

Julie was telling Doug about the life they had together, about his job and about his family, but it seemed none of it was getting through to him. For the next few weeks, they all took it in turns to visit him and tell him stories. Andrew had decided that, although, Jason wanted to visit Doug, he should wait a bit. He had told Jason about his first visit with Doug when he came out of the coma. Jason knew how that felt, his dad wasn't too thrilled when he told him he was gay.

Weeks had now passed, Doug had received lots of physiotherapy, and the big day for him getting home was tomorrow. Although he was now physically ready to go home, he was still withdrawn and showed no emotion to Julie or Grace. He was also rude to Andrew anytime he visited. Julie had noticed it a few times and asked

17

Andrew if something had been said between the pair. Andrew told her a white lie, that nothing had happened, but Julie sensed that something must have been said.

"Why do you continue to visit him? I can see that he's being mean to you."

"He's my big brother, Julie, he's lost his memory, just think how much we can tease him when he gets it back."

"Yes," smiled Julie, "I just hope it's soon."

"Me too," nodded Andrew, "he's not been too polite to Mum or Dad either. But they're just thrilled he's awake, time is a great healer."

"Yes, I've noticed he's been distant with them too, maybe when we get him home tomorrow and he gets himself reoriented to family life, it will jog some memories. When I spoke to the doctor this morning, he said this could be the best thing for him."

Julie and Andrew hoped the doctor was right, and Doug would start improving.

It was nine-thirty AM, the day Doug was getting home. Robert and Mary went to Doug and Julie's house, Julie answered the door, she invited them in. Julie had just put the kettle on for tea and coffee.

"Where's our little Grace?" asked Mary,

"She's asleep, thank goodness," said Julie, "she's not been sleeping well at all, I've hardly had a wink of sleep all night. What time are you getting Doug?" Julie asked Robert.

"Eleven o'clock," he replied.

"How do you think he'll be today?" asked Julie,

"Let's hope he had a good night, and he's in a fine form."

"God, I really hope so, I can't lie to you both, but I'm kind of wary being here myself with him."

"Oh, you won't need to worry. Doug's never been violent toward anyone except when he's boxing," said Robert.

"I know but he's not been the old Doug lately," said Julie.

"We'll visit regularly, and if you still feel this way, we'll arrange something else. He can come and stay with us," said Mary.

Julie made the tea for her and Mary and a coffee for Robert. They spoke about Grace for a while.

"I really hope Doug getting home today will help jog his memory, he hasn't even looked at Grace since he's came out the coma."

"Yes, we've noticed that too. This must be a very confusing time for him though."

It was soon time for Robert to go and collect his son from the hospital. When he arrived, Doug was ready to go, but he didn't seem too willing.

"Hi, Son, let's get you in the car and off home," he led the way, saying good-bye and thanking the nursing staff. Doug didn't acknowledge them at all, even when the senior nurse tried to shake his hand to wish him luck. Robert, seeing Doug's snub and feeling embarrassed, stepped over and shook her hand instead, thanking her for all they'd done for his son.

"I'm sure he'll be fine," she whispered to Robert.

It was a short drive home. Doug seemed anxious.

"Is everything OK, Son?"

"This doesn't feel right, I don't know any of you people."

"But you're my son, I've told you this already, Doug. You've had an accident and you've lost your memory, but the doctors say it could return anytime."

"The woman with the baby, she says she's married to me and that the baby is my daughter. Don't you think that if I had a baby, I would remember that? At least?"

Robert looked for somewhere to pull over the car, he saw an Asda store ahead.

"Let's stop here, and I will try and explain to you again."

"I'm not fucking stupid, mate," growled Doug. This stunned Robert, neither Doug nor Andrew had ever used swear words, but he let it go.

"I don't think you're stupid, Son." Robert drove into the car park which was only about half full and parked the car in a space well away from any other cars. Doug opened the car door and was about to get out the car.

"Please wait, Doug," pleaded Robert, "the reason you don't remember your daughter, Grace, is that she was born whilst you were in a coma. You've never seen her before. You and Julie have been trying for years to have children, Julie loves you more than you would ever dream of. Honestly, Doug, we're a very close-knit family, and maybe we've been coming on a bit too strong lately but it is only because we care about you. Please come with me, let me drive you home to Julie and Grace. Hopefully, something at home will help you remember."

Doug closed the door again, he agreed, somewhat reluctantly, for Robert to drive him home. Robert thanked his son, he drove out of the car park, and headed for Doug's house. When they arrived, and he parked the car, he'd expected Doug to get out, and go into the house, but he stayed in the car until Robert switched the ignition off.

Doug only got out when Robert did, his dad led the way. Mary had opened the door and was waiting to give her son a cuddle, but he walked straight past her into the house. Mary gave Robert a look of pity.

"He's been hard work," Robert whispered to Mary, "I'll tell you all about it later."

"OK," Mary nodded back, she closed the door and asked Doug if he wanted a cup of tea or coffee. He ignored her again, he was looking around and noticed Grace was sitting on Julie's knee. She was getting fed, she was sucking on a bottle of milk, Mary went over and took Grace from Julie. This allowed Julie to stand up.

"I will give you a quick tour of our house, if you'd like?" Julie said.

"OK," he nodded.

Julie led him to the kitchen, and then the downstairs toilet, and she opened the back door and let him see the garden.

"How long have you lived here?"

"We both moved in here about four months ago. We used to stay around the corner from your mum and dads." She closed the back door, and led him back into the sitting room, then she took him up the stairs. The first room she showed him was their bedroom, it had a big double bed in the centre of the room with a small bedside, two drawer cabinets, at either side of the bed, each with a small single bulb table lamp sitting on top. There was a four door, sliding mirrored wardrobe running the full-length from the floor to the ceiling.

"You fitted these yourself," she slid them open and an inner light came on to reveal on one side, six suits all on hangers, complete with covers about twenty assorted shirts and on the shelves, six pairs of shoes, two black pairs, two brown pairs, one grey pair and one pair that was a pale blue in colour. Julie saw Doug looking at the blue shoes.

"You have a suit that matches those shoes," she said.

Still no sign of emotion. The next room was the nursery/Grace's bedroom. It was a neutral colour, but the cot was white.

"We are going to decorate this with some pink wallpaper, we looked at pink and blue wallpaper. We never knew if we were having a boy or a girl," she said, "but we've got a beautiful daughter now, would you like to hold her?"

Doug's head stayed still, and he never spoke, his disposition never changed. Julie was doing really well holding onto emotions. The next door, she opened led to the bathroom, it was perfectly tiled both on the walls and on the floor. It was a wet room, and there was a big sunken bath with a shower above it. It looked great, even he looked slightly impressed.

"You did all this yourself too."

"I don't fucking remember any of this, and I'm not sure I can do all these things you say I can."

Julie was as shocked when she heard him using a swear word, "Why would I lie to you, Doug? You're my husband."

He was done with the tour, and he headed back down the stairs without any further interaction with her. Julie followed, and thought to herself, *this is not going to be easy.*

Once they were both back down stairs, Robert took one look at Julie and he knew it hadn't gone well.

"Would you like me to help you make lunch, Julie?" asked Mary.

"Yes, please, that will be great." They headed into the kitchen. "He said he doesn't remember the house or even the decorating. When I told him, he had tiled the bathroom, he looked at me as if I had horns growing out of my head. He even swore at me."

"Robert told me, when you were upstairs, that he swore at him too."

"What am I to do, Mum?" Julie pleaded.

"Hopefully, his memory will start to come back, remember, the doctor said this could be good for him."

"I know, Mum, but he's even more a stranger now than ever."

"Just give it a couple of days, love."

They made ham sandwiches for lunch. When they went back into the sitting room, Robert was trying, unsuccessfully, to have a conversation with his son and it seemed he was disinterested.

Robert asked him if being in his own house had jogged any memories, Doug just shook his head, and he looked like he would rather be anywhere else but here.

After they had finished their lunch, Robert decided it was time for him and Mary to go home and leave Doug, Julie and Grace to themselves.

"Maybe a bit of family time would do the trick for Doug." Julie looked horrified at the thought of being left alone with Doug. They both kissed Julie and Grace goodbye. Mary went over to give her son a kiss goodbye too, he let Mary kiss his cheek, but he didn't appreciate the gesture. This seemed very strange to Mary as her son was always affectionate towards her. He would usually pick her up and give her a big cuddle.

Robert offered his hand to Doug to shake but he was hesitant, he did eventually shake Roberts hand, albeit very reluctantly. About half an hour after they left, Doug decided he wanted to go for a sleep. He went upstairs and fell asleep on the big double bed. Julie fed Grace again, and she bathed and changed her too.

Three hours had passed before Doug came back down the stairs. Julie had just managed to get Grace to go to sleep. Doug scared her by demanding to know what kind of fucking game they were all playing.

"We're not playing any games. I can't imagine what's going on in your mind, but we're all telling you the truth."

"Well, I'm not getting anything from this fucking house, where did you say I work?"

"You work as an electrician at Smith Contracts."

"OK, if I work there, you can give me their telephone number, I want to call them now."

"Sure, I can do that, Doug." She gave him the number, he dialled it and the call was answered by a woman.

She said, "Good afternoon, Smith Contracts."

Doug put the phone down without speaking. He sat and stared into space for the next half hour.

"Would you like to ask me some questions about our life? Or would you like me to tell you some more about how we met?"

"Why, so you can tell me some more of your fucking lies?" growled Doug. "I feel trapped."

Julie was terrified and alarmed now, her husband would never raise his voice to her and he certainly would never constantly swear at her either.

"Well, nobody's forcing you to stay, you know where the door is," she blurted out and instantly regretted it. Doug's shouting had woken Grace and she was now crying again.

"Can you not shut that baby the fuck up?" Julie lifted Grace in her basket and ran upstairs crying. She had decided she was going to sleep in Grace's room. She cried herself and Grace to sleep, wondering how long her marriage could cope with Doug if his memory never returned. She guessed not very long at all.

If Doug hadn't mellowed in the morning, she and Grace were going to move in with her mother or Robert and Mary. She was certainly not staying here with Doug, not in his present state anyway. Never in a million years would she have imagined she would ever fear her own husband, her life had been turned upside down.

Just a few short months ago, she had the perfect life. Doug was never moody, she thought back to when she first met him. He was just so polite. She fell in love with a gentle giant, he was the exact opposite of who you thought he'd be, big scary looking guy, but he had a heart of gold.

The next morning, Julie popped her head into their bedroom. The bed didn't look like it had been slept in since she'd re-made it before going to sleep in Grace's room. She thought maybe Doug had fallen asleep on the settee. She quietly crept downstairs, hoping to see her husband, either asleep or at the very least in a better frame of mind.

When she entered the sitting room, he wasn't there. She looked in the kitchen, again no sign of him. She climbed the stairs again, and looked in the bathroom, he wasn't there either. This time, she went into their bedroom and she saw the bottom drawer of the dresser was missing. She looked at the far side of the bed and there it was lying on the floor, it contained Doug's socks, and boxer shorts, he also kept some money in the drawer for emergencies.

There was twelve hundred pounds in there the last time she looked, it was all gone. In its place now was his wallet, it contained his bank card, credit card, as well as some small photographs of Julie and one with them both taken on holiday last summer. She had the same picture in her purse. Doug had asked a passer-by to take the picture for them. The only thing she could see missing was his driver's licence.

"Why would he leave his bank card and credit card and only take his driver's licence and the cash from the drawer?" she was mystified. Grace was now awake and demanding some attention. Julie went in and lifted her daughter from her basket. She carried her into the bathroom, stripped off her clothes, and nappy, and gave her a bath. When she was done, she put a new nappy and a clean baby grow suit. She put Grace back into her crib and carried her down stairs. She sat it on the floor, in the sitting room, whilst she put the kettle on and made Grace a bottle of milk. When it had cooled down, she fed Grace with it, who hungrily finished it in no time at all.

Julie called Mary, told her about the confrontation with Doug last night and that he was nowhere to be seen.

"I don't know when he left, but his bed was unslept in and he took the cash that he kept in his sock drawer. The strange thing is, he left his wallet and its full contents, taking only his driver's licence."

"Yes, love, that is very strange. I will speak with Robert and we'll come over in about an hour."

This left Julie enough time to make some tea and toast and have a quick shower.

Chapter 3

Robert and Mary arrived about five minutes after Julie had finished her shower and had gotten dressed. She put the kettle on again, and made them all a fresh brew tea for her and Mary and a coffee for Robert. Just as they were finishing the hot drinks, Robert's mobile phone rang. It was his friend, John Smith.

"Hi, mate," Robert answered.

"I've just had a call from my brother, Ricky. He had a strange phone call from Doug late on yesterday."

"What was strange about the call?"

"Well, for starters, he asked Ricky what kind of game we were all playing. Ricky asked him what he was on about. Doug said the woman with the baby had told him she was his wife, and that he worked for him as an electrician. He said he was sure he would remember something about his job and this life he was supposed to be living, if it were all true. Ricky assured him that it was, indeed, all true, but Doug called him a fucking liar and he said he wasn't swallowing any of this shite, and that if he really did work for him, then he quit and then hung up the phone."

"I'm really sorry," replied Robert, "he swore at both Julie and I yesterday too, he never swears."

"Oh, don't worry about the colourful language, mate. Ricky and I have worked on more than a few building sites and the swearing on those would make your head spin."

Robert told his old friend about the journey home from the hospital yesterday, and the events with Julie last night.

"He's now walked out on her and baby Grace too."

"This is terrible, Robert," sympathised John. "Let's hope he comes to his senses sooner rather than later. If there's anything I can do to assist you, Robert? Please let me know."

"I will, thanks for the offer and the call. I'll see you later." Robert hung up the phone and relayed the conversation to Mary and Julie.

"He must have called Ricky from here when I went upstairs with Grace after he shouted at me. He asked me for his works telephone number, he dialled the number but never spoke. He must have hit the re-dial button, unless he memorised the number. I know he's really good with numbers, but that was before the accident."

Grace was awake again and seeking someone's attention. Robert lifted his granddaughter from her basket, he was bouncing her on his knee, and she was now gurgling away happily. They spoke about how Doug had been since he'd come out of the coma.

"He's been very aloof, and angry, very unlike Doug. And look at how he's been since he got out of the hospital, he's been grumpy and moody. It seemed like he was looking for an excuse to leave, and I'm not sure I helped matters. I told him nobody was forcing him to stay, he obviously took it literally, and left us," Julie sobbed, "some supportive wife I am."

"Look, love, none of this is your fault. We witnessed how he was yesterday," said Mary, comforting her distraught daughter-in-law.

"Maybe leaving you here alone with him yesterday was a bad idea. We thought some time with you and Grace would help. We were wrong," added Robert. They all knew Doug was never like this, he was always a happy go lucky sort, and his accident had certainly changed his temperament.

They stayed for a couple of hours, and they went back home, hoping maybe their son was there now. Robert asked Julie to keep them informed if Doug turned up again. Julie was still upset after Robert and Mary left, she called her own mum, Dot and asked if she could come over.

"Of course, you can, love, I'll put the kettle on." When she arrived at her mum's, she couldn't keep herself in check, and she burst out crying. She told her mum about the way Doug spoke to her, and that she was frightened.

"Listen, love, he's just in need of some time, he'll come around." Dot had always liked Doug. He was kind to Julie and adored her. Dot's husband, Julie's dad, Raymond, had died when Julie was just ten years old. He was a bit overweight and had a lot of health issues, he had a massive heart attack and died instantly. Dot never had another man in her life since Raymond passed.

Julie and Grace had stayed the night with Dot, and when they arrived home the next morning, she had hoped that her husband would have returned back home. But he hadn't. Julie called Mary to see if they'd heard from him, they hadn't. Mary told Julie to stay put, they would head over to her house shortly. When they arrived, Julie and Mary hugged each other, they were both very upset that Doug had now been gone overnight and they were crying. This started Grace again off, Robert lifted her from her basket.

"This is now getting serious," he said to Grace, she gurgled back at him. "Other than the call to his boss, Doug has fallen off the face of the earth. We know Doug's not been right since the accident." They all agreed, but this was just not in Doug's character to be this selfish. Now, they were all worried sick about his well-being.

"The doctors have told us that it may take some time for Doug's memories to return," said Julie, "but Doug's been very distant and cold, and he's shown no affection toward me or Grace. He has ignored his own daughter, apart from telling me to shut her up. Do you know how many sleepless nights we've had, discussing all the wonderful things Doug and I were going to do when this baby arrived? Now, it looks like it's all gone up in smoke."

"I know this is tough on you, Julie, but I know my son, he will come around. I'm sure of it," said Robert. "I just can't believe he's quit his job." Robert handed Grace over to Mary, he pulled his mobile phone from his pocket and called his friend. "Hi, John, has Ricky heard any more from Doug?"

"No, unfortunately not. I'm here at his office just now, he says hi to you all. I take it from this call that you haven't heard from him either?"

"No, mate, not a thing."

"Listen, I know Doug's been through a terrible ordeal. Ricky, and I have been discussing the recent events, and he says he'll keep Doug's job for him, for a while anyway, to see if he comes to his senses. He can do any urgent stuff himself meantime, and if needs, he can call on a mate of his who runs an agency." Robert asked his friend to thank his brother for him. "You can thank him yourself, he wants a quick word with you," and John put Ricky on the phone.

Robert thanked him for holding onto Doug's job, but Ricky reminded Robert that as well as Doug being his son, he is also a very good friend and colleague of his too.

"Remember, Doug was my apprentice, and as John has already said, we're here if you need anything. We mean it, Robert, if there's absolutely anything we can do to help, please call us." Robert thanked him again and hung up. Robert told them what the Smith brothers had said to him, regarding Doug, well at least that's some good news.

Mary made them another brew. Robert decided he was going to go to the local police station, more for advice than anything else. He finished his coffee and told the women he would be back in a couple of hours. When he arrived at the police station, he spoke with a young woman at the reception. She asked him what he was looking for. He explained his family predicament, she asked him to take a seat and she would see if she could arrange for someone to speak with him.

Robert was seated for about fifteen minutes when a plainclothes detective came to see him. He introduced himself as Detective Chief Inspector Craig, he was very senior in rank. He led Robert into an interview room.

"I'm not sure I should be troubling a senior policeman of your rank with this."

"It's absolutely fine, I'm the only one available at the moment," replied the DCI. Robert told the detective all about Doug, the accident, the coma, and about him disappearing. The DCI said this was known as skip tracing, this is when someone leaves the family home but doesn't want to be found. As Doug had not committed any crime and was not considered dangerous, the police were very limited as to what they could do, but the DCI assured him they would do as much as they could.

The DCI wrote all the relevant details onto a pad, took down a mobile number and handed Robert his business card, it had all his contact details on it. The DCI promised him he would get in touch with the other local police stations, and give a description of his son, and put some feelers out, but other than that, there was, unfortunately not much more they could do. Robert thanked him, and they shook hands.

Once outside the police station, he decided to call, and get an appointment to see Mr Robinson, the consultant that had looked after Doug. Robert wanted to know if Doug's behaviour was common among this type of injury. He managed to have a quick word with Mr Robinson, on the phone, to give him an idea of what he wanted to discuss. Mr Robinson agreed to see him at two PM later that day. Robert called Mary, and told her of his meeting with the detective, and his call to Mr Robinson.

"I'll be back in half an hour." When he arrived back, Mary had already boiled the kettle, and made him some lunch too, she gave him cheese and tomato sandwiches, and she'd also opened a tin of Lentil soup. Robert enjoyed the soup, then he ate the sandwiches, they hit the spot. He was hungrier than he'd thought he was, he had a coffee too. It was soon time to go and see the consultant. When Robert arrived at the hospital, he was shown into the consultant's room by his secretary.

"Hello and welcome." The consultant offered him a seat, Robert sat down across the table from him. "Please, tell me what's happened."

Robert told him of the events of the past couple of days, and that Doug had now shown aggression and hostility toward them all, he'd not done that before. He also mentioned the call to his boss and retold the incidents of Doug thinking they were all trying to con him, about the swearing, and then disappearing in the middle of the night, without warning or contact information. Robert asked Mr Robinson if his son should be out of hospital right now.

"Wouldn't it be better for Doug to be under some form of supervision? I'm scared, he will do something to himself, or God forbid, Julie or Grace."

Mr Robinson pondered over this question and he started by saying, "Doug has shown no signs that he would self-harm or harm anyone else for that matter.

"With the kind of injury Doug has suffered, it's very difficult, to be certain how quickly, or even when, if ever, he will get his memory back," but Mr Robinson re-assured him, it was very rare for a patient not to get some recollection of life before the injury. "Time is, as they say, a great healer. Has Doug been drinking much since he left Hospital?"

"No," confirmed Robert, "in fact, no drink at all."

"What about drugs?"

"No, again. Doug has never used drugs, and he only ever drinks very moderately."

"I must confess to you, Mr Clement. I'm only mildly concerned. Doug hasn't had a small glimmer of recollection yet, as I've said, there's no definitive time scale on memory returning, but this is mystifying, nonetheless, regarding Doug leaving in the middle of the night. We would normally expect patients to stay within the security of the family surroundings. So, let's hope Doug gets his memory back sooner than later.

"I spoke to a couple of colleagues, this morning after your call, just to get a fresh input and we are all in agreement that Doug's actions, although strange, are definitely not uncommon. Sometimes, the patient just needs time alone to reflect on the situation they find themselves in. One colleague told me of a patient that left home in similar circumstances to Doug, he returned home four days later, but couldn't remember where he'd been and was so sorry for the worry he had put his family through. That patient got his full memory back two days later. I think, if you don't hear from Doug by the weekend, you should maybe inform the police and report him as a missing person."

"I've already been to see the police, but they've told me there's very little, if anything, they can do other than notify other stations." Robert thanked him for seeing him at short notice.

When he left the hospital, he called Mary and told her the discussion he'd had with Mr Robinson. Robert asked her how Julie and Grace were doing. Mary said Grace was as good as gold and was sleeping and that Julie was so-so. He told her he was going to visit the gym that Doug was a member of on the off chance he'd been in.

It took Robert half an hour to get there. When he spoke with a staff member named Craig, he knew Doug, very well. Craig had heard about the accident, but he'd not seen him for a good few months. Robert left his contact number with Craig, he slipped him a twenty-pound note too, and asked him to call him if Doug appeared. He thought it unlikely, but he was running out of options. Craig thanked Robert and quickly put the money into his pocket, and promised he would call if he saw or heard anything relating to Doug.

Robert's next port of call was their own family doctor just in case Doug had gone there looking for medication, he knew the GP would most probably not divulge any information, but he had to try. He knew the doctor well, and he confirmed, off the record, that Doug had not been in or even called them.

Robert had run out of ideas. He headed back home, Grace was now awake, she'd awoke soon after Robert had called earlier. This poor little girl was none the wiser about her missing dad. This was more likely a good thing, he thought. He could see that Julie was starting to show signs of stress, the uncertainty of not knowing where her husband had gotten too was getting to her.

Julie wasn't getting much sleep either. The combination of Doug being missing, and Grace not sleeping were weighing on her heavily. Mary made them all a fresh brew. They spoke for a while about nothing in particular, the weather, how Dot was keeping. Mary asked Julie, to go and try and get a sleep for a couple of hours. She would keep an eye on Grace. Robert decided to go for a drive around some of Doug's old haunts in the hope of finding him or someone he knew.

Robert went into two local bars, and not that Doug was a drinker. *It was more desperation than hope*, he thought, but it made him feel as if he was doing something constructive, rather than sitting at home worrying, but none of the barmen had known Doug. *It was worth a try,* he thought.

Robert had never felt this low before, even after his own accident. He was putting on a brave face for Mary and Julie, but he was starting to feel desperate. He called Andrew, more for moral support than anything else. Andrew worked as a manager for a plant hire company, he invited his dad over to his office for a cuppa, which Robert greatly accepted.

Leave the woman folk alone for a while anyway and get another man's perspective on the situation, Robert thought to himself. Andrew was also worried about his brother, but he knew that Doug could take care of himself, he'd been to the boxing club with him a few times and had seen him fight, albeit Doug was not himself lately, but still he was confident he would be OK.

Andrew listened to what his dad had been told from the consultant. This was a trying time for the family but he was sure it would soon all end happily. Robert wished he had his son's belief. He thanked him for the coffee and the pep talk.

"I'd better go and collect your mum from Julie's. I will keep you posted if I hear anything."

"Ditto, Dad," replied Andrew.

Robert took the scenic route home, driving really slowly when approaching any pedestrians. He was still on the lookout for Doug. Robert collected Mary, and they were heading home for supper,

"I'm worried about Julie's state of mind."

"Yes, me too," he replied, "we'll have to keep an eye on her."

Mary made pie, beans and chips for their supper. He opened a bottle of wine and they had two small glasses each. They had an early night.

The next morning, around ten AM after breakfast, Robert called Julie to see if she'd heard from Doug. But alas, she hadn't.

"Listen, Dad, do you think this will end anytime soon? I don't know how much more I can take, I'm at my wits end. Grace hasn't slept a wink again last night, and I'm falling apart at the seams." Robert could almost feel the desperation in her voice, he could also hear in the background that Grace was crying again.

"I'm sure it'll all end soon and we can look back on this terrible ordeal as a character builder. Hopefully, not much longer now, it's taking a toll on Mary too. She's asleep now, but she was up all-night worrying. I think you both need to see a doctor to, hopefully, prescribe something to help you both get some decent sleep. We spoke last night, and we think it would be better if you came and stayed here for a while, just to allow you to get some rest. We can all muck in with Grace."

"I couldn't impose of you two."

"It would be no bother," Robert assured her.

"What if Doug's memory comes back, and he comes home, and we're not in?"

"Don't worry about that, if that happens, where do you think he would go next? Here, of course."

"OK, let me think about it, I will call you later. I need to go and attend to Grace, she is crying again."

"Yes, I can hear her."

Julie hung up the phone and went into Grace's room and picked her up out of her crib.

"Oh, my little darling, where would I be if I never had you in this time of crisis. Hopefully, one day very soon, your daddy's going to walk through that door and shower us both with hugs and kisses, just you wait and see." Grace just cooed back at her.

Julie bathed and dressed Grace then gave her a bottle, that took about an hour. She thought about moving in with Mary and Robert, would Grace settle there? Well, she'd hardly settled here, so that wasn't a reason not to go. Would Doug come to his parents if he came home and found the place empty? That was an emphatic yes. So, she decided, to take them up on their offer, she called them. Mary answered.

"Are you sure it's OK for us to come live with you for a bit?"

"Is it OK? Are you kidding, we'd love to have you both here. It's hard enough worrying about Doug without having to wonder how you two are getting on. To be honest, Julie, you'd be doing us a favour."

It was settled then, Robert would collect them at five PM, he arrived at a quarter to five. He always liked to be early, he helped her pack some things, and off they went. Mary had the kettle on, she made the brews and sandwiches, whilst Robert unloaded the car. Once everything was inside, they settled down and Mary poured the drinks and brought in the sandwiches. Robert was famished, he made short work of his sandwiches, and then his thoughts turned again to his missing son.

Chapter 4

It was mid-June 2012, Johnny Wilson, a Glaswegian and big-time gambler with a small-time income, had just lost another two hundred pounds he didn't have on an odds-on favourite at Ascot. He now owed moneylender and crooked businessman, Big Jim Cassidy, even more dosh. Johnny had already sold off everything he'd owned of any value to keep his head above water.

His marriage to the only woman he'd ever truly loved, Betty, had ended in divorce five years previously, due to his incessant gambling. Betty had given him chance after chance to change his ways, and he'd screwed them all up. The final straw came when all her Jewellery went missing, and it had transpired that Johnny had pawned it all to cover some of his gambling debt.

Betty was mortified that her husband had sunk so low, how could he do that to her? She managed to get the pawn ticket from him and she borrowed some money from her dad to get her jewellery back. She'd decided enough was enough and the next morning, she took their two young sons, Matthew, eight and Luke, six, to stay with her parents, in Manchester. She'd expected an argument from Johnny to make her stay, but it was not forthcoming so she left him.

Johnny had seen the boys once since then, last Christmas Eve, for an hour or so when they came to visit Betty's sister in Wimbledon. His sons barely knew him at all. Betty met a new man, she met him when she took the boys to Skegness a couple of years after leaving him. His name was Archie, and they were now married. He was a good man, and he'd taken the boys on too. This gave Johnny some comfort that, at least, his boys were being looked after.

Johnny was now thirty-four years old, he worked as a security guard mostly on construction sites. He was one of life's losers now, but when he was younger, he was a promising young architect student at the University of Strathclyde in his home town of Glasgow.

Johnny met Betty at a disco in town and they started dating, she fell pregnant soon after, and he had to drop out of university to get a job to support his soon to be family. Mathew was born first, then just under two years later, Luke followed. Johnny had worked as a building site labourer, a council bin man, but he soon got the sack from both jobs as he was always late or never turned up for work at all.

Johnny turned to drink and gambling and ever since, he has always looked for a quick way to make easy money. This led to numerous scrapes with the law and he was arrested for breaking and entering an electrical warehouse, trying to steal to support his gambling and drinking addictions. He was given a three-year custodial sentence in Glasgow's notorious Barlinnie Prison.

Betty vowed to stand by him if he gave up his addictions, which he promised to do. For the following two-and a-bit years, Betty worked as a cleaner in the local school. This led to a job as a classroom assistant. That job was a lifesaver as she managed to feed and clothe the three of them whilst he was in prison.

When Johnny was released from prison, he got a job in a shopping centre, as night-time security, and he even managed to stay sober and never had a bet for almost a year, but he started betting again, in small amounts, which steadily increased to larger amounts.

Betty was none the wiser until he came home, one Thursday night, with a few bruises and a black eye. He'd lost all his wages, gambling on greyhound racing, at Glasgow's Shawfield stadium, and then he demanded his money back from the bookmaker, saying the races had been fixed. The security guards got a bit rough with him resulting in the state he was in that night.

Betty gave him an ultimatum, stop the gambling once and for all or she was leaving him and taking the kids. Betty borrowed some money from her parents to get them by until Johnny got paid again the following month. This was turning into an all too regular occurrence, culminating in the night her jewellery went missing, and she had, subsequently, left him. He'd lost the cushy job he had in the shopping centre soon after. Johnny had nothing to keep him in Glasgow now that Betty had left for Manchester with his sons.

He hitchhiked down to London, managed to get a job as a labourer on building sites and met a fellow Glaswegian on a site who had a spare room to let. Johnny jumped at the chance, the guy returned to Glasgow soon after Johnny had moved in. He now rents the place himself. He left his labourers job, and for a while, he drifted from dead end job to dead end job.

Johnny was now working, off the books, as a security guard for a construction company. He'd met a guy in a bar, they got talking and the guy asked, him if he wanted a cash in hand job working a few shifts a week. The work was easy and Johnny agreed. He has worked there ever since ever, it was now eighteen months and counting. Johnny was gambling as much as ever.

Chapter 5

Johnny was playing a dangerous game, he knew the consequences of not paying Big Jim Cassidy. As well as being a moneylender, Cassidy also arranged illegal unlicensed fights, and he had his finger in a lot of pies, not one of them was legal. Johnny had heard a few scary stories about his big enforcer, JoJo, he was a thug, he enjoyed breaking bones and generally hurting folks. Johnny remembered someone telling him of an encounter with him, a broken arm and two snapped fingers were the outcome, just for forgetting to pay back an instalment of a loan. Johnny got queasy just thinking about it, and the mess he was in again.

For nearly two years, this was Johnny's life, working as many shifts as he could get, and gambling very badly, he was just about managing to pay Big Jim enough every week to stop JoJo beating him up. Johnny still owed Cassidy a right few quid, he was never too sure exactly how much it was though, as the interest on the money kept climbing, he guessed at approximately two grand. Johnny was paying around about one hundred and fifty pounds a month, and had been for the past year or so.

God only knows if he'll ever manage to repay it all. Johnny got the sense that Cassidy liked him, even though, he knew, he was never more than two missed payments away from a visit from JoJo. He was fortunate that he'd never missed two in a row. He came mighty close on more than one occasion, but by the skin of his teeth, he's always cobbled enough and no more to make the payment. But this month, he found himself in the awkward position of not having enough to pay the debt, as he'd already missed last months, he was shitting himself.

Johnny was definitely playing with fire, the last thing he needed was getting any of his bones broken. If he couldn't work, he wouldn't get paid. It was good getting paid cash in hand, and not having to pay any income tax, but the big drawback to that scheme was you didn't get paid sick money. Johnny would have to avoid Cassidy and JoJo until he had enough money to pay him a double instalment.

Where the fuck could he get three hundred pounds in a hurry? If only he could get that big elusive win, he would get his life back on track or, so he dreamt. Every horse he backed seemed to finish second or third but never first. He'd put his last forty pounds onto a nag of a horse, it was a six to one shot and was leading the race by a good ten lengths when it tumbled at the last fence. What a fucking arsehole of a jockey, he just needed to keep the horse on its fucking feet and he would have collected two hundred and eighty pounds.

Johnny's luck was due to change, he knew that. He was heading to work and wondered what loser they were going to palm him off with today. The last guy he was paired with chucked the job in, he was a young guy early twenties, he only lasted three weeks. *What's wrong with the youth of today, they're all lazy bastards,* he thought. He'd had to work his last shift on his own because that guy hadn't shown up for work and never gave them any notice that he was leaving.

"They better have somebody lined up to work with me today, I'm not doing another shift on my lonesome. It's not like they pay me double money, they're long enough shifts without having no one to talk with," he said to himself. He was currently driving an old, beat up, black Ford Focus. He parked in his usual space outside the compound and headed up the metal staircase to the security office. It was a block of four porta-cabins all stacked together.

There was, indeed, a new arrival in the security team when he got into the office. Johnny looked like a big lump of a man, but he didn't look to him, to be the type to last, this was not unusual as lots of guys took this type of job on as a stop gap, until they got something better. But not him, he'd remembered at least six different guys had come and gone in the space of just a single month, but Johnny liked the hours and the job was easy. The money wasn't too bad, and he'd never had to pay a single penny in income tax on it either. It got him by.

He was introduced the new guy, his name was Doug. He looked even bigger and scarier up close, *He was a huge man, easily over six feet tall and at least eighteen stones,* Johnny thought. He'd tried to strike up a conversation with the big guy, but all he got were one-syllable answers. *Oh well,* Johnny thought, it seemed to him, his initial assessment was right. He couldn't see this guy lasting too long, he was obviously the strong silent type.

It was much the same during the long shift, *This prick's hard work,* thought Johnny, *but there's no point in wasting my time trying to get to know the stranger. He probably won't even trap tomorrow, we don't need long, engaging conversation to look after this place, but it sure would help relieve the boredom if newbie opened up a bit, and managed to say two sentences worth of words at the same time.*

To Johnny's great surprise, the new guy showed up for work the next day, and he was a bit more talkative too, but he was still not giving too much away. As the week progressed, so did the talking. It turned out Doug had been in an accident and had ended up in a coma. He told Johnny that when he awoke, he found these strange people fussing around his bed, all telling him how much they loved him and how worried they were about him. They were too touchy feely for his liking.

One of them was an attractive woman. She told him she was his wife, and the little baby girl she was holding was his daughter, Grace, but he'd never seen her before, and he definitely didn't remember having a baby.

"That's not the kind of thing you forget, is it?" Dough asked.

"No, I suppose not," agreed Johnny.

Doug said, he couldn't fathom out what was going on, some kind of con trick. They kept coming to the hospital every day for about a month, hassling him to remember them, but he couldn't, he said. He didn't know what their game was, he also told Johnny, he was very suspicious and confused and when he did eventually leave the hospital, they took him to a house that he never recognised.

The woman had told him he was an electrician, she said he worked for a family run business and that he should go and see the boss, a guy named Ricky. Well, he never went, but he did call the number the attractive woman had given him. A woman who sounded a bit older than him answered the phone saying the name of the company.

"How may I direct your call?" the woman had asked.

Doug said he didn't speak, he just hung up the phone. "It just didn't feel right," he told Johnny. When the attractive woman went to bed, Doug called the number again and asked to speak to the boss.

"Is that you, Doug?" the woman on the phone asked him.

"Just put me onto the boss, will you?"

"Oh, OK, I will put you through to him."

The boss geezer tried to convince him everyone was telling him the truth but he told the guy to fuck off, he wasn't stupid and he wouldn't be coming to work for him. He slammed the phone back into its cradle, then he grabbed some money he had seen in a drawer in the bedroom and left whilst the woman and the howling baby were sleeping.

As the week progressed, Johnny warmed to Doug, and he looked like he could handle himself in a fight. He asked Doug, where he lived and Doug was currently staying in a cheap hotel.

"It's not the best, but it will have to do until I find something better." He told Johnny he'd checked in there the night he left the strange home they took him to after leaving the hospital. It was also the same day he quit his job as a so-called electrician. Doug doubted he could even wire a plug, let alone wire a whole house, it just felt beyond him. He definitely thought someone was fucking with his head.

Johnny asked him, "Why don't you move in with me? I've got a spare room you could rent, it would help us both out."

Doug said he would think about it. They agreed they would go out for a couple of pints. On Thursday night, it was payday, and they were on day shift, and best of all, they all would be off for three days. Johnny liked the four days on two days off rota.

After Thursday's shift, they arranged to meet at a bar in town. Doug arrived around seven-thirty PM. He told Johnny he'd meet him around eight o'clock. He ordered a pint of Guinness for no other reason than it looked like a good pint, and most of the guys in the bar were drinking it. He couldn't recall ever having been in this bar, or even what he liked to drink, this seemed very strange to him.

Doug took a sip of the Guinness, but it didn't taste as he imagined, still it was not bad. He looked around to see if he'd recognise anyone one, but doubted he would, he didn't. He finished his pint, and ordered another. Just then, Johnny arrived.

"What you having?" Doug asked.

"I'll have my usual," Johnny laughed.

"What the fuck's that?" asked Doug.

"Same as you're having big chap, a Guinness, to be sure," he said in a funny Irish accent, they both had a chuckle. Johnny said, "Hey, grab that table over by the door." He pointed to the table to the left of the door, "You bring the pints over." Doug took the pints over, and told Johnny he was just nipping to the toilet.

"Probably my starter for ten."

When Doug got back, he asked Johnny what he did when he wasn't working. Johnny told him he went to the odd, on the cobbles boxing fights. They were arranged mostly by a guy named Jim Cassidy.

"What does on the cobbles mean?" asked Doug.

"It means they're illegal, and unlicensed. You can have a bet on which fighter you think will win. There are sometimes, four or five fights each time."

"Do you win money?" asked Doug.

"Yes, you can win money." Johnny told him he used to be quite lucky and win a lot of money, but lately, his luck was pretty shite.

"Where do these fights take place?" asked Doug.

"There are two regular venues, one is in an old gym down by the old power house night spot in hackney, it's called Benny's. Sometimes, a fight night gets arranged at short notice and the location is that one, or in an old gym just on the outskirts of town. They're kept hush-hush because the police might find out. And as they're illegal, it's best they don't find out."

Doug was intrigued by these revelations. Johnny was some guy. He also told Doug about his divorce, and how he had only seen his two sons the one time since he'd split from Betty. Although he was glad they were OK, he still missed them. They had another pint each then Johnny told Doug he was going outside for a smoke, he was away for about ten minutes.

Doug was wondering where he was and decided to go outside and see what the holdup was. When he got outside, he heard a commotion in the alley next to the bar. He looked in and saw these two chunky guys, one of them and a fat, ginger-haired guy was giving Johnny some grief. He noticed Johnny had a burst lip, the guy must have punched him.

"Hey, what the fuck's going on here?" shouted Doug to him.

"You can mind you own fucking business, arsehole," the fat, ginger-haired guy barked back.

"That's my mate you're terrorising, so it is my fucking business, fatso," roared back Doug. The guy let go of Johnny, and he made a move toward Doug, but he was too slow. Doug moved to his left and the guy grabbed at thin air. H then turned and threw a punch at Doug, but it was telegraphed. Doug saw it coming a mile off, bobbed his head to the left and the punch missed. That was big ginger's second mistake, and Doug was not taking a chance that he'd get it right on the third attempt.

So, Doug stepped back slightly, and thundered a big righthander at big ginger, the stunned guy went down like a condemned building. His mate looked on in frightened amazement, as no one had ever lifted a hand to JoJo. And by the looks of him, he was out cold. Frankie's first impulse on seeing his big mate lying there unconscious was to turn and run as fast as he could. JoJo was the fighter of the two, he then thought maybe, it was just a lucky punch, and anyway, if he did run away, how could he explain that to Cassidy?

Frankie had to try and maintain the status quo with him, he thought he'd better try and keep a handle on this, before it got out of hand, or he'd get a big telling off from Big Jim for leaving JoJo and for not sorting out this stranger. He decided he needed to try and end this as peaceful as possible. He made an unenthusiastic dash for the big stranger, hoping he would turn tail and run, but he should have gone with his first impulse and ran away because as he arrived in the kill zone, the big guy was prepared for him. When Frankie tried to a grab Doug, he was all wrong and off balance. Doug skipped to the side and the bumbling Frankie went wide. Just as he did so, Doug skelped him right on the back of the head and for good measure, kicked him in up the arse and drove him straight in to the wall face first. Frankie joined his mate in slumber land.

Johnny was now as white as a sheet, "For fuck's sake, Doug, do you know what you've just done? Those two pricks work for Big Jim Cassidy."

"Who the fuck's he?"

"The guy I told you about earlier, there'll be serious repercussions for us," shrieked Johnny.

"Why the fuck were they beating you up?" asked Doug.

"I owe Cassidy some money."

"How much do you owe him?"

"I'm not sure, it's just over two thousand pounds, I think."

"For fuck's sake, Johnny, what do you mean you think it's that amount? How can you not know how much you owe this wanker?"

"It's complicated," said a still shell-shocked Johnny.

"For fuck's, mate, how did you end up owing him that much money?"

"It's like I told you earlier, gambling, especially on illegal boxing fights. I was winning then I hit a bad patch, and now, I seem to be always losing. I pay him a small amount every so often, but I've been a bit short of cash lately and have missed a couple of payments. That's why I suggested you move in with me, it would allow me to pay him off a bit sooner. I never thought he'd send those two goons after me. I thought he would just add a little bit onto my tab."

"Do think we should call an ambulance for these two?" Doug asked, pointing at the two unconscious geezers.

"I suppose we should, but I'm not hanging around waiting for it." Johnny went inside, and asked the bar man to call an ambulance, he told him that there were two guys lying knocked out in the alley.

The bar man asked, "What had happened to them?"

Johnny lied, shrugged his shoulders and said, "I don't know, mate, I'm just doing my civic duty."

They got the fuck out of there sharpish. Doug agreed to move into Johnny's spare room, to the massive relief of Johnny. They called in to his hotel on the way home from the bar. Doug collected his gear and settled his bill in cash. When they arrived at Johnny's gaff, Doug was shown to the spare room. It was as big as the hotel room he had just vacated, and he said it would do just fine.

They had a couple of beers and Johnny let Doug know a bit more about Cassidy. He was a general bastard and wow betide anyone that crossed him, and that they should probably expect a visit from him or even worse, more of his lackeys, he was terrified.

Doug didn't share his concern. "We'll deal with whoever they send."

This didn't help much to reassure Johnny. He told his new housemate some more about his life with Betty and his two sons. He did miss them, but he knew it was too late for regrets. Doug could not reciprocate as he could not remember a single thing about his life before the accident, but he was sure it would all come back to him soon though. They went to bed around one AM.

Chapter 6

The next morning, at eight thirty, Big Jim called Johnny's mobile phone. When Johnny saw from the display who it was calling, he was shitting himself. He knew he would be in even more trouble if he ignored the call.

Johnny answered and without listening to Big Jim, he blurted out, "Listen, Mr Cassidy, I can explain."

"Oh, fucking great, you've got an explanation that will cover that Frankie and JoJo got carted off to the hospital in an ambulance unconscious? I can't fucking wait to hear it, Son."

"I'll tell you what happened," Johnny replied, trying not to sound as panicked as he was feeling.

"Just you cool your jets, Son and bring your personal minder to me."

"I'm not sure I can bring him."

"Oh, I'm ever so sorry," replied Cassidy, in an apologetic tone, "did I put that over as a request?" Then he barked, "You just get your little, fucking sorry, Scottish arse over here tonight or else. I want to hear this story in person, and I want to see this guy, face to face. He must be some piece of work if he took out JoJo and Frankie."

So, instead of being angry, as Johnny had assumed he would be, he was more intrigued, and he was keen to meet the guy who had single handed, knocked the fuck, out of his two best guys. Johnny tried to downplay the situation, and told Big Jim, he was just a guy he'd met in the pub, last night. Cassidy was not buying this he'd went personally to collected Frankie and JoJo from the hospital this morning. They'd told him the full story.

"So understand this, Son, if you don't bring your mate over here tonight, you will regret it big style. Do I make myself clear?"

"Crystal." Johnny then tried to tell him exactly what had happened in the alley last night and far from attacking Frankie and JoJo, all his mate was doing was defending him from getting a kicking from them. "Why do you want to meet him? Is he in trouble for helping me?"

"We'll see what develops, I may have proposition that suits all parties, you included, so make sure you're here with your big pal at eight PM tonight."

Before Johnny could protest anymore, Cassidy had hung up. All Johnny had to do now was to convince Doug to go with him to meet Cassidy tonight. He waited until Doug got up, then he filled him in on the conversation he'd had with Cassidy.

"Why do you think he wants to meet me?"

"He says he might have something to offer you that will suit us both. You can be sure, anything he offers will need to suit him too. I guess we'll find out tonight."

"OK, we'll go and see him. If those two pricks, are his best men then we should be fine. I don't mind making some extra money, as long it's nothing too dodgy and I'm definitely not getting involved in scaring people to giving over money for him. And I'm not selling drugs either."

"Nor me," agreed Johnny, "but as far as I know, he never has anything to do with drugs, a niece of his died of a drug overdose, a few years back. He sent JoJo to break the drug dealer's legs, and he stole all his money and drugs too. He also threatened to kill him and throw him in the Thames if he didn't leave town that day. He's into pretty much everything, except drugs though, so we'll see what he's offering."

That night, at eight PM, they arrived at the gym. Doug was introduced to Big Jim Cassidy by Johnny; the stitched and bandaged Frankie and JoJo were startled when Johnny and Doug arrived. JoJo stood up, readying himself for round two, but Big Jim, who had obviously not mentioned to them that Doug and Johnny were coming, told him to sit on his arse. JoJo sheepishly did as he was told.

"Can you get him to roll over beg too?" asked Doug.

"Listen, big man, don't get too cocky, or I will let him have another go at you," grinned Big Jim.

"If you like? But it will be his loss if you do. I can't stand bullies like them, they think it's OK to beat the shite out a little defenceless guy like Johnny."

"They were just doing as they were told, if this little Scottish loser here had paid me when he should have, I wouldn't have had to send them out looking for him. He's been avoiding me for nearly a fortnight now. Your mate here owes me four grand."

Johnny looked a cross between despair and embarrassment.

"What kind of businessman would I be if I let that slide? As soon as word got out I'd gone soft on people that owe me money, nobody would pay me, would they? I need to keep a lid on this, so there will be no mention of what occurred last night in that alley. Is that clear?" Big Jim was looking around at the four of them.

Frankie and JoJo nodded instantly as did Johnny, but Doug had a rueful smile on his face, and was non-committal.

"Listen to me, big man," Big Jim now said directly to Doug. "If it got around my two enforcers got their arses handed to them, they will lose the fear factor and that can't happen. That's the first of the two reasons why I've invited you here tonight. To keep your mouth shut."

"What's the second?"

Big Jim had been sizing Doug up from the moment he walked through the door, "You can obviously handle yourself in street fight, but can you do it in the ring?"

"What do you have in mind?"

"I have a fight arranged for next week, and one of the fighters has pulled out due to having a broken finger, and I don't want to let the punters down. We have the venue and everything else is arranged. I just need a replacement fighter, and by the looks of you and judging by how you handled those two sorry looking pricks," he said, looking over to the now sheepish Frankie and JoJo, "you fit the bill. I will pay you two thousand pounds if you take the place of the guy that's pulled out, and you'll get another two thousand on top if you win."

"Who will I be fighting?"

"Tam Cranston, he is about fortyish and roughly your height and weight, he's experienced, but he's getting on a bit. He's had about 20 fights for me and won them all by knockout. If you're as good as Tweedle Dee and Tweedle Dum over there say you are," he was again, looking at his two damaged enforcers, "then I'm sure you're an even match. Do you think you can handle the fight? As a token of my goodwill and generosity, I will also knock off a grand from this little reprobate's tab, let's call it an introduction fee."

"What kind of fight will it be?"

"A full-scale boxing bout, consisting of as many three-minute rounds as it takes to have a winner. We don't do draws. There will also be a referee in the ring to ensure nothing too untoward happens like biting or kicking, but he will be there primarily to declare the winner after their opponent is knocked out or unable to continue."

"What about gloves?"

"Yes, there will be boxing gloves, I don't go in for those draconian bare-knuckle fights. The contest would be over too quickly without gloves, and that's just not entertainment for my guests? The winner takes the spoils. If you win this fight, I can guarantee you a better pay day for the next one, but let's not run before we can walk?"

"OK, I will take the fight. Where and when will it be?"

"In here, next Friday night, ten PM, you're now the top of the bill and the main attraction," scoffed, Big Jim.

"OK, now you listen to me, if I'm getting you out of a jam, and taking this fight then I want you to promise me that you'll keep those two wankers away from Johnny," Doug pointed towards Frankie and JoJo.

"OK," agreed Cassidy. "Just make sure you turn up, or there will be hell to pay."

"Don't you worry, I'll be here."

"Do I fucking look worried?" Then Big Jim smiled, at Johnny through gritted teeth, "You know the rules if there's a no-show, Son, don't you?"

"Yes," gulped Johnny, "I do."

Cassidy and Doug shook hands, and as he and Johnny were heading out the door, JoJo called after them, "I hope my big mate, Tam, knocks your fucking head right off, that will teach you for fucking with me."

"We'll see about that," laughed Doug, "maybe you can be my next opponent when I knock fuck out of your pal. That's only if you can get that big fat ginger arse into the ring." With that parting shot, they left the gym.

Once outside and out of earshot of anyone in the gym, Doug turned to Johnny, "What the fuck have you gotten me into? Have you seen this guy fight before? Is he any good? Do you think, I stand a chance against him?"

"Too many questions there. Cassidy's not the kind of guy you say no to and to answer your questions honestly, yes. I've seen him fight a few times. I won't lie to you, he's a good solid puncher, but most of the guys I've seen fight him have gone into the ring already beaten because they know his reputation. You don't, and he has far more to fear from you than you do from him. And yes, he's good, but no-where near as good as you. The answer to your other questions is yes again. I think you stand a great chance against him. Especially if way you handled Frankie and JoJo wasn't just luck."

"It wasn't luck."

"Good then that's settled, you'll win. Big Jim and all his buddies will have bets on Cranston. The guy he was fighting had next to no chance against him, he just had to turn up to win that fight. The guy was well past his best and had lost his last five fights. I should know, I bet on him to win them all, thinking he was due a win. That's why I'm in so fucking deep in debt to Cassidy, I didn't think I owed him that much though. The guy probably broke his own finger on purpose to get out of the fight. If you go in and suss him out in the first couple of rounds, see if you can find a weakness, you never know.

"Like I said, the way you took out Frankie and JoJo last night was pure class. If you can land a couple of those big punches on Cranston, it will give him something to think about. He's not used to getting hit back, he thinks he just turns up for a quick knockout and collects his money. He's in for a big surprise next Friday. Anyway, you're getting a couple of grand just for turning up."

"So, he says, but will he pay me the money?"

"Definitely, Cassidy cares about nothing more than his reputation as a hard man. He'll pay you OK, even if just to keep you onside, and remember, there's the little matter of him not wanting anybody knowing about his heavies getting fucked up last night. You heard what he said to you about keeping your mouth shut. Can you imagine that getting out in the streets the next time they go to frighten someone a bit bigger than me to pay up. I'm sure there'd be a few guys that owe him big money thinking what if and fancy their chances against JoJo. Remember Mike Tyson, everybody thought he was invincible, he won most of his fight before he even stepped into the ring. That was until he got knocked out by Buster Douglas, then everybody knew he was human and could be beaten. He hardly won another fight after that. And like Cassidy said, he deals in fear to get paid. Every dog has its day, as the old saying goes."

Chapter 7

"We had better start getting you into shape if you're going to have any chance against Cranston," Johnny said with a smile.

"What the fuck do you mean any chance? I thought you said this guy was past it?"

"Well, that was a lot of shit for a start just to boost your confidence, Tam Cranston maybe around about ten years older than you, but he's still a fucking brute. I've seen a few of his fights and he's won them all, but don't sweat. I've never seen him fight anyone as big as you, it's usually guys under six feet he fights. Cassidy always bets heavy on him, so it's never been in his interests to line him up against anyone with a chance of beating him."

"Then that begs the question, why would he want me in the ring with him?"

"Now that you mention it, it does sound a bit off. I did say to you, he never does anything that doesn't result in him making money. Maybe he thinks Cranston past it, and he's looking at you as his new cash cow. I just don't know how his brains wired, so until we can figure out the angle, let's still assume for now he wants Cranston to win."

"I have agreed to take this fight, but I'm not too sure about this being a regular gig."

"OK, let's just deal with this as a one off for the minute, but let's keep that to ourselves. I'm convinced you will find a weakness in Cranston, but you will still need to be in good shape, so no more booze for you until after the fight. You can start by going for a wee run tomorrow morning before our shift. I will see if I can find somewhere for you to train without any Cassidy's spies finding on how you're doing."

"OK, Mr Manager," replied Doug.

"I doubt there will be much money changing hands, betting on you to beat Cranston, even Cassidy's goons will be betting on him. We might get good odds on you to win."

Doug shrugged his shoulders, betting was not his thing, he didn't understand the odds thing. They watched a film on TV before bed, it was Star Wars.

The next morning, around five AM, whilst it was still very dark outside, Doug went for a run in Clissold Park, not too far from the flat in Brownswood where they were staying. The distance round the park was just over one mile. He ran around it six times, it only took him fifty minutes. He was taking it easy; he didn't want to knacker himself. He headed back to Johnny's place, and had a shower, and whilst he was doing this, Johnny made him three breakfast rolls with sausage and bacon and a big glass of fresh orange juice.

When they had finished breakfast, they went to work. It was a boring shift with nothing eventful happening. After work, they headed home and got changed. They jumped into Johnny's car, it started after a few attempts.

"I really need a better car, than this heap of junk, it's getting harder and harder to coax into life," Johnny said. He drove towards a gym called Semple's. An old pal of Johnny's, Eddie Semple, owned it, he was in this evening, as usual. Johnny introduced them.

"Doug, this is Eddie." They shook hands.

"Good to meet you," said Eddie, "so you're taking on Big Cranston then?"

"It didn't take long for the little secret to get out," interjected Johnny.

"Nothing stays a secret for long when there's money to be made from it," said Eddie.

"So, it seems, my little friend, Johnny here has managed to arrange it, pity it wasn't him fighting Cranston," said Doug.

"Even I would pay good money to see that," laughed Eddie.

Johnny looked indignant. "I am here you know, and I can hear you."

Doug looked around, it was a busy place, and there were around twenty geezers in tonight, all doing their own thing, some punching an assorted mix of punch bags, some of them were skipping. There was a couple of guys in the ring, sparring. Doug was shown to the changing room, and he got ready for some training.

When Doug returned, Eddie showed him the ropes. They spent a couple of hours there. Doug and Eddie lifted some weights, they did some skipping and for some reason, Doug took all this in his stride. He felt comfortable in these surroundings and he even enjoyed the weight lifting. The skipping came very easily to him, yet, he'd no recollections of ever doing it before.

"How about I get one of the guys to spar a couple of rounds with you now, Doug, are you up for that."

"Yes, I am, that would be good."

"Who'd you have in mind?" asked Johnny.

"Big Chick, him over there," Eddie pointed over to a corner where a guy was pounding a heavy bag dangling from the ceiling on a big thick chain. "Fancy your chances with him?"

"Why not," mused Doug.

Eddie shouted the guy over, he was a regular, and he was a big guy, nearly as big as Doug.

"Hi, Chick, do you want a few rounds of sparring with Doug here?" Eddie introduced them, "He's fighting Tam Cranston soon." Chick had heard some nasty things about Cranston, and he didn't think much of Doug's chances against him. He'd seen Doug doing some weights and punching the bag earlier.

"OK?" Chick said. "If you're sure you can handle it?" he said to Doug.

"Why wouldn't I?" asked, a now pissed off, Doug. "We'll see if you are."

Johnny was looking this massive guy up and down, and was mighty glad he wasn't going to have to fight him. He was huge, but Doug didn't look too intimidated though, which was a good thing. In fact, he looked angry. Trust this geezer to noise Doug up with that barbed comment. Doug and Chick climbed into the ring. Eddie spoke to them both, about tactics. Johnny wanted Doug's defences tested to the limits, and this massive guy looked just the man to test them, but this guy wasn't interested in any tactics. He was just keen to show Doug his knockout ability in the ring.

Eddie had decided on three, three-minute rounds with himself as the referee and Johnny as the timekeeper. There was a small bell at the side of the ring. Johnny rang the bell.

"OK, guys, round one," and they walked to the centre of the ring. Chick knew this would be over inside the first round. No way was this big lump going to give him any trouble, let alone last three rounds. He now wanted to show Doug how dangerous it was to think he could get into the ring with him and stand a chance. He had decided to put Doug out of his misery early on with a couple of big thundering blows. It was all right throwing punches at a stationary pad, but now he was in the ring with a fighter that would hit him back.

That was a costly mistake on Chick's part because as he went to land his first big punch, Doug saw it coming and moved his legs slightly towards the left and ducked under the oncoming right-hander. Chick was now off balance, and Doug caught him bang on the chin with an uppercut and down he went. Chick looked embarrassed as well as surprised. Lucky for him, Doug never put all his power into that punch. The big regular got quickly to his feet, Johnny had counted to six.

"Are you OK to continue?" asked Johnny.

A nod was enough for the round to continue, Chick had decided after that mistake he would change tact and try to get some body shots into Doug. He approached the centre of the ring to meet Doug, but before he knew what had hit him, he was on his arse again. Doug had hit him flush on the nose, poor Chick had been so annoyed at himself for going down so early, he was too eager to try and get Doug with some body shots. He'd forgotten the cardinal rule in boxing, always protect your head. The big guy's nose was bleeding badly, and he couldn't continue. Eddie managed to stem the bleeding.

They sat down and discussed what had occurred. Chick admitted, he'd had grossly underestimated Doug's ability, and asked him where he had learnt to fight like that, as he was now more than impressed.

"I don't know," answered Doug, "it just feels natural."

"Well, if you can hit me that easily, and I can assure you, I'm no mug, you've got a great chance against Cranston. I hear he's a bit of a handful, but you've got youth on your side, so good luck, mate." They shook hands and both headed to the changing rooms.

Whilst Doug was in getting showered, Johnny and Eddie discussed them coming back the next night, they'd also spoken a bit about the upcoming fight with Tam Cranston. Eddie had heard of him and was convinced he'd even saw him fight once before.

"Are you sure your mate is up to the task? If Cranston's the same guy I'm thinking of, then he's a fucking animal, and he takes no prisoners."

Johnny asked Eddie if he'd come across Big Jim Cassidy before.

"Yes, I think so, does he usually have a couple of gorillas with him?"

"Yes, their names are Frankie and JoJo, and take a guess who punched Frankie and JoJo out of their fucking shoes? It was Doug, and you just saw how he took apart your man Chick in the ring just now. So yes, I'm pretty sure he's up to the task. He just needs a little bit of refining, and some decent sparring to get him into shape for next Friday. Any help you can give in that direction would be brilliant.

Do you have anyone better than Chick, Doug can spar with?" Johnny practically begged.

"Wait here, let me go and make a couple of phone calls."

Doug came out of the changing rooms and saw that Eddie wasn't there.

"Where's your mate?"

"He's away into his office, he's trying to arrange a better class of sparring partner or two for tomorrow night."

Eddie returned, about fifteen minutes later, all sorted.

"I've just spoken with one of my mates, Brian, he's done some fighting at these events arranged by your man Cassidy and would you believe it? He's even fought Cranston. It was about five years ago, and he lost badly too, I might add, but he's coming here at eight PM tomorrow night, and says he'll spar a few rounds with you, Doug. He says he'll be able to let you know if you stand a chance against Cranston, he did ask if you were mad wanting to fight Cranston. I said no, you looked quite sane to me, but he says he'll make up his own mind when he meets you tomorrow."

Doug turned to Johnny and asked him, "What the fuck have you really gotten me into? The more I hear about this geezer, Cranston, the less I'm liking having to fight him."

"Don't worry, Doug," Johnny reassured him, "you'll take him, no problem. Remember Frankie and JoJo?"

"Yes, but I was an unknown quantity to them. I'm sure Cassidy will put Cranston straight, and I won't be going into the ring with Cranston without him knowing something about me."

"I'm not so sure Cassidy will let on about you, anyway let's not worry about them, and let them worry about you."

They got up to go, they shook hands with Eddie and were headed toward the door to go home. Eddie said he was going to lock up soon. The last couple of guys had not long finished their sparring match and were now in getting showered. *They were lightweights, at best,* thought Doug, he'd passed them on the way out of the changing rooms.

"See you both tomorrow night," shouted Eddie as they departed down the stairs.

As Johnny drove home, he noticed Doug wasn't saying much. They'd agreed earlier they were having a Chinese take away for supper. Johnny told him there was a good one not too far from the flat. They both had a breast of chicken curry with fried rice. They were home around half an hour later, Johnny put their meals onto plates, he had a beer and Doug had bottled water. After they had finished, Doug collected the plates and cutlery, he took them into the kitchen where he washed, dried and put them into the cupboard. He grabbed another beer and a water from the fridge, he took then into the sitting room.

Doug asked Johnny, to tell him as much as he could remember about all the times he'd seen Cranston fight. Johnny recounted the previous two fights. The first being a one rounder where Cranston had risen from his stool as soon as the first bell had sounded, rushed straight over to his opponent and he managed to thunder a few punches straight into the poor guy's face before he'd even managed to get his arse off his own stool. The fight was over inside twenty seconds, the guy was knocked out cold, and he had to be stretchered out.

"Thanks," sighed Doug, "that's really cheered me up. What about the latest one?"

"Well, this one lasted four rounds, the guy was quite a decent fighter, and his name was Rob Martins. I'd won on him before, and I thought he might just do Cranston as he was long overdue a defeat, but alas, it was not to be. Cranston tried the same tactic, but Rob had either seen Cranston's last fight or he'd heard about it. As soon as the bell for round one rung, Rob was off his stool right away, and he was prepared for the onslaught. He managed to ride out the storm because let me tell you, mate, Cranston was relentless. For the first two rounds, he was throwing everything but the kitchen sink at Rob. He even tried a couple of sneaky headbutts too. I've just remembered that about the cheating bastard. He will try and do that to you, so make sure, you keep an eye out for it."

"Thanks again, Johnny, you're a fucking Jedi master of deceit, do you know that? You could have shared these things about him before I agreed to take this fucking fight."

"Don't worry, big man, you'll be sound. Anyway, it's not all bad news, late in the third round, Rob somehow managed to land a powerful blow to Cranston's jaw. I'm sure I saw him wince, the bell saved him, and I can remember thinking the bell was a good bit early too. Someone was obviously keeping him safe, so the moral of this story is making sure that when you hurt him, it's early enough in the round to stop the time keeper, ringing the bell early, to save him."

"How did round four go?"

"Unfortunately, for Rob, that wee scare must have given Cranston a wakeup call that he needed to get Rob out there, and quickly, before he had the chance to land another big shot, it was all Cranston and Rob was hanging on. It looked like he would see the round out. But that wee, fat bastard time keeper, he made up for the short round three because he added enough time on round four for Cranston to finally knock Rob out. I reckon at least another thirty seconds were added on."

"What the fuck, Johnny?" said an exasperated Doug, "do you have any fucking good news, you'd like to share? It sounds to me, Cranston's not the only fucker I'll be fighting. As well as the timekeeper, I suppose the referee will be on his side too."

"Probably," conceded a sheepish Johnny. "He can have as many people on his side as he wants, it won't make a blind bit of difference, Doug, when you knock the prick out, and I am convinced you will."

The next night at Semple's, Doug met Brian, the guy, Eddie had arranged a sparring session with. He was a solid looking guy, about six feet tall, and around eighteen stone. They got changed, and headed into the ring. In the first round, Brian was tasked with trying to find weaknesses in Doug's defences, it proved pretty futile. Brian never managed to hit Doug with any purpose.

The second round, it was Doug's chance to see if he could find any way past Brian's defences, he had a raw power that Brian didn't possess. Doug managed to connect with a few punches and jabs. He found, quite early in that round, he could most likely knock him out without too much difficulty, but he didn't want to dispatch him in this round.

In the third round, Doug had decided to see if he was right, and to find out just how good Brian's defence was. As they both had on head protectors, Doug decided he was going to throw some heavy punches Brian's way. He successfully landed a very big punch that knocked Brian off his feet, he was momentarily stunned, and stayed down for a ten count. He was helped up by Doug and Eddie. He was a bit unsteady on his feet, he hadn't been hit that hard, not for a long time, probably not since the Cranston fight. Doug had a powerful punch, and Brian never saw it coming, it was well disguised.

It was decided by Eddie that the remainder of the session should be with Doug working out on the heavy bag. Brian had gone into the changing rooms for a shower, when he returned he went over to speak with the guys.

"I've just called one of my friends, Syd, he's a bit younger than me and a far better boxer than I am. He says he will come in tomorrow night, and give Doug a better workout, if you like?"

"Yes, that would be great," said Johnny. "The better prepared he is for Cranston, the better his chances are of winning. Can Syd be relied upon to keep his mouth shut? I don't want Cassidy finding out how well Doug's getting on."

"Yes, he's sound as a pound, he'll not tell anyone anything about this."

"Good, I don't care if you guys all get a piece of the action, they're offering odds of 4/1 against Doug to beat Cranston."

Eddie asked Brian how he rated Doug since he'd already fought Cranston albeit four years ago. Could he gauge in the three rounds if Doug had a chance?

"I certainly don't remember Cranston having the power Doug has, and if you look at it this way, Cranston's four years older now, so I reckon, Doug's definitely got a chance all right." They all arranged to meet back here in the gym the next night at eight PM.

Johnny and Doug had the next day off. Doug had a bit of a lie in until nine AM, then went for a run. He didn't go to the park this time. He went for a run around the estate to see if anything jogged his memory, he felt good in the ring last night, he ran for about an hour, but couldn't seem to recognise anywhere. This all seemed very strange to him, that they could remember being in the hospital, but not before then. Also who were the strangers that came to visit him in the hospital? He was convinced it must have been some elaborate con, he couldn't fathom exactly what it was they were after from him, though, why couldn't he remember anything before the hospital? Doug arrived back at the flat, Johnny had eggs, bacon and sausages in the frying pan.

"Breakfast will be ready in ten minutes. You've got time for a quick shower."

It was a lazy day, they stayed in and watched some TV, about four PM, they had an early supper, and they watched some more TV until it was time to head to the gym at seven-thirty PM. When they arrived, Brian was already there with his mate, Syd, he was about six foot four tall, and as big as a house. Johnny thought he looked mid to late twenties, and he looked in good shape. Brian introduced them all, they spoke for a short while and discussed some methods of sparring and then the three protagonists got changed, and climbed into the ring.

Johnny had spoken on the way to the gym about the need for Doug to get some ring time, under his belt. He'd suggested that Doug not go for a quick big knockout should Syd not be as good as Brian had suggested. He wanted him to try and box a bit and get the feel of a boxing ring before his big fight with Cranston. Doug agreed as he thought this was a good idea.

So again, as the previous night, Johnny acted as timekeeper, and Eddie as the referee. They were going for five rounds tonight. Johnny rang the bell to start round one. As Doug had expected, Syd came straight for him, Brian must have told him to get some revenge for his knockdown last night. Doug seemed to know how to deal with this and effortlessly dodged Syd's big early bomb punches. He also managed to block an uppercut, he weaved and bobbed about the ring, and made Syd chase him a bit then he changed tact. He went into the centre of the ring, and kept the big Syd in tight and as they moved apart, Doug caught him in the ribs, with a solid punch, just hard enough for Syd to realise Doug could punch a bit too as well as block. This was an early lesson for Syd to stay back a bit and not rush in, unless he wanted another sore one in the ribs.

Doug managed to land a couple on Syd's head but nothing too hard. Halfway through round two, Doug thought he could easily knock Syd out if he needed to, but as he'd discussed with Johnny earlier, he fought out the five rounds winning them all comfortably, only landing a couple of semi-hard punches around Syd's head guard, just to keep him alert.

They removed their gloves and shook hands. Syd complimented Doug on his performance and asked him where he learned to box like that.

"You certainly know your way around the ring. You read most, if not all, my punches."

"I can honestly say to you, I'm not too sure, but it felt good in there."

Eddie asked them, "Are you up for some more tomorrow night?"

"Yes," agreed Syd, "if you want, I can bring along one of my other pals, Andre, he's a bit younger than me and maybe can give you an even sterner test."

"That sounds good to me," replied Doug.

They went and showered, and afterward, they all sat and spoke about Doug's upcoming fight with Cranston. Syd said he'd seen the fight Brian had with Cranston.

"And no disrespect mate," he said, turning to Brian, "but I think Doug may give him a harder fight."

"That's cool, mate," said Brian, "I agree, but it's no good just giving him a harder fight, we need you to beat the bastard," he said looking at Doug. "I think, seeing you tonight, you are solid in defence, and you'll will need that, as he'll come right at you from the off. He's not as young as he once was, and he won't want a long fight for the obvious reasons. Once he sees your size, and that you're a good ten years younger than him, he'll want you out of there as quickly as possible. But, from what I saw in there earlier, I'm sure you can handle that, and with your power, you can hurt him, and that's what you will need to do, the sooner the better. If you can land a decent punch early on, that will give him something to think about, it will also stop him rushing in, that's the way he always likes to fight. A big early landed punch should, at least, slow him down a bit. I know from my three rounds last night and I'm sure Syd will agree, you winded him a couple of times. You've definitely got the ammunition to hurt Cranston, and I could see you were still holding back a bit, you won't get away with that with Cranston."

"Oh, don't worry, I've no intention of holding anything back with Cranston. I'm just trying to build up a bit of stamina. I don't know how long the fight will last, but I can assure you, if I get the chance to knock this prick out, in the first round, then that will suit me just fine. There's no gain, for me to knock any you guys out, in the first or second round. I'll probably need all the help I can get from you guys."

It was time to hit the road homeward. They all shook hands, and agreed tomorrow was another day, Doug and Johnny left and headed home. Doug was getting up early in the morning to go for a run.

When they arrived back at the house, Johnny made them macaroni and cheese for their supper.

"This will give you stamina," he said.

When they had finished, and the dishes had been cleared away, they watched a film on TV. This time, it was Rambo, staring Sly Stallone, there was plenty of action in it. When it finished, Doug, headed for bed. He'd set his alarm for five AM. The next morning, when it went off, he shook himself awake, and went for a run. He made his way to the park again, this time he ran around it four times. He felt no ill effects of yesterday's run, or last night's visit to the gym.

Once back home, Johnny had the breakfast on the go. Doug was quite hungry after his run, he had four sausages, three rashers of bacon, two fried eggs and some orange juice. He could get used to this, he thought. They got ready for work, their shift started at ten AM, ten till six PM. They both agreed this was the worst shift, there were all sorts of tradesmen working on the construction sites, and you couldn't skive at all during the day. You could take it in shifts to grab a couple of hours sleep on night-time shifts, but not on days.

They were taking over from an old guy named Bob, and another newbie on the team, he called Justin. He was early twenties, and he didn't look the type to stick around too long, probably using this, as a stop gap until he found something better. Johnny couldn't see him lasting long. They had nothing to report.

Once Bob and Justin had left, they had a brew, and then set off for a wander around the site. Johnny was telling Doug how easy it was, to get some extra cash, there was always a moneymaking opportunity. He'd gotten to know most of the tradesmen on a first name basis, they'd usually turn up on most the sites he'd worked on, an odd time. They'd need something or other, for private jobs, known as homers, usually from the secure stores area.

Johnny would often let them help themselves, and he would turn off the CCTV camera. He hoped one or two of them needed some kit, as they always paid him handsomely for turning a blind eye. They weren't employed to stop the workers thieving. Their job was to stop the materials from getting stolen at night-time, or weekends by people breaking into the site and they were also responsible for preventing the big plant hire equipment, getting stolen or vandalised.

During the walk round, Johnny noticed Stan. He was a joiner, and he'd gotten some stuff from him before. He hoped he needed some today. He was in luck, Johnny introduced Doug to Stan.

"All right, Johnny, how's tricks?"

"I'm good, mate, how are you?"

"Tip top, can I have a word in private, Johnny?" he asked.

"You can say anything in front of Doug. He's more a friend than a workmate."

"OK then, I need to make twelve sheets of 10mm plyboard and a couple of worktops, two base units, and two sinks complete with taps disappear from the stores and re-appear in the back of my van tonight."

"No problem, I happen to have my magic wand with me today, we're on until six. Come and see me when you're done, and I'll make sure the camera is off."

"Same deal as usual?"

"It sure is, buddy."

"OK, I'll see you just after five PM then," replied Stan.

Doug and Johnny continued their walk around. Once they were out of earshot of any eave's droppers, Doug asked him how much stuff goes missing?

"Quite a fair bit, but not too much that would cause any suspicion to come our way."

"OK, it sounds like you got us covered."

They headed back to the security office. On route, they were intercepted by the site manager, Brian Cooper.

"Hi, guys, everything good with you two?"

"Yes, all good. How about you?"

"I'm good too, but I need to be out of here at three PM today, I have a meeting with the architect. Can you be on the lookout for a delivery of two more MEWP's? They were supposed to be delivered this morning but my purchasing department forgot to place the order. I need them to be here for the roofing guys for first thing tomorrow morning. I spoke with a guy named Andrew at the plant hire company, and he has promised me one of his drivers will deliver them between four and five today."

"Yes, that's cool, we'll sign them in. We're here until six o'clock today," said Johnny.

"OK thanks, and can you make sure they're left around the back, next to the new building on the left-hand side?"

"Yes, no problem, mate," said Johnny.

They left the site office, and went into their security office.

"Time for a cuppa?" suggested Johnny. Doug filled the kettle from a tap in the small but functioning kitchen area. He plugged it in and pushed in the button. "I used to go to college when I was younger," said Johnny. "I was studying Architecture. Brian could have been coming to meet me today if things hadn't turned to rat shit for me, but let's not dwell on the past eh, always best foot forward."

Doug made them a coffee each, there was a packet of cheap supermarket brand custard creams in the drawer next to the teaspoons. He grabbed them and took six out of the packet, three each, he twisted the packed closed again, and put it back into the drawer.

"Hey, Johnny, look what I found," Doug said as he handed him his biscuits.

"These biscuits are shite," he replied, "but they're not as bad tasting, if you dip them in your coffee."

"That's fucking disgusting," said Doug as he threw his straight into his mouth. He was now laughing so hard that he ended up spluttering crumbs everywhere because one of Johnny's biscuits had broken in two, falling into his coffee, and Johnny was trying to fish it out with his fingers.

Johnny laughed too, "I take that back, they're still shite biscuits."

The rest of the day was uneventful until the MEWP delivery driver appeared. Johnny gave Doug the delivery note to sign, whilst he directed the driver to where Brian had wanted them sited. Doug signed the delivery note as required and the driver also asked him to print his name too. He printed his name as B Cooper, after all he was the one that hired them.

The site started to empty from about four PM onwards. All the workers had to come into the security office, and signed out the contractors' book by five PM. All were gone except Stan and his mate, they came into the office, and signed out. Johnny handed Stan the key to the secure cage, and then he pulled the plug on the camera, looking over toward it. Stan handed him some money. When Stan left the office, Johnny looked at the money, and there was one hundred pounds. Three twenty-pound notes and four ten-pound notes.

Johnny took fifty and handed the other fifty to Doug, and said, "It's been a pleasure doing business with you."

Doug put the money in his pocket. A couple of minutes later, Stan tooted his horn. Johnny went out and Stan handed the keys back. Johnny let them out of the vehicle gate, then closed and padlocked it. He went back inside and put the keys back onto their hook, in the key cabinet, in the security room. Johnny plugged the security camera back in, it took about a minute or two for it to flicker back into life and then the picture steadied itself.

"Won't anybody notice the camera was off for half an hour?" asked Doug.

"It's never been an issue before, it could have failed because the generator was playing up. Don't get yourself stressed, mate, these things happen all the time. Who's going to miss a couple of bits of wood? This site is massive, there is always wastage. The skips are full of off cuts, no hassle will come our way, trust me, this is not my first rodeo."

They both laughed, "Time for another cuppa before changeover."

Doug filled the kettle to make them a coffee, Johnny couldn't remember who was on tonight, he'd gotten a rota, but he never memorised it. He knew his and Doug's shifts and unless there were any guys leaving or calling in sick for the next two weeks, it was very unlikely they would not be split up. When the coffee was ready, they had decided, not to have any more of those cheap biscuits.

At five minutes to six, the two guys on duty next arrived. Johnny knew them both. He called them the two Ronnie's, Ronnie Sweeney and Ron Baker. They had a quick hand over, nothing to report.

"All quiet on the western front," said Johnny.

He drove them straight home, the car starting after only a couple of attempts. They had a light snack of a pot noodle and a cheese sandwich. They'd have supper after the gym tonight. An hour or so later, they headed over to the Semple's Gym.

Chapter 8

Between them, Mary and Julie managed to settle Grace down for a nap.

"OK, now you two go get your heads down for a sleep, I'll keep an ear open for Grace," Robert suggested. So, off Mary and Julie headed to bed. He was deep in thought, where would Doug go to? He couldn't just disappear off the face of the earth. He must be living somewhere, how was he for money? He knew from Julie that he'd taken twelve hundred pounds from his own sock drawer, but how long would that last? He'd decided if Doug hadn't showed up by tomorrow lunchtime, he was going to the police. He wasn't too sure if they could help, but it was clutching at straws time, and he had to do something.

Although he couldn't show it to Mary or Julie, he was really starting to worry about Doug's fragile state of mind, and the aggression he had shown to both Julie and him. What if he hurt himself? Or God forbid, someone else? He knew Doug could look after himself, but the problem, as he saw it, was Doug just wasn't himself.

About three hours later, he was distracted from his thoughts by Grace crying, this also woke Julie and Mary. Julie boiled a kettle and made Grace a bottle of milk, whilst Robert made the three of them a brew. After they had their hot drinks, they decided they would have a take away dinner. Robert went to the local Chinese, he bought two portions of spare ribs, two chicken curries and two fried rice for the three of them to share.

When he got back home, Mary had the plates and cutlery ready. They ate their supper, mostly in silence. Robert cleared up and washed the dishes and forks and put them away. He told them of his plan to go and see the police, if Doug hadn't been in touch by tomorrow. They all agreed it was a good idea.

When it was bedtime for Grace, Julie and Mary bathed her. Robert had decided he was going for a drive, and then he was going to pop over and see Andrew and Jason, let them know the up to date situation, and see if Andrew had any clearer thoughts as to where his brother might go. They were really close, and always seemed to get on. Robert had called Andrew from his mobile phone to ask if it was OK to pop round.

"Of course, you can come over." Andrew lived with his partner, Jason, they had a nice house. Robert and Mary had known, from a young age, that Andrew was gay and when he told them, it was no big surprise. They had accepted it, without question, as had Doug, as long as he was happy, that was the main thing. Andrew and Jason seemed to be very happy.

Jason was an assistant manager for a security recruitment company. Unfortunately, Jason's dad, Gary, was not as understanding and supportive as Robert and Mary were. When Jason told his parents that he was gay, his mum, Sheila, was fine, she'd had an inclination for a few years, but his dad Gary, went berserk, and threw him out and called him some very hurtful names. They hadn't spoken a word to each other in nearly ten years. His dad was known to have a volcanic temper, as Jason and Sheila used to call it, he could erupt anytime, without warning, over the slightest thing, and he did so regularly.

Sheila often visited, her son and Andrew albeit without Gary. She always told him, when she visited them, as Jason was their only child, she thought in time, one day, her husband would eventually come around, but as of yet, he hadn't. *Such a pity,* she thought. He seemed to be a bit mellower these past couple of years, maybe that day was getting nearer, she hoped and he would finally accept their son for the man he was. He didn't erupt much nowadays.

Sheila knew he missed his son, but he was still not admitting it. She was in visiting the boys when Robert arrived, she was just leaving, and they had a quick friendly chat. She asked him to give her best regards, to Mary and Julie. Jason had told her about Doug's accident, and subsequent disappearance. She had met him and Julie a few times, and had liked them both instantly. Robert thanked her and assured her he would pass on her regards.

After Sheila left, Jason put the kettle on and made them all a coffee. They discussed Doug, and places he maybe goes to. Robert couldn't help but feel sad for Jason's situation with his dad. Jason was a lovely guy, and he was thankful his own son had found a loving partner, his dad was missing out. It was his loss, maybe in time, he will see the error of his ways and let his son back in his life.

Jason said he would ask around to see if Doug's name came up within his company books, Robert thanked him. They discussed the places Robert had been to and he told them about leaving his mobile number, with the guy form Doug's gym. Andrew asked his dad if he wanted him to go the police with him the next day, but Robert said, "No thanks." He would rather Andrew kept as normal a routine as he could on the off chance Doug tries to get in touch with him at his work.

Robert finished his coffee, bid them both good night and headed home. Julie was asleep, on the floor, in a sleeping bag in the spare room with Grace next to her in her crib. Robert told Mary of his visit to Andrew and Jason's place and about meeting Sheila. He passed on her regards.

"Oh, how's she getting on? Is there any sign of Jason's dad coming around?"

"She's good, and no such luck on that front, just yet. It's such a pity, Jason's a great guy."

"Yes, I was thinking that myself earlier, but unfortunately, people are strange, especially when it comes to beliefs, but you never know though, stranger things have happened."

It was now ten-thirty PM, they went to bed hoping upon hope to be awoken during the night by Doug, they weren't.

Next morning, Robert, after a shower and shave, went to the local supermarket and bought some fresh milk, bread and a packet of biscuits when he got back there was mad panic, there was an ambulance, and a police car in the drive. Mary and Julie were hysterical, his heart sank, he thought something must have happened, to Doug, but it wasn't, it was Grace.

"Oh my God, what's happened?" asked Robert.

"When Julie got up to make Grace her bottle, she was unresponsive, we both tried to wake her but we couldn't. I tried to call you but you'd left your phone charging in the sitting room. I called an ambulance. Oh my God, Robert, I think there something seriously wrong with Grace."

Just then, there was a commotion in the house. Julie had collapsed. The paramedics put Julie on a stretcher and lifted the crib, with Grace in it and left for the hospital with their blue lights, and sirens on. Robert and Mary went into the house. Mary ran up the stairs in tears, Robert spoke to the police officers.

"Do you know what's happened?" asked Robert to one of the police officers.

"Please take a seat, we need to ask you some questions."

"What kind of questions?"

"We just need to try and get some basic information, how old is the baby?"

Robert told him the baby's name is Grace, and she's six weeks old.

"Are you related to Grace?"

"Yes, she's my granddaughter."

"What about Grace's mother what's her name?"

"Her name is Julie, she's my daughter in-law."

"When did you and your wife last see your granddaughter?"

"Last night, around eight PM. Julie, put Grace down to sleep around that time. I went out to visit my son, Andrew."

"Is he Grace's dad?"

"No, my other son, Doug, is her dad."

"Can we speak to him?"

"Unfortunately, he's missing."

A quizzical look appeared on the officer's face. "How long has he been missing?"

"Look, son, I have already reported my son is missing to DCI Scott Craig. I think I have answered enough of your questions. I need to see to my wife, and then we'll need to get to the hospital."

"I know this is difficult for you, sir, but its best we get as much information as we can whilst it's still fresh in your mind."

"I'm sorry, but I disagree. I think this is getting out of hand now, what kind of information do you need right this minute? My granddaughter, and daughter in law have just been taken to hospital, unconscious, my son is missing, my wife is upstairs breaking her heart, and you're giving me the third degree. You're acting like there's been a crime committed here. I will need to ask you to leave."

The police officer, PC Harper, reluctantly, agreed with Robert, "I'm sorry sir, I'm just trying to get some information, but we can do this another time. I'll let you and your wife get to the hospital to see Julie and Grace. I hope everything turns out OK with them. I will speak with detective Robinson, and see if there's any update on your son, Doug."

Robert thanked the PC. Robert then showed him and his colleague out. He went upstairs, to comfort Mary and make sure she was OK. She'd only just managed to compose herself; it had been a huge shock to her finding Grace unconscious, then seeing Julie collapse. They were going to head over to the hospital, they got into their car, and he drove to the hospital. When they arrived, Robert asked the main reception, where Julie and Grace had been taken? They were shown to a private waiting room. After about fifteen minutes, a doctor came in and calmly informed them that their precious little baby granddaughter had passed away, most likely from Sudden Infant Death Syndrome, or SIDS as it was commonly known.

They were devastated by this shocking news. Robert tried and failed miserably to console his wife, he was only just keeping himself in check, and he asked the doctor about Julie's condition.

Julie was still unconscious and had not yet, been told about her daughter's death. The doctor said he was going to find out the latest update, regarding Julie, and said he would come back to see them ASAP. He left then in the private room, and promised he would have some tea and coffee brought in for them. When he left the room, Robert called Andrew and told him the dreadful news about Grace. Andrew said he was coming straight over to the hospital, he arrived twenty-five minutes later and he hugged his mum.

"Oh my God, we've certainly been put through the mill this past few weeks. I take it there's still no word about Doug?"

"No, we haven't heard a word, Son, poor Julie."

"How's she going to cope with this?"

"I've no idea," sobbed Mary, "but we'll all be here for her."

Andrew called Jason, and told him the bad news.

"Do you want me to come to the hospital?" he asked.

"No, thanks for the kind offer, I will stay here awhile, and I'll call you when I'm coming home, I love you, see you later."

"I love you too. I'll call my mum, and let her know, she keeps asking me when she's going to meet Grace." He rang off, just as the doctor returned. He informed them that Julie was now awake.

"She's been asking to see Grace, she hasn't been told of her passing yet."

Robert introduced his son, Andrew.

"I'm very sorry about your daughter, sir," said the doctor.

"Grace was my niece; my brother, Doug was her dad."

"Oh, I'm sorry for jumping to the wrong conclusion."

"Its fine, you weren't to know."

"Is he on his way here?"

"My brother is missing, he's had a serious car accident, and has vanished, for the time being, he seems to have lost his memory."

"I'm very sorry to hear that," replied the doctor. "We think it best if Julie has some family in the room when we tell her about Grace, is that OK?"

"Yes, that's probably best," said Robert, "lead the way and we'll follow."

As soon as they all walked into Julie's room, by the look on her face, she knew there was more bad news coming, but she wasn't expecting to hear her beautiful daughter was dead. There was an almighty scream from her that rocked them all, and then she fell silent for a minute, then she sobbed and sobbed and was inconsolable.

"What have I done to deserve this?" she cried, "A few months ago, I had everything I've ever dreamed of, now I have absolutely nothing. No husband and now little Grace has gone. What am I to do? I don't want to live anymore." Mary hugged her, as tight as she has ever hugged anyone.

"Listen, love, Doug will come back soon."

"I don't want that bastard back, this is all his fault."

The doctor, with the help of a nurse, managed to get her sedated, then he took them back to the private room. They sat down, and had some tea, and coffee that was brought in by a young nurse.

"That was the grief talking," the doctor, said to Mary. "Julie feels as if her life is over right now, I wish I could tell you this will soon pass, but I can't, everyone is different, but given a few days for this to sink in. Hopefully, her heartache will lessen a little and she may have a different outlook."

"We're all heartbroken," she replied.

"Yes, I'm sorry, I'm sure, you all are," he gave them some leaflets about SIDS and tried to convince them that it was nobody's fault, these things happen. "Usually, you have a healthy baby and then suddenly, without any warning, the baby is found unresponsive, usually dead, even with all the data they have collected, these deaths are unexplained. There's no rhythm or reason to the deaths, this is the hardest thing for a parent to comprehend. Often, they feel guilt, and resentment, even anger."

"It looks like anger and resentment are taking hold of Julie just now," said Andrew, "surely, with all the cases of SIDS, you have some idea how this can be prevented?"

"Unfortunately, no, we don't. We're no closer to understanding this than we were ten years ago. This is a worldwide mystery, not just here in England."

Chapter 9

Robert suggested Andrew take his mum home, he was going to call Julie's mum, Dot and go collect her and bring her to the hospital. In all the commotion, and as it had all happened so quickly, none of them thought to call her. Mary went with Andrew. This was not the kind of phone call anyone wants to have to make, but he managed to get a hold of Dot, and he relayed to her the sad news. She, like them, was crushed that her one and only granddaughter was dead, and her poor daughter was now in the hospital, without her husband and daughter.

Robert arranged to collect her in an hour, this would give her time to get home from work and get changed out of her uniform. She worked in the local superstore. He had a quick look in on Julie, she was still sleeping. *God help her*, he thought, he was distraught about losing Grace. How the hell was Julie going to cope? He just wished, more than ever now, that Doug would show up.

Robert left the hospital soon after. He headed over to Dot's house, they hugged on the doorstep and she invited him in. He told her he'd looked in on Julie just before leaving the hospital, and that she was still sedated and would probably be asleep for a good while.

"In that case would you like a coffee?" Dot asked.

"Yes, please, that would be great."

Dot put the kettle on and made them a cuppa, she asked him, if he wanted something to eat. He gladly accepted, it seemed ages since he last eaten anything. She made him a cheese and tomato sandwich. He told her of Julies outburst about not wanting to see Doug again, he omitted the swear word.

"The doctor, told us this was probably a mixture of grief and anger." Robert gave her the leaflet about SIDS. Dot looked at it, but couldn't take in its contents. She was still numb about the loss of her granddaughter.

"Listen, Robert, Doug has been very good to Julie, and me. I think the world of him, I'm sure if Doug turned up right now, Julie would be the first in line to welcome him back." Robert thanked her for the kind words about his missing son.

She asked him, "What happens now with Grace's body?"

"I'm not too sure, I suppose we can ask at the hospital."

"How's Mary coping?" she asked.

"Much the same as you, I think, it's a terrible shock to us all, but I believe we need to try and put brave faces on for Julie's sake."

"Yes," she agreed.

They finished their coffees and headed to the hospital, they arrived and went to ward six. They spoke with one of the nurses at their station and were told Julie was still asleep. They went into her room, it was number three. Julie was, indeed, still sleeping, Dot went over, and hugged her daughter, tears were streaming down her cheeks.

"Do you think she can hear us?"

"I'm not sure, but let's assume, she can."

They pulled a chair up to either side of her bed and Dot started telling Julie that everything might look bleak just now, but things will get better.

"It's a crying shame, what's just happened to little Grace, but we need you to get well enough to get home and we can start helping you rebuild your life."

They stayed for about an hour and a half. When they were leaving, they both kissed Julie goodbye, and promised they would be back tomorrow. They went to see if they could have a word with a doctor to discuss Julie, and to ask how they would go about arranging a funeral for Grace. They managed to see the doctor Robert had spoken with earlier, his name was Dr Davidson. He informed them they were going to keep Julie sedated until the morning. They thanked him. He told them the death certificate was signed and it was SIDS that was the cause of death. He went to fetch it from his office. He gave it to Dot and told them they would need to speak with an undertaker, and have them collect the remains.

"They will arrange the burial or cremation. Hopefully Julie will have peaceful night tonight," Dr Davidson said

"Can I come back in the morning, and see Julie?" Dot asked.

"Yes, that will be fine, but please wait until after ten AM, doctors' rounds will be completed by then. What we'll probably do if Julie's still upset is put Julie on a mild dose of Citalopram. It's an anti-depressant."

Robert and Dot both thanked Doctor Davidson, again.

As they got to the car, they decided to head for Robert and Mary's house. Robert called Mary, to let her know they were on their way. When they arrived, about half an hour later, Andrew and Jason we already there. They all hugged one another. Mary made them a brew and brought out some sandwiches and biscuits. Andrew, asked his dad, if Julie was awake when they were at the hospital.

"No, she was still sedated, the doctor has told us he will assess her in the morning and if she's still really upset, then he will prescribe her an anti-depressant. He has also given Dot Grace's death certificate, it was SIDS," Robert replied.

This was a sombre moment, Mary and Dot had tears streaming down their cheeks.

"If it's OK with you all," said Andrew, "Jason and I have discussed this, and we would like to arrange the funeral. We've both booked the day off work tomorrow. It's the least we can do in the circumstances. I know if Doug were here, he'd do it, but he's not here, and as his brother, I would like to take some of the burden off you guys."

They all agreed in principal.

"Let's see if Doug turns up, and if not, we'll speak with Julie tomorrow, if she's up to it." Andrew said.

Dot handed the death certificate to Andrew. "Have you not heard a thing from Doug?"

"Not a thing at all," replied Robert. "I've decided to go looking for him again in the morning. As we need, more than ever now, to try and find him, he'll need to know Grace has died. I realise, I probably won't find him, but I need to keep trying. How can a silly disagreement with us end with Doug walking out on his entire family without so much as a bye or leave?"

"Where could he be?" asked Dot.

"If only we knew," said Mary, "Robert's been all over town, looking for him. Andrew told them he and Jason, have asked everyone they know to be on the look-out for him."

"How's he surviving?" asked Dot.

"We have no idea, he took twelve hundred pounds from his bedroom cabinet, but he never took his bank card. We're mystified," said Mary.

When the brew was finished, Andrew, Jason and Dot left together. Jason was driving, and they dropped her off at her home, it was one the way to their house. Before they left, Dot had agreed to call Mary from the hospital in the morning.

Chapter 10

At eight-thirty the next morning, they Googled funeral directors. There was one local to them. Jason and Andrew went there, it turned out it was a family run business. It was a first for them both. They spoke to a woman on the reception desk, and she showed them to a lovely little waiting room. She told them one of the undertakers will be with them very soon, and she asked if they wanted a tea or coffee but they both declined as they had not long had one.

There were some leaflets on the table, they were browsing through them when the door opened and in came one of the undertakers, he introduced himself, as Brendan, and they introduced themselves too.

"What can I do for you, gents?" he asked.

"My niece, Grace, has just died, and we need to arrange her funeral, but neither of us has done this before and we don't know where to start," Andrew answered.

"That's not a problem, I can talk you through the whole thing, it's not as scary as you would imagine, and how old was grace?"

"She was only six weeks old."

"Oh my goodness, that's dreadful. Have you got the death certificate?"

"Yes," said Andrew, and he handed it to Brendan.

He perused it, "SIDS, that's dreadful. The first thing you need to do now is go to the registry office. It's in Islington Town Hall on Upper Street and register her death. This is fairly straightforward, you'll be given a green form. You need to bring that to me, then I can fill in the correct forms. Have you thought on a casket for Grace?"

"No, we haven't really given much thought to anything like that yet. We decided we would try and take the burden off my parents and my sister in-laws mum by arranging Grace's funeral. As my brother, Doug, Grace's dad, is missing." He gave Brendan a brief run-down of the events of the past few months, culminating with, Doug's disappearance.

"My word, your family have certainly not had their troubles to seek, have they?"

"We certainly haven't," agreed Andrew.

"Well, let's have a look at the various options. For baby caskets, we have some really gorgeous wicker coffins. These are quite new on the market. I think these are a better option than a wooden casket. If you come with me, I can show you a couple of different ones to choose from." Brendan showed them, a couple of different styles he had.

"Oh, they are lovely," Andrew and Jason both agreed when they saw them. Andrew asked Brendan if he could take a couple of photos on his phone to show the family the options.

"Yes, that's fine," replied Brendan.

Andrew took four photos. The three of them went back into the waiting room, Brendan got some details from them, and they spoke about the type of funeral service that would be best suited to them. As they weren't overly religious, Brendan advised them that humanist funerals were more common nowadays.

"Where a celebrant, rather than a priest or minister, will conduct the funeral service, this may be better for the family and can include as little or as much of Grace's short time here on earth, as you like. I have a celebrant guy I use quite frequently, I can contact him for you, if you want," Brenan said.

Andrew told him he would get back to him on that aspect, of the funeral. He was a little out of his depth and didn't want to commit to this until they'd discussed this with Julie and their parents. Brendan asked which hospital Grace was in. Andrew told him. He said he would call the mortuary at the hospital, and find out when he could collect Grace. He informed them he would bring her here to be prepared for burial and that he would call Andrew when that was arranged.

They thanked Brendan for his assistance and they left. Once they were back in the car, Andrew said, "I'm glad we don't have to do this very often."

Jason agreed it wasn't the best way to spend your morning. They headed to Hackney Central Train Station, and parked the car. They had decided on a train to the registry office would be less stressful that driving around looking for a parking space at this time of day. The journey time to Islington was only six minutes, the registration of death was really straightforward. The woman that dealt with them was amazingly helpful, she practically filled in the form, and all Andrew had to do was sign it. They were in and out with the certificate, and the green form for Brendan in just under an hour.

They went to costa, and had a coffee and a sandwich. They were pretty exhausted, but the worst was over for now. They got the train back to Hackney, and they were back in the car less than two hours after they'd parked their car. Andrew drove them, back to the undertakers, Brendan was out. They left the form with the receptionist, she assured them she would pass it to Brendan.

They got back into the car, Andrew again driving, headed to his parents' house. It was now just gone twelve-thirty, they relayed, the information that Brendan the undertaker had given them, and told them about the visit to Islington to register Grace's death, and then back to drop off another form to the undertaker.

"It sounds like you two have had a busy and productive morning," said Mary.

Andrew showed them the photos he'd taken of the baby burial baskets. They all agreed one of those would be much better than a small white wooden coffin.

"Let's hope Julie and Dot prefer this too," said Robert.

"Speaking of Dot, have you heard from her today?" asked Andrew.

"No, not yet," replied his mum while she was on the way to put the kettle on. Whilst she was in the kitchen, the house phone rang. Robert jumped up, and answered it. It was Dot, she said she was still at the hospital, and told him Julie had been awake, but she was still very distraught and despondent.

"She'd asked to see Grace, and the doctor had arranged to have a nurse take us down to the hospital mortuary. It was very distressing seeing Grace's dead body. Julie got really upset again, and was sobbing uncontrollably, which was to be expected. The nurse and I managed to comfort her a little. When we got her back to her room, the doctor gave her some medication to calm her down a little, she's now asleep again. The doctor has told me she should be all right in a day or two and that she will most likely be released tomorrow, or the day after. How did the boys get on at the undertakers?"

They've only just recently gotten here, they got on fine, and they've even managed to register Grace's death at Islington Registry Office. Without doing that, we couldn't have her funeral. We've much to discuss, how about I head over to the hospital to collect you, and bring you here?"

"I suppose that will be OK as Julie's asleep. The doctor said she will be until around five PM. I don't want to put you to too much trouble, you've been doing enough running about, as it is."

"Of course, it's not too much trouble. I'll be there in twenty-five minutes; I'll get you at the main entrance."

"OK, Robert, I'll be outside waiting on you, and thanks again. I don't know if Julie and I would get through this without all the help you lot have given us.

"We're all family, and we're in this together, Dot.

"I'll see you soon," she hung up the phone.

Chapter 11

Robert drank his coffee, and put the empty mug in the sink, grabbed his coat and car keys, kissed Mary goodbye and headed for the door. He told them all he would be back with Dot as soon as he could. He drove to the hospital, in deep thought, *Just where could Doug be?* he wondered. Robert looked at nearly every person he passed on the way to the hospital, but to no avail. He turned into the hospital, and he soon saw Dot waiting outside the entrance as agreed.

Dot was speaking to another woman, she saw him approaching, and finished her conversation. She opened the car passenger door and climbed in.

"Hi, Robert," she said, "thanks again for coming to get me."

"It's no bother," he waited until she'd fastened her seat belt before moving off.

"Was that a friend of yours, I saw you speaking with?"

"No, she was a total stranger. She'd just nipped out for a breath of fresh air, her son's in intensive care. She was telling me he'd been knocked off his motor bike by an articulated lorry. Poor sod, him and the lorry driver."

I used to drive one of those lorries, it's sometimes difficult to see cyclists and motor bikes. It's so sad to think of all the accidents, and deaths that happen every single day, and all the poor families that have to deal with them, and we never give them a seconds thought, until it comes to your own door."

"Yes," she agreed, "it's very sad indeed."

He relayed some more of Andrew and Jason's visits to the undertakers, the photos of the burial baskets, and the registry office. They arrived back at Robert and Mary's house just under an hour after Robert had left. He'd made good time, he thought. When they were inside, Mary put the kettle on again, her kettle was getting well used lately, *More so than ever before*, she thought.

Mary said, to no one in particular, "I don't think any of us could get through any kind of crisis if we didn't have a kettle."

They all smiled at this, which was probably the first time in two days they had managed this. Once the tea and coffee were made, they settled into their chairs. The boys told Dot their full story of how they got on today. They showed her the photos they'd shown to Robert and Mary. She did agree, the wicker type basket was less intrusive than the coffin type. They also discussed the humanist service which, again, Dot thought would be less stressful for Julie than a full-on religious funeral.

It was as settled as it could be for the minute. They all agreed that Andrew should call Brendan and arrange for the celebrant to come to the house the following day at around three PM, if he could fit them in. This would allow him to gather some information about Grace to allow him to make a funeral speech. He called the undertakers, Brendan was still out, he left his mobile number with the receptionist, and asked for Brendan to call him ASAP. Andrew and Jason left to head home, they dropped Dot off again on route to their house. They arrived home twenty minutes later.

Chapter 12

They had been home for about an hour. When there was a knock at the door, Andrew answered it, and when he opened the door, there was a smartly dressed, middle-aged man looking back at him.

"How can I help you, sir?" asked Andrew.

"Can I speak to Jason, please?"

Just then, Jason popped his head out the sitting room door, he'd recognised the voice instantly, and his heart sank when he saw his dad standing at the door. The last thing they needed right now was him having another fight with his dad.

"If you've come here to call me some more names, now is not the time."

"Can I please come in?" pleaded his dad, "I'm not here to fight, Jason. I'm here to beg your forgiveness," he had big tears in his eyes. Jason had never seen his dad show any emotion, ever, except anger, of course. He looked at his partner who nodded his head.

"Well, in you come then," offered Andrew. Jason was wary, but crumbled, as soon as his dad stepped over to him, and hugged him, they both cried. Even Andrew had to control his own emotions. Was this really happening? Jason and his dad released their embrace.

"This is my partner, Andrew."

"I'm very happy to meet you, Andrew," he hugged Andrew too.

"It's really great to finally meet you too, I've heard Sheila mention you a few times."

"Nothing good, I reckon?"

"You'd be surprised," said Andrew.

"What brings you to our house now?" enquired his son.

"I've been an old fool, I saw you guys come home earlier, and I've been sitting in my car, plucking up the courage to knock on your door. I'm truly sorry I hurt you, Son," he said to Jason. "If you allow me, I am going to try and win back your respect, and hopefully, your love, the both of you." He turned to Andrew and said, "I'm sorry to you too, it's been far too long. I know, what you must think of me, and you've every right to show me the door. Sheila told me about your niece, Grace. You and your family have my sincerest condolences. When she told me this, I was embarrassed, and ashamed of myself, it's kind of put some things into perspective for me. Life is too short, and precious, and I've wasted ten years of my life being bitter."

He was crying again, he looked at the son he hadn't seen for nearly a decade. "I've lost my son, and I want him back." Jason was crying too, "And I want to be a part of his life, in fact, both your lives, it you will let me."

Andrew gave him a hug and said, "If it's all right with Jason, it's all right with me."

Jason nodded his approval.

"Dad, you have no idea, how hurt I felt, when you couldn't accept I'm gay. But if you're serious, then you have no idea how happy you have just made me. I forgive you, and yes, if you have really accepted me for who I am. Then yes, I would love to have you in our life."

"I can assure you, Son, I do accept you for who you are. You're my son, and I love you." They hugged again, and cried.

"Does mum know you're here?"

"No, she doesn't, she's been telling me all about you lately, even told me your address. She probably thinks I wasn't listening to her, but I was. I'd decided a few months ago to try and contact you. This is my first step, on a long road, to convince you two that I'm very serious about being part of your lives." He turned to Jason, your mum isn't aware that I've been seeing a councillor for a few months to get my head straight before I contacted you. I know, I wasn't the easiest to get along with, always flying off the handle. Your mum says, I've got anger issues, but I'm trying to change. It's going to take time, but I'm feeling the benefit already. I know it was wrong of me to judge you, and if I could take back the horrible things I said to you, I would. But I will promise you here and now, in front of Andrew, I'm not the homophobic man I was. I've had the scales removed from my eyes now, I am trying to be more tolerant. I've even been out for a drink with a couple of gay men from my work, you guys aren't any different from anyone else, Christ, nearly every celebrity you see on television is gay. I've been living in the past for far too long, I'll freely admit that I've decided. I would rather have a son that's gay than not have a son at all, and for the past ten years, I haven't had a son. And through no fault of yours, you've not had a dad, that's so wrong, and it's all my own fault."

He hugged his son again. There were more tears.

Andrew said, "OK, you two have a seat, and I will put the kettle on,"

Jason, sat next to his dad, and asked him how he was doing.

"I'm feeling much better for seeing you. I can't believe how grown up you look. You were just a boy the last time I saw you, my fault, I know, and please believe me, Jason, I really do regret my actions." Just then Andrew came into the sitting room carrying a tray with three mugs of coffee and some biscuits.

"Do you need sugar for your coffee?" asked Andrew.

"No, just milk is fine, thanks," replied Gary.

"Just like your son then?" smiled Andrew.

"This is a nice house, how long have you stayed here?"

"Six years now," replied Jason.

"Your mum says you work at an employment agency."

"Yes, I've been there for eight years now. I am head of engineering recruitment."

"That sounds great, what about you, Andrew?"

"I manage a plant hire company, we hire out all kinds of equipment, we specialise in access plant, like scaffolding, and MEWP's."

"What's a MEWP?"

"It's a Mobile Elevating Work Platform, or a scissor lift, as it's also known as."

"I've heard of scissor lifts, is there a big demand for them?"

"Yes, we hire out about fifty a week."

"What have you been up to today?"

"We've had a particularly difficult day, first we went to see an undertaker, we're arranging little Grace's funeral, then we had to go into Islington, and register her death."

"I am really sorry to hear you both had to do that today. It can't have been easy."

"No, it wasn't," they both agreed.

"Grace's mum, Julie, my sister-in-law, is in hospital, and my big brother, Doug, has disappeared. He had an accident a couple of months back, he suffered a blunt force trauma injury and he can't remember anything, not even his family. It's really been a difficult time for my mum, dad and Julie lately. If Jason wasn't here, to keep me sane, I don't know what I would have done."

Gary smiled and said, "Yes, his mum keeps telling me the same thing. He's a good man, pity it's taken a tragedy for your family to jolt me to my senses. If there's anything Sheila, or I can do, please let us know, thanks, sir."

"Don't call me sir, I don't deserve it. Call me Gary."

"It's good that you came by tonight, Gary, this is the first positive thing, that's happened lately."

They had finished their coffee, Gary got up and thanked them both for giving him a chance to apologise.

"I'd better get home now, it's getting late. Can I come to see you again?" he asked Jason.

"Yes, that would be nice," they hugged again, and he shook Andrew's hand.

"I'll tell your mum I have been to see you, hopefully it will make her as happy as it's made me."

They waved him goodbye from the window.

"Well, that was a turn up for the books, can you believe that?" said Jason. "Miracles can happen; did you hear him call me son? I don't remember him ever calling me that." Jason now had tears of joy in his eyes. Andrew hugged him. "Let's hope he's serious," said Jason and not a flash in the pan gesture.

"I'm sure he is," he sure looked happy and relieved that you were willing to give him another chance. "I'm going to call my mum and dad, if it's OK with you?"

"You bet it's OK."

Andrew dialled their number, his dad answered after three rings.

"Hello, hi, Dad, you'll never guess who just left our house."

"Please tell me it was Doug."

"No, sorry, Dad, I wasn't thinking, getting your hopes up like that. It was Jason's dad, Gary."

"How did that go?"

"Very well, he came over to apologise to Jason, and begged for a chance to make up, and be a part of his life, in fact, our lives, that's how he put it."

"That's fantastic, if he's really going to accept Jason for the great guy he is."

"He certainly said all the right things, apparently, he's been seeing an anger management councillor for a few months now, and he says he's got a different outlook on life. He even called Jason son, and declared he loved him, and told us he'd been an old fool for saying, and doing what he'd done."

"How's Jason?"

"He's on cloud nine, and he seems to be happy enough, let me put him on."

"Hi, Jason, I'm glad, your dad's finally seen the error of his ways."

"Yes, me too, I just hope I can meet his expectations."

"Jason you've no need to meet his expectations, you're a fine young man, and I couldn't be happier you're with my son. Your dad is the one who will need to meet your expectations."

"Thanks for those kind words, Robert, we'll see, it was a big shock when he knocked on our door tonight, albeit a good shock. He says he's changed, his whole demeanour was different to the one I remember. Only time will tell though, as he said to us earlier, small steps, I will put Andrew back on."

"OK, good night." Jason handed the phone back to his partner.

"How's Mum?"

"She's sleeping, I'll tell her about Gary in the morning. If he's seriously changed, then it's great, but be careful, a leopard doesn't often change its spots."

"Yes, I agree, but, Dad, I saw him crying, if he's putting it on, he's a seriously good actor, and he looked truly ashamed of his actions. He stayed for about an hour and I was trying to gauge him. I think I can read people pretty well, and I think he was genuine, but as you say, we'll see."

"I am going to ring off now, Son, I will see you tomorrow. I have arranged to collect Dot at ten AM. We're heading over to the hospital, and hopefully, Julie will be getting home, have good night," he said, and hung up.

Just as Andrew put his phone down, it rang. He picked it up, "Hello," he said thinking it was his dad again.

"Hi, Andrew, it's Sheila, I've been trying to get through to you guys for ages. Did Gary really come to see Jason and you tonight? He just told me he did? Please, tell me he did?"

"Yes, Sheila, he did, indeed, come to see us, and no angry words, just a whole lot of hugging, and crying."

"That's brilliant, how's Jason?"

"He's great, Jason," he called out, "it's your mum on the phone."

Jason took the phone, "Hi, Mum, I take it dad told you he came over to our house?"

"Yes, he did."

"Mum, are you crying?"

"Yes, of course I'm crying. Ten bloody years it's taken to have my family back together, it's just a pity it's taken the death of a baby for him to come to his senses."

"I don't think it was just that, he told Andrew, and I that he'd been thinking of coming to see me for a while. He just plucked up the courage tonight."

"I'm so glad, love, he's been a different man of late. I just had to call you, to be sure he wasn't telling me a fib." She told him she was going to have a happy night's sleep and wished her son and Andrew a good night.

Chapter 13

Next morning, during breakfast, Robert told Mary about Jason's dad, Gary, going to see him and Andrew.

"He says he's a reformed man, and wants a second chance, he wants to be part of Jason's life. He apologised to him, for all the terrible things he said and done."

"Do you think he's serious?"

"I don't know? Andrew and Jason seem to think he is. Only time, will tell though, let's hope for the boy's sake, he is." Robert finished his coffee, and got his phone from the sitting room, he'd had it on charge. He kissed Mary goodbye and headed to go get Dot. He'd called her when he got into his car, telling her he would be there in quarter of an hour. She was ready, and waiting for him, he told her about Jason's dad coming over and making peace, just as he had told Mary this morning. She too was thrilled for Jason.

"It must have been difficult for him, living with the knowledge his own dad resented your way of life?"

They arrived at the hospital, and managed to find a parking space fairly easily. When they got to Julie's room, they discovered that she was awake and sitting in a chair by her bed. She looked up, but she didn't get up when they entered her room. Her mum leant down and kissed her cheek, as did Robert.

"How are you today?" he asked.

"As good as can be expected," she replied dryly.

"Are you getting home today?" he asked her.

"I don't know, the doctors on his rounds, the nurse said he was running late and that he will be here shortly. I've just asked her where he was, just before you came in."

Dot sat, on the edge of the bed, and held her daughters' hand. Ten minutes, or so, later, the doctor came in, he asked Julie how she was coping.

"I feel better than I did yesterday, but losing my daughter is not going to be easy to forget." She was now crying again, her mum comforted her.

"We don't want you to forget," said the doctor. "We just need to assure you it's wasn't your fault."

"Well, good luck with that because I feel responsible," sobbed Julie.

"That feeling will pass soon, as I explained to you yesterday, your daughter died from Sudden Infant Death Syndrome. This is not something you could have foreseen, these deaths, are unexplained and occur all too frequently."

"I just feel, if I my husband hadn't run off, Grace would still be alive."

Robert felt her pain more than ever now, that her daughter was dead, but she was his granddaughter too. How could Julie be blaming Doug, he was hurt and a bit shocked by her statement, but he knew it wasn't his sons' fault. But there was no point adding to Julie's stress levels, so he kept quiet.

"Come now, Julie, if your husband had been right here by your side, it would have made no difference," said the doctor. This had little effect on her, the doctor asked the nurse to give Julie her medication and took Dot and Robert outside. "I think Julie should stay here for another night, she's still a bit angry and blaming herself and your son," he said looking at Robert. "I think we may have to up the dose of her medication, if she shows no improvement soon."

"Fair enough," Robert sighed. We're in the middle of the process of trying to arrange Grace's funeral. I don't suppose we should broach this with her just now."

"No. I think it's best if you don't. She's still too fragile to handle that at the minute. In past cases, the families have organised them and the patient goes along with those arrangements."

Dot and Robert went to the canteen and he bought them both a coffee, Dot offered to pay, but Robert was insistent he pay. They sat at a table by a window.

"Robert, I know none of this is Doug's fault. Julie's just feeling isolated, and a bit lost. She's had far too much tragedy to deal with in too short a time. I'm sure when she's a bit better, she will apologise for the way she spoke about Doug."

He thanked her, and said he really hoped she was right. His mobile went off, it was Andrew. He was confirming the celebrant had confirmed he was OK for three PM today.

"OK, thanks, Son, I'm with Dot, I'll let her know," he hung up. He told Dot what Andrew had said, confirming that the celebrant was coming to his house at three o'clock this afternoon.

"It's a pity Julie won't be there."

"Yes, but at this moment in time, I don't think she could handle it, we'll go back to see her before we leave."

They both finished their coffee, and then he headed back to Julie's room. She was now lying on the bed, and was asleep.

"Poor Julie," said Robert, "I just wish Doug were here for her."

"Yes, me too, have you still not got any leads on where he could be?"

"Not a thing, it's like he's disappeared into thin air. I'm really getting worried about his wellbeing, but I daren't tell Mary and the police have been little or no help at all. I've been in touch with or visited all the places I can think of that he would go to, our GP, his boxing gym, his work. I spoke with a regular at his gym, who knows Doug well. I gave him my phone number and asked him to call me if he saw or heard from him. I'm kind of at a loss where to turn to next."

They both kissed Julie's forehead and left her sleeping, and they headed for the car. He arranged to drop her off at home, then he would collect her around two-thirty to be at his house in plenty of time for the celebrant coming at three PM. He drove in silence; they were both trying to collect their thoughts. It seemed, neither of them was looking forward to this afternoon, but it had to be done. They arrived at Dot's.

"OK, thanks, can I give you some money for fuel?"

"There's no need, Dot, I've got it covered, but thanks for the offer anyway." She got out. "I'll see you shortly," he said, and drove off towards his own house.

He called Mary on route home, and gave her a rundown of the hospital visit, and told her what Julie had said about Doug.

"She's just angry and confused, she'll come around eventually," Mary said. He'd just decided that, rather than coming straight home, he was now going back to see if he could get a hold of the guy he spoke to at Doug's gym.

"I'll be home in about an hour."

"OK," replied Mary, "I'll make us some lunch."

"Oh, when Andrew called to tell me the celebrant had confirmed, he said Jason's couldn't stop talking about his dad's visit last night, he's really chuffed he got in touch. Andrew said they had a long conversation about it last night. They both agree, they will be very wary and take this slowly, and they agree with you, that only time will tell if Gary really has changed his stance. Well, I don't mind telling you, I'm far from convinced yet. But let's give him the benefit of the doubt, I really hope for the sake of the boys, he's genuine. We could certainly do with a little bit of good fortune. We've not had any of that for a while."

"You'll get no argument from me on that statement," replied Mary.

"I will see you shortly," he said, and then he rung off.

Fifteen minutes later, he was at the gym, he asked the receptionist, if Craig was around.

"I'm sorry, it's Craig's day off, can anyone else help you?"

"Is the manager available please?"

"I'll go see if he's available, can I ask what it's regarding?"

"It's a private matter, I will only take a couple of minutes of his time."

She left the reception, then returned a couple of minutes later.

"If you come with me, Robert Smith, the manager will have a word with you."

"Thanks," he said, and followed her through two doors and up a set of stairs. She stopped at another door and knocked on it.

"In you come," someone shouted.

"In you go," the lady said, she had a name badge on, it said her name was Janice.

"Thanks again, Janice," he said. She looked puzzled and Robert pointed to her badge, she smiled, "My names Robert."

"OK, Robert, good luck," and she disappeared back down the stairs.

Robert entered the office, and a slim guy, around fiftyish, was smiling back at him from behind a metal desk. There were two piles of paper on the desk. He got up, and came from behind the desk and introduced himself.

"I'm Rob Smith, the manager here. How can I help you?"

"I'm Robert Clement, I'm her to ask if you've seen or heard anything from my son, Doug."

"I know Doug," said Rob, "have a seat." They both sat down. "Craig told me you were in a couple of days ago, I'm sorry about Doug, we heard about his accident. He's not been in here since. Has he not been in contact with you?"

"No, he's gone missing," Robert gave him a quick run through recent events including the unfortunate death of Doug's daughter, Grace. Rob listened in silence until Robert had finished.

"Oh, my word, that's a terrible tale," voiced Rob. "I can assure you, if Doug comes here, or gets in touch, I will personally, call you. You and your family must be at your wits end?"

"Yes, we are, but we're trying to keep strong for Doug's wife, Julie."

69

"I've met her, she's been here once or twice, she's a lovely woman. Please pass on my condolences to her, your wife, and your other son.

"I will do, and many thanks for taking the time to see me today."

"It's no bother at all, I've got two grown up children too. If anything like that happened to either of them, I would like to think anyone that could assist, would do, without too much trouble."

Rob took Robert's mobile number and promised him he would be in touch if he heard anything about Doug. Robert thanked him again, and they shook hands.

"Are you OK to find your way back to reception?"

"Yes," replied Robert. He left Rob's office, went back down the stairs, and through the two doors back to reception. He thanked Janice again and left the gym.

Chapter 14

Robert limped back to his car, he thought that Rob was a kind man, and that he would call him if he saw or heard anything about Doug. Just as he arrived at his car, he heard his name being called, he turned around and saw it was Rob, jogging toward him.

"I've just had an idea, I wanted to run by you."

"I'm all ears," said Robert.

"How about this, we get a picture of Doug? Then we make a few copies, and then we make up a missing person poster? I can hang one in the gym, I get quite a lot of members from other gyms pop in from time to time to use our facilities. It may be worth a try."

"That's a fantastic idea, Rob, we could put a few up around different places. I'm sure we've got a recent picture of Doug at home."

"Good, if you have one, bring it back here. I've got a scanner in the office, we can add a little information, and put your phone number down as a contact."

"Thanks, Rob, you're a star." They shook hands again. Robert climbed into his car, and headed toward home. Once again, as he was driving, he was scanning everyone he passed. *Where on earth could Doug be?* he wondered. This was like a waking nightmare, he could hardly comprehend it all. *Would a missing person poster work?* he thought. Well, it was better than nothing, and who knows, it may just work. He arrived back home, he told Mary about the meeting he had just had with Rob Smith, and the idea of the poster.

"I'll go get a photo of Doug," she said. "I'm positive there's a recent one upstairs in my photo album," off she went upstairs. She came back down a couple of minutes later with a picture taken in the garden a couple of months ago when Doug was fixing the back gate after it had been blown off in a storm. "Do you think this will do?" she asked, as she showed it to him.

"This is perfect," he told her that he thought Rob was a genuine sort. "The idea for the missing person poster must have just came into his head as I was nearly back in the car when he came running after me."

"Do you think it will work?" she asked.

"I hope so, Doug's a very popular guy, even Rob said so. Nobody's a bad word to say about him."

"Except Julie, of course," she reminded him.

He half-smiled, "I forgot about that. I'm running out of places and ideas. Hopefully, he will come to his senses soon, I really fear the worst for Julie, she's not handling any of this well, and who can blame her?" They had a quick lunch of a cuppa soup and toasted sandwiches.

Andrew and Jason called to say they were on their way over. Robert left, and headed over to collect Dot. They got back to the house with about ten minutes to spare before Jack Mullen, the celebrant, knocked on the door. Andrew opened the door and invited him in. He was introduced to all present, the usual small talk about the weather was conducted. Mary put the kettle on again. Dot helped in the kitchen, and they soon returned to the sitting room with tea and coffee and a plate of chocolate biscuits. When they were all seated, Jack asked the family what type of service they wanted for Grace, he said Brendan had only given him the name and age of Grace and how she'd died.

"What different services are available?" asked Robert.

"I can conduct non-religious, semi-religious or spiritual."

Robert suggested something along the line of a semi-religious funeral as they weren't regular churchgoers, but they were no atheists either. Mary and Dot agreed this would be best. Andrew and Jason were happy to go along with the majority.

"OK then tell me a bit about Grace, and the family, can I take some details of Grace's mum and dad, and what relation you guys are to Grace, and possibly a little bit about her time with the family?"

"Well," said Robert, "I'm Grace's grandfather, Mary's her grandmother, Dot's Grace's other grandmother. Andrew, and his partner, Jason, are her uncle's. My absent son, Doug, is her father, Grace's mother is Julie, she's in the hospital. We're very hopeful she will be present at the funeral. We really hope Doug turns up too."

Jack, asked about Doug. Robert told him the story in near enough its entirety.

"This is all rather unfortunate, tell me as much as you can about Grace, and I will put together a small concise service, do you want to choose some music?" asked Jack to the room.

"Let's have a word with Julie and see what she thinks?" said Dot. "She's a bit delicate at the moment."

"That's understandable and it's not a problem, we can add that later."

They all took some time to think, then they shared, with Jack, their own little time snaps that they'd each spent with Grace. About an hour later, Jack said he had enough to go on for the present. He asked for an email address to which Andrew gave him his. Robert asked the awkward question about payment, but Jack said his costs would be included in the package cost from Brendan.

"That's great," said Andrew, "I'll speak with him tomorrow."

With that, Jack thanked them all for their input, said he would send a draft of the service to Andrew to allow them to read it over and discuss any alterations or additions they wanted. He shook all their hands and left.

"He seemed like a really nice man," said Mary.

"Yes, I thought so too," agreed Dot.

"Right, we're going to head home now," said Andrew. "We can drop you off, Dot, if you'd like."

"Yes, please, that would be great, if you're sure it's no trouble."

"None at all," said Andrew.

"Robert and I will go and visit Julie tonight," said Mary, "I'll call you later, Dot."

"I'm going to be working tonight, six till midnight, but I'll call you in the morning, unless anything happens that you think I need to know about this evening," replied Dot.

"OK, no problem."

With that, they all hugged, Andrew, Jason and Dot left, Mary and Robert talked a bit about what they thought Doug might want added to the service for Grace, but they couldn't think of anything. It's not something they would have discussed.

Robert called Rob Smith to see if he was still at the gym, he was and said he would be for another couple of hours.

"That's great, I've got a recent photo of Doug for the poster."

"Brilliant," replied Rob, "bring it over now, and we'll get to work on it. The sooner we get some posters up here, the better chance we have of finding Doug."

"OK I'll be there in twenty minutes."

"I'll see you when you get here."

When he arrived, Rob, took the photo from Robert. He looked at it, "This is perfect." He handed it to Janice, he'd recruited her to assist. She was a genius on computers. In about half an hour later, she had produced ten missing persons posters with Doug's photo and Robert's mobile number just below, and a couple of sentences asking anybody who recognised Doug Clement, or had any information regarding his whereabouts could they please call his dad, Robert.

"They look great," they both said to Janice.

"Just wait until you see them laminated." She got her laminator, from her stationary cupboard, she plugged into a socket on the wall. It took a couple of minutes to heat up. Janice then counted out ten clear plastic looking, floppy pocket type sheets from a packet and placed each poster inside one. She then fed them through the machine, one at a time, and as they passed out the other side they were now stiff. Robert and Rob, marvelled at this, as neither of them had ever seen laminating done before.

"This looks tremendous," said Robert, I'm very grateful to you for doing this."

"It's no trouble," replied Janice, "I've got a soft spot for Doug, he's always cheery, and he never passes me without asking how I am." He's a real credit, to you and your wife."

"Thanks," said Robert, "I'll pass that onto Doug's mum, Mary."

They left the office, and Rob taped one of the posters up in the main reception area. He also put one in the changing rooms, that way, if anybody missed one, they would most likely see the other. Rob handed Robert six of the posters. He kept two, he said his friend was the manager, at a bookstore in town, he had already spoken with him, and he'd agreed to put them in his shop.

"That's most helpful of him, please thank him for me, and thanks again to you both, I'll ask the owner of our local newspaper shop if he will allow me to put one in his window. I will also ask my friend to put a couple around his business place." With that, Robert shook hands with Rob and kissed Janice on the cheek, and said he was humbled by their generosity.

He left and headed home to Mary. Robert couldn't wait, to show the posters to Mary and the boys. He called her and told her he'd be home shortly. She had dinner almost ready by the time he got home. He showed her the posters.

"These are great, I hope they work." She put the dinner out, and she'd made macaroni and cheese. Robert's favourite. When they'd finished, he helped Mary with the dishes. She got changed into a blouse and skirt, she'd been wearing kick about the house clothes. He locked up the house, and they got into their car.

The drive took about half an hour. It took about another ten minutes to find a parking space. They walked into Julie's room, at quarter past seven. She was sitting

73

on the chair beside the bed, she got up, and greeted them. It seemed, to him that she was in better spirits than she'd been this morning when he and Dot visited her.

"How are you feeling now?" asked Mary.

"I'm feeling much better," she went over to Robert and cuddled him. "I owe you an apology, Dad. I wasn't thinking straight this morning when I was blaming Doug for Grace's death. I know it's not his fault. He can't help that he was in an accident. Is there any word of him?"

"Unfortunately, no, we've heard nothing yet." He told her about the missing posters, "We can only pray someone will see Doug somewhere. I believe, if we can find him, the doctors will help him get some of his memories back."

"Yes, I hope so too," nodded Julie.

"I do too," said Mary.

"Sit down, love," asked Robert. "There's no good time to bring this up, but we've been preparing for Grace's funeral."

"What's been decided?"

"We've not got any firm arrangements yet. We want to make sure you agree with everything before it's settled. Are you feeling well enough to discuss her funeral?"

"I'm not sure I'll ever be, but I'm as well as can be expected under the circumstances. I've accepted that Grace is dead, if that's what you mean."

"This is an extremely difficult time for us all," chimed in Mary, "but more so for you, love. We were thinking it will be best if Grace has a humanist funeral, we've spoken with a celebrant, he has agreed to give her a semi-religious funeral, but only if you agree. We thought you would like this better than a full-blown funeral. We were thinking of just immediate family, and a couple of close friends. What are your thoughts on this?"

"That sounds fine, have you picked out a coffin yet?" she asked, tears were now starting to run down her cheeks.

"No, not yet, we want you to have the last say on any of the arrangements. We've looked at a white wicker basket type of casket. It looks lovely, maybe we can go and visit the undertakers soon?"

"The doctor has told me I'll probably get home tomorrow. I think I will move in with my mum for a bit."

"Yes, whatever suits you," said Robert, "I will come and collect you tomorrow with your mum."

"That would be nice, thanks," said Julie.

They discussed the celebrants visit to the house. "He sounds OK, can he come back to see us again?"

"Yes, absolutely, he can, he's very accommodating. Have you told your mum you're getting out tomorrow?"

"Not yet, the doctor just told me five minutes before you came in."

"Your mum's working tonight, I'll call her later and let her know," said Mary. "I'll come and visit you tomorrow afternoon at your mums, and we'll see if you're up to going to see the undertaker. How does that sound?"

"It sounds OK, but I'll see how I am tomorrow before I agree to go. Andrew and Jason have done all the legwork. Please thank them for me." She had a great relationship with Andrew, he was the brother she never had, and she couldn't have been happier for him when he met Jason. "How are they two getting on?"

"Jason's dad, Gary, has been to see them, and he said he now accepts Jason as gay and he's asked for forgiveness. He wants to try and repair the relationship he broke. He seems genuine, but you never know, why wait until now, it's been years and years since he threw Jason out."

"I remember Jason telling me all the horrid things his dad said to him. Can you imagine getting called a fagot by your own dad?"

"Yes, it was a dreadful and spiteful thing to say. He knocked on their door and practically begged for a chance to speak to Jason. Apparently, when Jason's mum told him about Doug being missing, and what has happened to Grace, it put things into perspective for him, and he wants a second chance. Andrew is happy for Jason, but I'm not so sure, the last thing we need is more grief from him, if it turns out he's not serious about accepting his son's lifestyle. I don't know how that would go down with Jason."

"Why would he do that?" asked Julie.

"Who knows? Human nature's a funny thing," said Robert. They spent the remainder of the visit talking about not much at all. Julie was starting to yawn, probably the pills she was now on. At eight thirty, the bell rang to sound the end of the visiting time. Robert and Mary kissed and hugged Julie, she waved them, goodbye.

When they left Julie's room, and they went to the nurse's station, Robert asked to speak to a doctor. They were shown to a small family room, it was not the one they were in previously, when Julie got admitted. A few minutes later, a young doctor came in, he introduced himself as Doctor Brown.

"What can I do for you?"

"We're Julie Clements, parents-in-law, Robert and Mary Clement, we were just informed by her that she's getting home tomorrow, it that correct?"

"Yes, we feel she'll recover a lot quicker, if she's home with her family. We've put her on a stronger anti-depressant, and it seems to be working."

"I agree, it seems to be. She is a lot brighter and not as morbid as she was this morning when I saw her."

"She's been a lot more settled this afternoon, but it's imperative Julie takes these tablets. She's had a very big shock. I'm sure you all have, but with the situation with her husband and the death of her daughter, it seems to have thrown her right over the edge. These tablets will help her to cope in the short-term, but she may need counselling. They say time is a great healer, we can hopefully reduce the dosage over the next few weeks. I will only be giving her two weeks supply when she gets home tomorrow."

"OK, thanks, doctor, we'll keep an eye on her, and between us and her mother, we'll make sure she takes her tablets. What time shall I come to collect her?"

"Tomorrow morning, doctors' rounds are finished by ten thirty, probably best to leave it until about eleven o'clock. That will give the pharmacy time to get her medication ready."

"OK, thanks for your time," Robert said. He shook the young man's hand as did Mary. When they were in the car, Robert said Julie was looking and acting a lot better tonight.

"Yes," his wife agreed.

Chapter 15

They drove home, both Robert and Mary were scanning everyone they passed the whole journey. When they arrived home, Mary called Andrew. She told him of their visit tonight, and how well Julie was.

"That's fantastic that she's getting home tomorrow, do need me to do anything?"

"No, your dad's going to collect her, he's going to pick up Dot on the way."

"Is she staying with you, Mum?"

"No, she's going to Dot's, probably best for a few days."

"How's Jason? Has he spoken with his dad again?"

"He's over at his parents' house just now. He left here about seven PM. I asked him if he wanted me to go with him. He said he would go himself first time, just in case, there were any fireworks. He called me an hour ago, and said everything was fine, they're just catching up for lost time."

"That's good then."

"Do you think Julie will be up for visiting the undertakers tomorrow?"

"We're hopeful, Son. Your dad spoke to her about the funeral, and gave her a brief outline of the arrangements. She seemed to take it well, but I'm still not sure if she'd be ready for a visit to the undertaker just yet."

"OK, Mum, let's play it by ear."

"But she was definitely a lot better tonight, although, it was probably the tablets the doctor has her on." She told him about the missing posters that Rob Smith from the gym had suggested to his dad.

"That's a brilliant idea, strange that none of us thought of that, so simple, but they may just work. What we need, Mum, is a little bit of luck. If it wasn't for bad luck just now, we wouldn't have any luck at all."

"I feel a change of fortunes is coming our way."

"I hope and pray you're right, we could certainly do with some luck. It seems good luck has deserted us right enough. I'm going to ring off now, Mum. Jason will be back soon. Have a good night, and I'll talk to you tomorrow."

"OK, good night to you too, Son," she put the phone back in its cradle. She spoke for a while to her husband. They discussed Julie's better spirits, and they both wondered how she would cope with a visit to the undertakers and, speaking with Mr Mullen.

"We'll just have to be here for her, it'll take her a while to adjust. I can only imagine what she's feeling, losing her child. We feel terrible and Doug's only missing, I couldn't even contemplate losing Doug or Andrew." They had a small glass of wine, then they went to bed.

The next morning, Mary was up at seven AM, she felt she'd had a decent sleep, must have been the wine. Julie was due out of the hospital today, she wondered how she was feeling today, she'd no doubt find out soon enough. Robert was still asleep. She had a shower and made herself some tea and toast. Robert got up around eight AM, he'd arranged to collect Dot at ten thirty, and then head over to collect Julie at eleven. This would give the doctors time to conclude their morning rounds in the hospital, and to arrange any medication Julie needed to take home with her.

He had a shower, Mary made him a coffee, and two slices of toast. When he was finished, he'd decided to go and see Doug's boss, Ricky Smith. Primarily for a catch up, and to see if he would put one of the missing posters up. Robert arrived at Doug's workplace at five past nine. Ricky's secretary made them both a brew and put a plate of chocolate biscuits on the small table between the two comfortable black leather chairs in the visitor's office.

"Thanks, Emily," said Ricky. Robert gave him a quick rundown of the past few days' events, including little Grace's passing. "Oh, my goodness," exclaimed Ricky, "that's terrible news, how's Julie coping with that?"

"Not great, to be honest, she's been in the hospital for a few days, they've put her on anti-depressants."

"You're right, that's not good at all."

"I'm collecting her today; she's going to stay at her mums for a while."

"How's Mary bearing up?"

"She's a bit like myself, putting on a brave face. But I can tell, she's really worried just how Doug will react when he discovers the daughter that he's been longing to have for goodness knows how long has died, and he never even had the chance to meet her."

"I don't envy you the task of telling Doug about Grace, that's for sure. Is it OK if I let Emily know about Grace? She and Doug are fairly close, they both started working here around about the same time."

"Yes, that's fine."

"Thanks," he said and left the office. Robert could soon hear Emily crying. A couple of minutes later, Ricky came back in. "She got a little upset with the news, it's to be expected, like I said, she's very fond of Doug. How's Andrew fairing up," he enquired.

"He's really stepped up, I can tell you. He and his partner, Jason, have been absolutely fantastic. They've been to see an undertaker, and have managed to, more or less, arrange the full funeral."

"Will it be OK if I attend the funeral?"

"Yes, mate, that'll be fine, it's only going to be a small funeral, immediate family and a few very close friends. You fit the bill, as does John. I'm going to call him shortly."

"He's on his way over just now," replied Ricky. "When I heard you come in earlier, I thought it was John."

A couple of minutes later, Robert's good friend, John, arrived.

"I thought that was your car I just saw there in the car park." Robert shared the horrible news about Grace, his mate gave him a hug.

"My Christ's sake, Robert, how the hell are you still standing, you've had enough blows to knockdown a gorilla."

"I've no option, John, I have to keep standing, and look forward. If I'm honest with you both, I'm terrified to stop and think the worst. I keep thinking, our lucks got to change for the better. I should find out, later today, when the funeral will be. I just hope Julie's, up to visiting the undertakers later on today."

John gave his mate another man hug, and assured him he would be here if he needed anything at all, even if it's just to get something off his chest.

"You're a good friend, John," then he remembered why he was there. Robert then told the brothers about the missing posters. He showed it to them.

"This is a good likeness, when was this picture taken?" asked John.

"A couple of months back. Mary took it when Doug was mending our gate. Would it be OK to put one up on the notice board in your reception?"

"Yes, it's absolutely OK," said Ricky, "and I'll do better than that, I'll ask Emily to make some more of them and get some up on the sites we're working on. If it helps find Doug and get him back to full health, I would be happy to do so; my customers keep asking when he's coming back. They miss him too, as I've said to you before, Robert, Doug is very well liked."

He called Emily into the office, she had managed to compose herself a little. Ricky showed Emily the poster, and asked her to make a dozen copies. When she saw Doug's photo, she looked quite sad and some more tears rolled down her cheeks.

"Don't you worry, Emily," said John. "We'll have the old Doug back her in no time at all. You mark my words."

Emily forced a smiled, "I really hope so, John." With that, she was away to print off some copies as her boss had asked.

"I've taken up enough of your time guys," said Robert.

"No, not all," they replied in unison.

"I'd better be making tracks, I promised Dot I'd get her at ten thirty."

"It's only just gone ten now, you'll be fine," said John. The three of them shook hands, and as he was leaving, he thanked Emily for the tea and for helping with the posters.

"No problem, Robert, I am just glad to be of any help and say hello to Mary for me."

"I will do that, Doug's very lucky to have a work colleague like you, and a boss like Ricky."

He arrived at Dot's at twenty-five past ten. He was glad he'd made it on time. He was old school, and he hated being late for anything. He called Dot, and he let her know he was outside, waiting. She said she was ready, and she would be there in a minute, and she was. She climbed, into the car and they set off towards the hospital. They got there at five past eleven, and Robert found a parking space, no bother, the parking only seemed to be a problem during visiting hours.

They walked to the main entrance and took the lift to the floor Julie's room was located on. When they entered Julie's room, she was dressed, and all packed up. She told them she was just awaiting her prescription; the nurse was away getting it from the hospital pharmacy. Robert and Dot hugged her. Robert asked her how she was feeling today.

"So-so," she replied. Not exactly the response, he'd hoping for, but, he supposed she was just anxious to get out of the hospital.

Ten minutes later, the nurse arrived with Julie's medicine. "Now, Julie, you must take these tablets as prescribed by Dr Brown."

"I won't forget," she promised.

"OK, then you're all set, remember, if you encounter any issues, you know where we are." She handed her a leaflet with the contact numbers to get in touch if needs be. Julie thanked the nurse. Robert followed the nurse out of the room.

"Is Doctor Brown available for a quick word?" asked Robert to the nurse. She showed Robert to a small waiting area.

"If you kindly take a seat, I will go and see if the doctor is around the ward."

"OK, thanks," and he sat on an uncomfortable wooden chair.

"Doctor Brown is available," said the nurse, returning. "He will see you in five minutes."

"That's great, and thanks again, nurse."

A few minutes passed, and in came the doctor. He was a short man with cropped greyish hair.

"Hi, I'm Doctor Brown," he said extending his hand for Robert to shake.

"I'm Robert Clement, I met you yesterday, I'm the father in law, of Julie Clement," he said, shaking the man's hand.

"I'm sorry, I never recognised you."

"That's OK, I'm sure, in your job, you meet a lot of people. I'm just a bit concerned about her. She seems rather distant, and not very talkative today. She was better yesterday, are you sure she should be getting home today?"

"Yes, I'm sure," said the doctor, "we've given her some good medication, and although she seems distant, the past two days, we've seen a great improvement in her. What you have to remember is that she has been through a very traumatic episode lately. And I can sympathise with you, that your whole family has been going through this too, but what we need to consider is this, keeping her in the hospital will have a negative impact on her mental well-being. Our experience tells us yes, Julie will be better served out of the hospital and into the bosom of her family, so to speak. This will lead to more interaction and ultimately a better healing process. We've given her strong anti-depressant tablets, and it's vital she takes them at the correct intervals. We've seen a drastic improvement in her condition these past two days."

"Well, if you're sure it's for the best, then so be it," Robert said, "and thanks for your time, doctor." They shook hands.

Chapter 16

Robert returned to Julie's room.

"Where were you?" asked Julie.

"I just nipped to the toilet, are you're ready to go now?"

"Yes," she replied. He carried her bags, and Dot took Julie by the arm and led the way to the lift. Once in the car, he waited until they'd both put on their seat belts before he started the car and drove back to Dot's. He was as he's been doing for the past while, subconsciously scanning everyone they passed, again without any success of seeing Doug.

They arrived at Dot's and he took her bags from the boot of the car and carried them into the house. Dot got Julie settled, and then she put on the kettle. Robert stayed for about an hour. The concerning thing for him was that Julie had hardly said a word the whole time he was there. He spoke with Dot in the kitchen out of earshot of Julie, and asked Dot if it was a good idea to have Julie stay here alone whilst she was working? She assured him she was going to call her line manager and book a week's holiday.

"I'm due some holidays, and I've already spoken with him. I told him I may need to take some time off at short notice, depending on how Julie was. He said, that was OK. I'll call him later when Julie's asleep, I don't want her thinking she's putting me to any trouble."

"OK, that sounds wise, remember, Dot if you need anything? Just call, I mean, it, Dot anything at all?"

"OK, thanks," Robert went back into the sitting room where he saw Julie fast asleep on the couch. He went back into the kitchen and let Dot know. She went into one of the bedrooms and returned with a duvet and laid it on top of her daughter. Robert kissed Dot on the cheek and left.

He called Mary and let her know the situation with Julie and of this morning visit to see the brothers Smith. He said it was very unlikely Julie would be attending the undertakers today. She told him she was not long off the phone with Andrew, he and Jason, were on their way over. They'd both managed to get another day off work to finalise the funeral arrangements.

"OK," said Robert, "I will be home in fifteen minutes, can you please make me a sandwich? All I've had today, since I left this morning, is a biscuit from Emily, Ricky's secretary, she said to say hello and passed on her condolences."

"That was kind of her, see you soon."

He hung up the phone. When he got home, he saw Andrews's car parked outside the house. He opened the door, Mary was just coming from the kitchen to the sitting room with a plate full of sandwiches, and four mugs of tea and coffee. Robert shared his concerns with them regarding Julie, he suggested it would probably be best if all four of them go to see the undertaker together. Andrew called Brendan to see if he would be available this afternoon.

"Yes, I'm free between three and four, how does that suit?"

"That's perfect, we'll see you then," and he rang off. "OK," he said to the others, "Brendan will see us at three PM." They had their lunch.

Mary asked Robert, "What did the doctor say to Julie before she left the hospital?"

"I'm not sure if the doctor spoke with her directly. But the nurse that gave her the medication reminded her how important it was to take them as prescribed. I went and spoke to Doctor Brown, the guy we met yesterday."

"Yes, I remember him, short greying hair."

"Yes, that's him, you've got a better memory than he has, he didn't remember me. Anyway, he assured me Julie returning into a family environment would much improve her metal state, his words, not mine."

"We must take their guidance, Dad," said Andrew.

"Yes, I know, Son, but I'm just not convinced Julie's ready yet. You should see her, she's like death warmed up, and she hardly spoke a word to me, or Dot."

Jason spoke up, and volunteered to go and sit with Julie if Dot wanted to go with the others to see Brendan.

"That is kind of you," said Mary.

"It's the least I can do."

Mary called Dot, she wanted to find out how Julie was. Dot answered right away.

"Hi, Dot, its Mary, how are you? And how is Julie?"

"I'm doing OK, thanks, Julie's been sleeping more or less since Robert left here earlier. She woke up briefly and I've managed to get her into her room. I keep checking on her every half hour or so, I think the medication she's on is making her very drowsy."

"I'm sure once she gets used to the tablets, she'll be fine," replied Mary. We're going to head over to see the undertakers shortly, do you want to tag along? Jason has said if you like, he'll come over and sit in and keep an eye on Julie."

"Thank Jason for his kind offer, but I'd rather stay here with Julie for the time being. I'm sure you're all more than capable of making the best arrangements, Julie's just not up to this."

"Fair enough, we'll head over, and finalise the arrangements and hopefully, Julie will be happy with them."

"I'm sure she'll be fine with them."

"Can I come over later?"

"Yes, that'll be good."

"OK, I'll see you, about seven PM."

She finished the call, and turned to Jason, "She thanks you for the offer, but she'd rather stay at home with Julie."

It was soon time to head over to the undertakers. Andrew suggested they all go in his car, they all climbed in, and they were at the undertakers at five minutes to three. The receptionist asked them to take a seat, and told them that Brendan would be with them shortly. He was just finishing with another bereaved family. Less than ten minutes later, his office door opened, and out came what looked like a father and son similar ages with Robert and Andrew. They all nodded a polite gesture in passing one another. Brendan came out a minute or so later.

"Hello, Andrew, Jason, how are you both?"

"We're well, thanks. This is my mum and dad."

"I am very sorry for your loss Mr and Mrs Clement, please come in and have seat," he gestured to his office, "would you like tea or coffee?"

"No, thanks," said Robert. "We collected baby Grace, from the hospital at lunch-time today. I have put her into one of the baskets you looked at the other day, but please feel free to decide on a different one, if that's your preference. Would you like to see her?"

"Yes, please," replied Mary.

"Just give me a couple of minutes to get a viewing room arranged for you all."

With that Brendan left them sitting in his office. A few minutes later, he was back, and he showed them to a door marked Viewing 1. Once inside, there was a small wicker basket with little Grace lying there. She had been dressed in a pink floral design outfit, she looked so at peace. It looked more like a crib than a coffin which pleased them all.

Mary now had tears streaming down her cheeks at the sight of her dead grand-daughter. Brendan was right on cue and handed her a tissue. Robert, Andrew and Jason hid their own tears well.

"This is a good choice," said Robert. "You have done a marvellous job," they all nodded in agreement.

"I have also managed to get a time and date for her funeral. It will be held at two thirty this Friday afternoon."

"So soon?" asked Mary, "that's only three days away."

"Yes, it is," agreed Robert, "but we don't want to put this off any longer than is necessary."

"I suppose not."

Andrew suggested they give his mum and dad a few moments alone with Grace. That way he could discreetly speak to Brendan about the payment. Robert nodded his approval, he and his son had already discussed this privately, and he'd given Andrew his debit card. When they were back in Brendan's office, he told Andrew the whole cost of the funeral, including Mr Mullen, the celebrant, was two thousand and nine hundred and fifty pounds.

Andrew asked if debit card payment was acceptable. It was. Brendan got up and left to go to the reception and when he returned, he had a card machine. He pressed a few buttons and handed the machine to Andrew. He checked the amount and inserted his dad's debit card and pressed the four-digit number his dad had given him. He handed the machine back to Brendan, he pressed a button and the machine started printing out a receipt. He handed this to Andrew along with the debit card. Andrew then put them into his wallet. They headed back into viewing room 1. Robert and Mary turned as they entered the room.

"Are you ready to go now?" Andrew asked.

"Yes," nodded Robert, "we are."

They thanked Brendan again, and left. They headed back to their car.

Chapter 17

After leaving Brendan, Mary asked her son to stop by the florist.

"We'll need to get some flowers, and a wreath arranged." He drove the short distance to the flower shop. Mary and Jason went inside first, this gave Andrew a chance to give his dad his debit card back and the receipt. Robert looked at the receipt completely nonplussed and put it along with his card back into his own wallet.

"Listen dad, do you need Jason and I to give you some money towards this?"

"No, thanks, Son, come on, let's catch up with your mum and Jason." They both climbed out the car and entered the shop. Mary and the woman behind the counter were looking at flower arrangements in a small brochure. She had settled on one she liked, and was about to pay for it when Andrew suggested that he and Jason pay for the flowers two arrangements. One each, from the uncles, and from the grandparents. Jason nodded in agreement. She conceded, but said, she wanted to buy a pink Lilly bouquet.

"This one will be from Doug and Julie."

"OK, Mum, I just hope we find Doug before Friday."

"Yes, me too," she said.

They paid the woman, she would arrange for the flowers to be delivered to Brendan's on Friday morning, she knew Brendan well. Mary thanked her. When they were all back in the car, Jason suggested they go and get some dinner from a restaurant instead of Mary having to cook, this has been a stressful day. They all agreed, and they headed into a restaurant they'd been to on many occasions.

Once there Mary and Robert had decided they were having the steak. Robert ordered his rare, Mary was going for well done, Andrew ordered a rack of ribs, Jason had a mixed grill, he liked his medium rare. They all had soft drinks. Robert would be driving Mary over to see Julie and Dot later, Andrew was driving home, he had a coke. Jason was most likely going to see his mum and dad later, he had a coke too. The drinks came before the meals. They all spoke about how lovely and at peace little Grace looked, they hoped Julie and Dot would agree with the choices they had made.

Andrew's mobile phone started ringing, it was a number he never recognised. He stepped outside the restaurant and answered the call. It was the Jack Mullen, the celebrant.

"I'm just calling you to see if you received the email that I sent you this morning with my thoughts for Grace's funeral?"

"I'm sorry, Jack, I haven't checked my emails today," he told Jack of today's events.

"That's fine, I can appreciate it's a busy time for you and your family, do you think you will get a chance to look at them tonight?"

"Yes, for sure, Jack. I'm with my parents and partner just now, we're just having dinner then we'll head home. I'll print them off and get them approved or let you know of any changes. I will call you later, if that's OK?"

"Yes, as long as you can call me before ten PM."

"Yes, it will be well before ten, I promise."

"Thanks," said Jack, he hung up.

Andrew saved the number into his phone contacts. He went back into the restaurant, just as the food was arriving. He sat back down, and he told the others who the call was from.

"We'll get a look at his notes when we get home."

They ate their meals without much more conversation. When they were finished, Jason paid the bill, much to the protestations of Robert.

Andrew drove them home, he noticed his dad, sitting in the front passenger seat, was, as usual, scanning left and right looking for any sign of his brother. His mum seemed deep in thought, he could see her face, in the back seat, directly behind his dad, in his rear-view mirror.

"A penny for them, Mum," he said.

"What?" asked Mary.

"Your thoughts," he replied.

"I'm thinking about your brother, again, it's only three days until the funeral, what if we don't find him in time?"

"We can only hope, we do, Mum, but if not, then we'll just have to tell him all about Grace, and how she died. There's nothing more we can do. It's just difficult to know what to do for the best. I know Doug's always been the reliable one."

"Don't put yourself down, Andrew. You're both the best sons any parent could ask for."

"Yes, I second that," said Robert.

"I would third that too, if you were my son," smiled Jason. This brought a smile to Andrews face for the first time today.

"I don't deserve you lot, you all say the nicest thing to me."

Chapter 18

They arrived at Andrew and Jason's house, Jason nipped into the kitchen and put the kettle on, whilst Andrew logged into his Gmail account on their home computer. He quickly found the email Jack Mullen had sent him, it had an attachment on it. He opened it, briefly read it, then he went to the print option. He noticed he had another four new emails, he read them, whilst waiting on the printer warming up. Three were from friends expressing their condolences about his niece's death, the other was from his dentist reminding him he had an appointment next Thursday at nine AM. for a check-up. The printer burst into life and out came three pages. He scanned them again and handed them to his dad, he read them aloud. It was extremely distressing to them all, listening to the sombre words for the first time.

Three pages of heart-wrenching words. There was nothing they could think of that Jack had missed.

"He's done a marvellous, if very sad, job with the short memories we'd had of little Grace," said Robert. Andrew asked if anyone wanted anything added or removed. Robert, Mary and Jason agreed this was as good a sermon as they could have imagined. They all agreed there was nothing to add or subtract.

"Let's have a brew, and then I'll call Jack and tell him we're all OK with this."

"Do you think we should consult Dot before we give Jack the green light?" asked Robert to Mary.

"I don't think it's necessary, she said to me earlier that she was giving us full control over this and she would trust us and agree with what he arranged."

"OK, if you're sure, I think what Jack has given us is perfect and the arrangements at the undertakers, especially the wicker coffin is lovely."

"I don't think Dot will have any issues with anything we have settled today."

"Tell you what, Mum, I'll call Mr Mullen and let him know we're ninety five percent good with this. You can take a copy to Dot tonight, and let her read it and comment on it, that way she feels involved."

"That's a good idea," said Robert. "OK, let me drive you two home."

Mary kissed Jason, on the cheek, goodbye, Robert shook his hand. Andrew drove then, the short distance to their home. He didn't go in, he'd decided he was going to ask Jason if he could go with him tonight to visit his parents.

When he got home again, he asked Jason if he'd mind if he went along with him to visit Gary and Sheila.

"Yes, my dad's either going to have to accept that I love another man, or he can go back to hell."

"I'm sure he'll be fine with it, he seemed genuine enough when he said he'd been a fool when he kicked you out."

"I suppose so, I'm going to call my mum, not for his blessing, but just so there's no surprises when we show up together." He called his her and let her know of his plan to bring Andrew with him tonight. His face was a picture when his mum informed him she was about to call him and suggest Andrew came with him tonight, and it was his dad's idea. "That's great," he said, "we'll be there in about eight-thirty PM," he hung up the phone. He told Andrew what his mum had just said.

"See, what did I tell you, your dad wants to be part of your life again."

"Yes, and part of yours too." Jason went down on one knee and asked Andrew, to marry him. Andrew was gobsmacked. He said yes instantly. "Let's keep this under wraps, until after the funeral though," said Jason. "We don't want to take centre stage."

"Yes," agreed Andrew, "sometimes, I'm surprised by your maturity, that's why I love you to bits." They kissed, and headed upstairs. A couple of hours later, they came back down stairs, having been showered, changed and ready to head over the Jason's parents' house.

When they arrived at Jason's mum and dads, it was Gary that opened the door and surprisingly, hugged his son and warmly shook Andrew's hand. He asked how today went at the undertakers. They told him and Sheila about the little wicker coffin, and how lovely and peaceful Grace looked. Sheila asked Andrew if they could attend the funeral.

"I'm sure, that'll be fine, it'll give you a chance to meet my parents, if you'd like?"

"Yes, that'll be great, if you're sure, we'd be welcome to attend."

"It'll be fine, Jason and I are partners, that makes you both part of the family. I hope you don't mind, I've told my mum and dad you've contacted Jason, and like me, their delighted, and they would like to meet you too as they are as fond of Jason as I am."

"I don't mind at all, mate, it would be my honour to meet your parents. I'm sure they got a lot of questions to ask me about why I did what I did."

"I can assure you, Gary, my parents are live and let live types, and as you may well appreciate, they have got enough on their plates to deal with at the moment."

"Yes, you're right, Andrew, I'm sorry. How are your mum and dad coping with this horrible set of events?"

"They seem to be holding up well, but I'm not sure how much of that is smoke and mirrors."

"Well, if there's anything we can do, please let us know."

They spent the next two hours talking about Jason's time at university and how the two of them met, it was easy conversation for a change. Andrew got the impression Gary was genuine in wanting to be part of his son's life again. Andrew liked him, maybe time was a great healer. They left to head home around ten thirty PM. Andrew asked Jason if he minded them calling in on his mum and dad before they went home. He wanted to find out how Julie was.

"No problem, I'd like to know too."

They arrived at his parents' house just as they were getting out of the car. His dad unlocked the house, Mary went in first to put the kettle on. He asked his dad what he got up to whilst his mum was visiting Julie. He went for a drive, he went a bit further afield than he'd been, looking for Doug, but he was unsuccessful.

Mary came out of the kitchen with four steaming brews. She told them, how her evening went. When she arrived, Julie was awake, she'd just had a sandwich and a bowl of soup. She was a little bit more talkative than she supposed she would be, but was still not her old self. She confided in Mary and her mum that she couldn't rid herself of the feelings of guilt as to why Doug had left and how Grace had died. She thought if she was more supportive of Doug, and if she could have taken better care of Grace.

"No matter how much we tried reassuring her none of this is her fault. We reminded her that Doug suffered a traumatic head injury, it's not her fault or even Doug's fault this had happened. Grace died from 'SIDS', again, it wasn't her fault. These tragedies happen. She asked why everything bad was happening to her. I just feel responsible, she said, and she got so upset, we nearly called a doctor. We eventually managed to get her calmed down a bit, Dot gave her one of her tablets, and then she went to bed. She was asleep in no time."

"Poor Julie," said Andrew, "she must be suffering terrible, can you imagine thinking you're responsible for your own child's death and that your actions drove your husband away?"

"Yes, it's very sad that she blames herself. If there's one thing we can agree on, it's that none of this is her fault." They all nodded in agreement. "Once Julie was asleep, I spoke to Dot about the funeral, I let her read the email from Mr Mullen, we both cried a bit, and Dot agrees with what he wrote. She's happy to go with it, without and changes."

"Good, at least that's settled, I will confirm to Jack in the morning."

"How did it go with your dad tonight, Jason?" asked Robert.

"He's definitely a changed man, he and my mum have asked if they can attend the funeral, will that be OK?"

"Yes, I don't have any problem with that."

"He's also keen to meet you both."

"Good, I look forward to that," said Mary.

"It's time we headed home," said Andrew, turning to Jason.

"Yes, let's go, we've both got work in the morning."

They hugged and kissed Mary, and hugged Robert and bid them goodnight.

"I will call you tomorrow from work," said Andrew.

"OK, Son, see you soon."

When they left, Robert asked Mary if she was up for a glass of wine.

"Yes, that would be lovely." He poured them both a generous glass each. "Where can Doug be?" asked Mary.

"I don't know, love, but I really hope we can find him before Friday, he'll be destroyed if he misses Grace's funeral. It'll be hard enough for him to cope, just knowing she died, but to miss her funeral too, it will be a lot to bear. Julie could really do with him being here."

They finished their first glass of wine, he poured them another. They spoke some more about Julie and then the conversation turned to Gary.

"I think I may have been too quick to judge him," said Robert.

"Everything we've heard about him seems to be good. Maybe the last ten or so years have been hard for him, and now the penny has dropped that the only way to get his family back is to accept his son for the man he is. I can't imagine us ever throwing out Andrew, can you?"

"It never even crossed my mind for a second, we knew from an early age about Andrew, it just shows you Gary obviously never paid close attention to Jason, or he would at least have suspected he was gay."

"True," agreed Mary. "I'm sure once, when I was speaking to Sheila, she told me she knew, from when Jason was in his early teens he was gay."

They finished their second glass of wine and Robert took the empty glasses and washed them and put them back into the cabinet. Mary went upstairs to bed whilst Robert locked up. She fell asleep pretty quickly. Robert just couldn't get to sleep. He had thought the wine would help him sleep, but it had the opposite effect, he tossed and turned all night. He was racking his brain, was there somewhere he had forgotten to look? Did Doug have any friends he'd had forgotten to ask if they had seen him? He just couldn't think of any he'd missed, maybe tomorrow the tide would turn in their favour. He eventually fell asleep.

Chapter 19

The next morning, Mary was up first. This was unusual as Robert was generally the early riser. She'd already showered and was downstairs in the kitchen on her second cup of tea when Robert came down. She made him a cup of tea and some toast.

"How did you sleep?" she asked him.

"Not great, how about you?"

"I had a good sleep, I think those two glasses of wine did the trick. I was just about to call Dot and see how Julie's night was when I heard you moving about upstairs. I will call her now."

Dot answered after about four or five rings, "How are you both?"

"I'm doing as well as can be expected, I suppose," replied Dot, "but Julie's not, she's still in bed. I'm thinking of calling our own doctor to see if he'll come out and look at her. I'm not convinced these tablets she's on are doing her any good."

"Wait until later on this afternoon, just in case they're slow to kick in."

"OK, I will, but if I don't see any improvement later, I'm calling Doctor MacLean at our own surgery."

"Fair enough, I'll give you a call around mid-afternoon to see if Julie's up."

"OK, thanks."

Mary hung up. She turned to her husband and told him, "Julie's still not up yet, she's been in bed since I left last night. We shouldn't be too concerned, they do say a sleep's as good as anything."

"I know she's struggling to cope, the doctor at the hospital did say it could be a slow process. He said that as the funeral was now only two days away, it was important, for Julie's sake, that everything goes smoothly. We don't need any more dramas."

"Yes," nodded Mary, her thoughts drifting back to Doug, all this uncertainty surrounding her missing son was playing heavily on her mind. He discussed visiting gyms to see if their son had been into any of them.

Together, they looked on Google to see how many gyms were located within a ten-mile radius of their house. To their great surprise, there were eleven. He wrote down their addresses, and postcodes. He was going to visit them all and take the picture of Doug with him, on the off chance someone would recognise him. It was a long shot, but it was better than sitting around doing nothing. He called Andrew and told him of his plan.

"You never know, Dad, you may just get a lucky break."

Robert kissed Mary goodbye, she called Dot and said she would go over to her house for a while, whilst Robert was out visiting the gyms. Hopefully, Julie would be feeling a bit better. They were all gravely concerned that she was not dealing with her grief, as well as they had expected. It must be very difficult for her, losing both her husband, and daughter, in quick succession, albeit Doug was still alive, just missing.

Mary tried to imagine Julie's pain, she was having a hard-enough time dealing with Doug's disappearance and Grace's death without the added stress of thinking it was your fault. What a mess. Robert had offered to drop her off at Dot's house, but she'd decided she was taking the bus. She wanted to stop off at a shop and buy a gift to try and cheer Julie up a bit. Maybe a small bunch of flowers, she knew Julie loved flowers.

Mary got a bus into town, and did some window-shopping for an hour or so. She changed her mind and bought Julie a box of chocolates rather than the flowers she'd thought of earlier. She'd gotten Julie flowers when she was in hospital and they hadn't been much use in cheering her up.

She managed to catch a bus, pretty much straight away. It would take her twenty-five minutes to get to the bus stop that was just around the corner from Dot's house. It was an uneventful journey, she even managed to catch her own reflection in the bus window, scanning everyone the bus passed. Robert had told her the other day that he has gotten subconsciously into the habit of looking at everyone he passed on all his journeys now, on the off chance that she catches sight of their son.

Chapter 20

The bus arrived at Mary's stop, she got off and walked to Dot's house, she knocked on the door and to her great surprise, it was Julie that opened the door.

"Hi, Mum," she said, "in you come." They had a quick cuddle.

"You're looking a bit better today, love."

"Yes, I had a long sleep, and now I feel a little less tired today than I did yesterday." She called out to her own mum that Mary, was here. She guided Mary into the sitting room, "Have a seat, Mum's upstairs, she'll be down in a minute. Would you like a cup of tea?"

"Yes, please, that would be great," she took the box of chocolates from the carrier bag and handed them to Julie, "these are for you."

"Oh, thanks, Mum," and they hugged again. "I hope you're going to help me eat these or else I'll get fat, and Doug will run a mile when he sees me. I'll put them in the kitchen for now, whilst I put on the kettle."

Mary thought, *My goodness, Julie's on fine form today.*

Dot came into the sitting room and gave Mary a hug. "Julie's looking better and sounding more upbeat now, isn't she?"

"Yes, she had a good long sleep, maybe the medication was as Robert said, taking it's time to get into her system."

"How do you think she will be discussing Grace's funeral?"

Without warning, Julie came into the room with a tray with three cups of tea and a plate with some biscuits. She caught the tail end of the conversation. Mary was a bit embarrassed that Julie had heard her mention the funeral, but again, to both Mary and Dot surprise, she said, "I've been thinking about the funeral, I know I have to be grown up about this, I am not the first mum to lose her baby, and I won't be the last, and I need to do this. Doug is missing, Grace is dead. I've decided, I want to go and see Grace at the undertakers, and I want you both to come with me. Can you do that for me?"

"Yes," said both her mums in unison.

"Good, have we got a date for the funeral yet?"

"Yes, it's arranged for Friday."

"My God, that's soon."

"We wanted to tell you yesterday, but we didn't think you were up to the news."

"You were probably right, but now I'm just going to have to be up to it. Thank you both, for arranging this."

"Andrew and Jason arranged most of it. They wanted to do as much as they could in Doug's absence."

"I'll call them both later and thank them. It can't have been easy for them."

"I'll call Andrew, he'll arrange, with the undertaker, for us to visit Grace this evening, if you're OK with that?" said Mary.

"Yes, please do," replied Julie.

Mary took her mobile phone from her bag and dialled her son. He answered straight away.

"Hi, Mum, is everything OK?"

"Yes, love, are you OK to speak or are you too busy?"

"I'm never too busy for you, Mum."

"I'm over at Dot's with Julie's just now."

"How is she?"

"She's fine, I've just called to see if you can get in touch with the man at the undertakers, I can't recall his name."

"It's Brendan," said Andrew.

"Can you please give Brendan a call and see if Julie, Dot and I can have a visit with Grace at seven o'clock tonight?"

"Yes, I will call him now, and call you back to confirm its OK."

Just then Julie asked Mary, if she could speak with Andrew.

"Julie wants a word with you."

"Great put her on." Mary handed the phone to Julie.

"Hi, Andrew, how are you?"

"I'm fine, Julie, more importantly, how are you, big sister?"

"I'm coping, but not much more than that at the moment. I just wanted to thank you and Jason with all my heart for arranging little Grace's funeral. I know how difficult this must have been for you both." There were tears, running down her cheeks now.

"Yes, it was difficult, but you're my sister and I love you to bits. I thought I should take that dreadful task from you." He, too, now had tears escaping from his eyes, and flowing, down his cheeks, just thinking of the turmoil poor Julie was dealing with.

"I love you too," she replied, "you're the little brother I never had and I couldn't have asked for a better one. I will speak to you later, please thank Jason for me."

"I will."

They said goodbye. She handed the phone back to Mary, she was about to say goodbye to him too, but he'd already hung up. Dot made them all another cup of tea.

Andrew called his mum about fifteen minutes later, she nipped outside out of earshot.

"Hi, Son, and how did you get on?"

"All good for tonight, Brendan will make sure you're looked after."

She told him that Dot had just given Julie the printed sermon notes that he'd given to her the other night. "We think she's strong enough now to read them and take in their contents."

"I hope so, she sounded really sad earlier."

"I think that was just because she was speaking with you about the arrangements. She was really good just before that, I thinks she'll be OK, Son. She's usually the strong one, between her and Doug, when it comes to things like this, you know how soft-hearted Doug is."

92

"Yes, you're right, Mum," he replied.

"OK I'll let you get back to work now." She ended the call and went back inside, Julie was nearly finished reading the notes. She had floods of tears falling down her cheeks again.

"This is good, it sounds as if this man knew Grace." When she'd finished reading them, her mum asked her if she wanted to add anything to them. "No," sniffed Julie, "this is a beautiful sermon. I don't think I could improve it." They all agreed it covered Grace's short life well. "Do we know how many people will be attending the funeral?" Julie blubbered out.

"We thought that it would be best if it's a small family funeral with a very few non-family members, probably no more than twenty people."

"That sounds OK," said Julie.

"Doug's boss, Mr Smith, wants to attend too, along with his brother, John," said Mary. "Are you OK with them attending?"

"Yes, they're welcome to come along, they've always been good to us."

"That was Andrew on the phone just now, he managed to speak with Brendan at the funeral home, he says he'll make the necessary arrangements for us to visit Grace at seven o'clock tonight."

"What time is it now?" asked Julie.

"It's quarter to three."

"OK, I'm going to go for a little nap."

"Fine, love," said Mary, "I'll ask Robert to collect you two at half past six tonight and we'll all go visit Grace tonight," Mary hugged and kissed Julie, and then she went upstairs to her bedroom.

Chapter 21

Doug and Johnny were getting ready for their shift, it was ten AM to six PM today. This had given Doug the time to go for a five-mile run this morning. He was starting to feel the benefit of the morning runs, and the evening sparring sessions and he was already looking forward to tonight. He wondered if Syd's pal would, indeed, give him a test, maybe he'd be a bit harder to hit. He thought to himself that he needed a test. He didn't doubt he could handle himself, but it was better to be sure than to find out in the ring with Cranston. He couldn't wait to get this fight over with, he wasn't nervous or afraid, just a little apprehensive.

They arrived for work, the site was a buzz of activity, and they spoke with Sammy and Stew, the two guys they were taking over from.

"Anything to report?"

"Yes, there was a couple shagging up against one of the fences last night after closing time in the pub. We saw them on the CCTV, and sicko Sammy here waited until they were right into it and rushed round and gave them the fright of their lives," they all laughed.

"Poor guy," said Johnny, "that'll teach the cheap skate, he should have gotten a room."

When they left, Johnny and Doug spoke again about the fight with Cranston. "Tell me again, Johnny, why you really think, I can win this fight?" Doug asked.

"Listen, mate, I'm so convinced that you'll win that I'm betting every bit of cash that I have on you to win. Cassidy is giving your odds of 4/1."

"How does that work?"

"Have you never put a bet on?"

"No, never."

"Well, you must've had a sheltered life. I wish I'd never had a bet, I'd be a millionaire. I will try and explain how it works. If I put on one hundred pounds, that's called my stake on you at 4/1 and you win, then I collect five hundred pounds, I get my original hundred pounds back plus I win four hundred pounds on top of that because your odds are 4/1."

"How much do you get back if Cranston wins?"

"If he wins then I get fuck all back, so it's best you don't fucking lose," laughed Johnny.

"What price is Cranston?"

"He's 1/2 odds on."

"What does that even mean?"

"It works the same way, if I put one hundred pounds on him and he beats you then, I get my original one hundred pounds back, plus I get fifty pounds on top."

"I don't understand that so you will win less money than you put on? That's just plain stupid."

"No, it's just the way gambling works. Cranston's been made the favourite, everybody who puts their money on him thinks he's a sure thing. What they don't know is, you're going to fucking win this fight. They'll all lose, and we'll win. Once you beat him, your odds will reduce for your next fight, that's how it works. Cranston was probably about four to one the first time he fought, there's always a favourite and an underdog," explained Johnny.

"So, they all think Cranston's a sure thing then?"

"Yes, mate, but by fuck, they're in for a big shock. Listen, I've seen so many fights, I've lost more bets than I've won but let me tell you this, if I was making the odds for this fight, I'd be making you the favourite. Cassidy thinks you will be cannon fodder for Cranston. I wouldn't be surprised if come tomorrow night, your odds have went out to five to one and Cranston's have shortened. I'll wait until then, before I place my bet."

The remainder of the day, Johnny kept telling Doug, to forget about being the underdog. "You can look at the history books; some mighty big underdogs have had their day. Have you never heard of David versus Goliath, who won that, eh? Nobody gave David a chance, but he won."

Their shift ended without incident, they handed over to Bob and big Kev, and they told them the story about the drunks from last night trying to have it off.

"I hope we get some entertainment tonight," smiled bob.

They headed home, via a Greggs. They both had a cuppa tomato soup and two tuna crunch sandwiches. They chilled and watched some TV for an hour or so.

Chapter 22

Robert had decided to go to the furthest away gym first, and work his way back toward home. It took him forty minutes to get to the Full Fitness Gym. It was a small cheerful looking place, he entered through a set of automatic sliding doors. There was a thin, young woman early twenties sitting behind a wooden counter with a pile of clean towels to her left-hand side

"Hello and good morning," she said, as he entered, "are you a member?"

"Good morning, no, I'm not a member. I'm looking for a little bit of assistance please. My son is missing, and he likes to keep himself in shape, he's been in a car accident and he's lost his memory." He showed the young woman Doug's missing poster, but there was no flicker of recognition in her eyes.

"I haven't seen him come in here before. I am sure I would remember a good-looking guy like that." This made Robert smile. "I only work here part time, I can ask the gym manager though, if you like?"

"Yes, please, that would be great if you could, thanks."

She picked up her desk phone and pressed a button. "Hi, Mark, can you please pop down to reception. I have a man here looking for your help."

"OK, I will be straight down," came a reply. A minute or so later, the manager came into reception. He was a young guy, about Doug's age, and he introduced himself as Mark Guthrie. Robert did likewise. "How can I help you?" Robert re-layed his story again and showed him the poster, again no sign of recognition. "Would you like a coffee, whilst I show your son's picture to the customers we've got in just now?"

"If you're sure it's not too much trouble?"

"None at all." He showed Robert into the café. He asked him how he took his coffee.

"Just milk please."

"Have a seat there," he pointed to a table and chairs right next to a glass observation wall, overlooking the gym. There were rows, of running machines, fixed bikes, rowing machines and a few weight lifting benches. Mark came back with one coffee, and one bottle of water. "Hang fire here," he said, and he disappeared through a door into the gym. Robert could see him a minute later, through the glass wall, he was showing Doug's picture to everyone in the gym, they all shook their heads. He arrived back at the table, a few minutes later. "Unfortunately, no one recognised your son. Tell me a bit about him."

"He's thirty-two years old."

"He's just a year younger than me then," said Mark.

It seems I was almost spot on with Mark's age, Robert thought to himself. "He's a member of our local gym, it's run by Rob Smith."

"I know Rob," said Mark, "we've been on a couple of courses together.

"That's handy, he's agreed to put a couple of the posters up for me, he knows Doug well."

"Have you got a spare poster, I don't mind putting one up in here, if you like."

"You can keep that one. Thanks for doing this."

"It's no problem. How does your son generally keep fit, is it the running machines or the weights?"

"He's mostly into boxing and sparring."

That's interesting, maybe you'll have better luck with a gym that has a boxing ring, like his own gym."

Robert pulled the list from his pocket and showed it to Mark. "Do you know if any of these gyms have a boxing ring?" The gyms were numbered one to eleven. Mark looked over the list, and his was number one.

"Numbers two, three, four and six don't have a boxing ring. This one here," he pointed to number five, "Semple's gym has got one. It's a bit down market, old school, more a boxing club than gym. A guy called Eddie Semple owns it. He was in here a year or so ago and he bought some old weights that we were selling. This one here number seven, shut down about eight months ago. I'm not too sure about the others."

"Thanks again for your time and information."

"It was no trouble at all, say hello to Rob for me."

"I will, Mark."

He was led back out to reception, they shook hands and Mark wished him good luck on finding Doug. When he was back in his car, he called Mary, her phone rang out and went to voice mail, he didn't leave her a message.

Chapter 23

Robert headed to gym number five, Semple's. It was about four miles away, he arrived there about eleven forty-five, it was closed. There was no sign on the door informing you what time it opened. He went into newsagents' shop, a few hundred yards down the street and enquired if the guy that ran the shop knew what time the gym opened. An Asian man, about fifty years old, told him the gym was only open at night-time. He said he usually saw lights on after seven PM. He told Robert it should be open later.

Robert called Mary, but it rang out again then it went to answer phone, again. He didn't leave a message; he hated those things. Mary will call him back when she notices the missed calls. He decided to go and grab himself some lunch, he went back into his car and drove to the local superstore he'd passed on the way here. He was hoping it had a cafeteria, he parked his car, then went into the store, and found they did have a cafeteria. He needed to visit the loo, he looked around until he saw the sign for the toilet, he needed to go there first.

When he was finished, he bought himself a large coffee and their lunchtime special of fish, chips and mushy peas. It looked nice, so he ordered it. The lady that took his order made his coffee, took his money and then handed him a small paddle with a number on it. She told him to sit at any table that he wanted to and to put the paddle in the holder on the table and that someone would bring his meal to his table when it was ready.

He picked a table that enabled him to see the main part of the store, this allowed him to look around at all the shoppers coming and going. He was scanning a new batch of customers coming into the store when a young man arrived at his table with this lunch.

"Would you like a top up on your coffee, sir?" he said, "It's free refills." Robert noticed the young guy had a name badge on his uniform, his name was Robert too. He glanced down to his near empty cup, he'd been so engrossed in the shoppers that he hadn't noticed his coffee was almost done.

"Yes, please," he replied to the young guys offer. He drank the small amount of coffee left in the cup and handed it to the young man.

He returned, a couple of minutes later, and put the new steaming coffee cup on Robert's table, and said, "Enjoy your meal, sir, and if you need anything, please, let me know."

What a polite young man he was, thought Robert. *He wouldn't look out of place as a waiter at one of the fancier restaurants in town.* Robert had now decided he was leaving young Robert a handsome tip. The fish and chips were delicious too, he wasn't expecting much from a supermarket café, but it had exceeded his expectations.

When he'd finished his lunch, and his coffee, he saw young Robert clearing a table two down from his. He beckoned him over and handed him a five-pound tip.

The young man was very pleased, "Thank you very much, sir, you enjoy the rest of you day."

"You too," replied Robert. Before he left the store, he decided to show the young man a photo of Doug. "Have you ever seen this man before?" he asked him, showing him the photo.

He studied it for a few seconds and said, "No sir, I don't recall ever seeing this man. Is he a friend of yours?" he asked.

"He's my son, and he's missing."

"I'm sorry to hear that, sir, I do hope you find him soon."

"Yes, me too," he thanked the youngster again and headed back to his car. He'd made up his mind, he was going to visit one more gym on his list.

Robert was just about to get into his car when his mobile phone started ringing. He looked at the display, it was his wife. He answered.

"Hi, Robert, I'm sorry, I've just noticed got a couple of missed calls from you, I hope it wasn't anything urgent?"

"No, it wasn't, I just wanted to give you an update."

"How did you get on?"

"At the first gym the manager, a guy named Mark was sympathetic and very pleasant, but he'd never seen Doug around his gym. He showed Doug's picture to his staff and the members that were in but none of them had seen or knew Doug. He knows Rob Smith from Doug's gym, he gave me a couple of pointers about the list of gyms I've got, most don't have boxing facilities. So, if Doug was attending a gym, it's unlikely he would go to one without a ring, and he's kindly taken a poster form me, and agreed to put it up in the gym, so it wasn't a complete waste of time. I'm just about to leave the second one now, it has a ring, but it's only opened a night. I'll go back there tonight or tomorrow night, have you been to see Julie yet?"

"Yes, I'm still here now."

"How is she?"

"She's great."

"That's fantastic."

"Yes, it is, she seems to be a bit more alert today, and she's even asked to go see Grace at the funeral parlour tonight. Are you OK to collect her and Dot at six-thirty tonight?"

"Yes, no problem. OK, I will ring off now, I'll collect you a bit later."

"OK, love, thanks," she said.

"I'll see you later. I'm going to visit another gym before I come to collect you." He hit the red end call button.

He headed for number eight on his list. He arrived at a very upmarket place named Saracens Gym. There was a swipe card access system that released a magnetic lock on the aluminium glass door. Next to it was a three-button buzzer type intercom with a sticker on each button. The top sticker had the word 'office' on it, the centre sticker had the words Saracen Tattooist and the bottom button had the words Saracen Gym. Robert pressed that button, and the door buzzed open. No one spoke through the intercom as he'd expected someone to. *Some security this was,* he thought.

He pulled the door open and entered. About five paces in, to the left, was a large open plan reception. There were three women working there, two were sitting facing each other and the other was facing the front. He noticed a large colour screen monitor that was depicting the front entrance. It had a very high-resolution picture; it was crystal clear. The woman that pressed the release button had obviously saw Robert at the door and considered him no threat to them, that's probably why she released the door to let him in, without conversing with him. He went to the woman facing him, and asked her, if the gym had a manager. One of the women behind the desk, stood and walked over to him.

"Hi, I'm Samantha, I'm one of the duty managers. What can I do to assist you?"

"Hello, my name is Robert Clement, I'm looking for my son, Doug. He's missing, he's had an accident, and he suffered some memory loss, he's always keeping himself fit. I'm doing a tour of all the gyms in the area." He looked at Samantha and the other two women to see if Doug's name had sparked any reaction, but it hadn't. He showed them Doug's picture, but none of them recognised him.

Samantha turned to the woman that was sitting opposite her and asked her to type in Doug or Douglas Clement into their database to see if he was, or had ever been, a member. Both names came up blank.

"Do you have a boxing ring in the gym?"

"No, we don't, I'm really sorry, we can't be of any help to you, sir."

"Thanks anyway, it was always going to be a slim chance, at least, I can cross you off my list. Is there any chance you could show this picture to the members you have in now? Just on the off chance someone recognises him?"

"I don't see why not. Ruby, can you give Mr Clement a quick tour of our facilities, whilst I show this picture around."

They both came out from behind the counter, through one of those lift up hatches at the far end.

"If you come this way," said Ruby, she showed Robert the male changing rooms first. She knocked on the door before entering, in case there were any naked men in there, she said. It was empty, she smiled, and said to Robert, "No luck for me today."

Next, she showed him into the main gym area. It was a bit like the first gym he visited this morning but on a larger scale, a lot more machines. It was about three times the size, all the running machines had a television monitor at the front to allow the exerciser to watch movies, the news or TV shows whilst they were hard at it. That would certainly relieve any boredom.

Ruby told him that they had over five hundred members, and the gym was open from six AM until ten PM. She also boasted they had twelve personal trainers you could hire and they could put together a training plan to suit all ages and all levels of fitness. She noticed Robert had a limp.

"Is that an old sporting injury you have there?"

"No, unfortunately, nothing as exciting as that, I used to be a tanker driver and I had a serious fall from atop of one. I smashed my hip and my knee."

She said she could offer him a starter membership for only forty pounds per month, if he signed up for twelve months. It was usually fifty pounds per month, but they had a special offer on at the minute. Robert thanked her for the tour, and said he thought his running days were over, but he would consider her offer.

Samantha was heading over in their direction now. She said one member thought he may have seen your son in here last year but he couldn't be certain.

"I'm sorry, again, we can't be of any more help. Did Ruby manage to sign you up for a membership?"

"No, she didn't, it's a tempting offer though."

"She's hopeless." The two ladies were laughing now. "I should have got her to show your son's picture around, I'm sure I would have sold you a membership."

"I'm sure you could have," he laughed too. Samantha and Ruby led the way back out to the reception, Robert thanked them again for their time and efforts.

"Just press the release button at the side of the door to get back out."

He waved at them as he left. *What lovely women*, he thought as he opened his car door and climbed in.

He decided he was going to visit Rob Smith to see if he had any news relating to the posters and to tell him of his encounter with Mark Guthrie. He arrived at the gym about half an hour later. He asked the girl on reception if Rob was available. It wasn't Janice, the girl that helped with the posters, *This girl was quite young, late teens, very early twenties at most*, he thought.

"Who shall I say is looking for him?"

"My names Robert Clement."

"Why does your name sound familiar?" she asked.

"Ah," said Robert pointing to the missing poster, "maybe this poster?"

"Yes, how silly of me, I've been looking at it all day, that's where I recognise your name. Have you had any luck finding your son?"

"No, not yet, hopefully he'll turn up soon."

She didn't have a name badge. She saw Robert looking. "My name is Angela I'm new, this is only my second day, I've not got a badge yet," she said. "I'll call Rob now."

"Thanks again, Angela," he said.

Rob came into the reception a couple of minutes later. "Hello, Robert." He greeted him like an old friend. He led Robert up the stairs, into his office, "How's Julie coping now?" he asked.

"She's getting better by the day."

"That's good."

"The rest of us seem to be coping a little better than her, but if I'm honest, it's probably the old smoke and mirror trick."

"Yes, I can understand that, you tend to put on a brave face for others."

"I won't lie to you, Rob, I've been having feelings of doubt, if we'll find Doug any time soon. His daughter's funeral is in two days' time, and there is no sign of him at all. Have you had any luck with the posters?"

"Not yet but, as you can see, it's in a very prominent position in reception and we have another in both changing rooms."

"Thanks, Rob, I can't fault your efforts."

"No luck on your end either, I assume?"

"None at all at this end either, I'm afraid. I spent this morning on a tour of some other gyms in a ten-mile radius."

"I would think there's quite a few."

"Yes. Eleven, would you believe, but only a few of them have a boxing ring. First on my list was Full Fitness Gym. I met a friend of yours."

"Let me guess, Mark Guthrie?"

"Yes, it was."

"How's he doing?"

"He asked me to give you his regards, he seems to be doing well. He's a nice guy, he said he hadn't seen Doug around his gym, but he did show his picture around the place, and thanks to knowing you, he also agreed to put a poster up for me."

"Yes, he's a very nice and helpful guy."

"Other than that, I never really accomplished much, but I did get to meet some nice people and it's certainly better than sitting at home waiting on my phone to ring."

"Would you like a brew?"

"No, thanks, Rob, just thought I'd call in on my way home to see if you had any news."

"It's still early days, I know it doesn't feel that way to you, but maybe someone will see the poster, tonight or tomorrow, and come up with a location." He led Robert back down to the reception. They shook hands.

Robert climbed back into his car, he looked at his watch, and it was already half past two, so he called Mary on route to collect her. He told her he'd be there in half an hour, and as he drove toward Dot's house to collect his wife, he was doing his usual scanning the people. He was careful not to take his eyes off the road too much, the last thing they needed was another accident.

He arrived shortly before his half hour estimate, just the way he liked it, never late, always on time, that's what he'd like on his tombstone. He parked the car and got out, he just arrived at Dot's door and was about to knock on it when Dot opened the door. She gave him a hug.

"Come in," she beckoned.

"You're looking great," he said to her. She half smiled.

"Well, maybe not great, but I'm getting there. Just having Julie back in the land of the living is a great load lifted from my shoulders."

"Mary was telling me earlier Julie's much better today."

"Yes, she is, and you've just missed her. She's away upstairs for a nap. You'll see her tonight. Mary's just put the kettle on, sit down, and when Mary brings your coffee in, and you're sitting comfortable, you can tell us how you got on today." Mary came into the room carrying a tray with two tea's and one coffee. *How would the world function without a brew,* he thought. Robert re-told his story.

"Are you hungry?" asked Dot, "I can make you a sandwich."

"No, I'm fine, thanks, Dot. I had some fish and chips and lunchtime today in a cafe in a big superstore."

"How was it?"

"Very nice, surprisingly, the fish was cooked to perfection and the chips were crispy enough, far better than I was expecting, that's for sure."

Mary told him of Andrews call earlier, and that he'd called Brendan, and arranged a visit to see Grace tonight. "I hope you don't mind, but I've volunteered you to collect Dot and Julie at half past six tonight?"

He smiled, "No trouble at all."

When they'd finished their tea and coffee, Dot got to her feet and put the empty cups back onto the tray to take into the kitchen to wash them. Mary also stood up and said they had best be heading home for their dinner and to get changed for tonight. The three of them hugged and kissed goodbye, arranging to see each other again at half past six. When they left Dot's, it was nearly half past three, just about enough time for dinner and a quick shower.

When they were home, Robert called Andrew, whilst Mary put on something quick for their evening meal.

"Hi, Dad."

"That's us home now," said Robert. It was nearly finishing time for Andrew, only another three quarters of an hour to go before he was heading home too. "What are your plans for tonight?" his dad asked him.

"I think Jason and I are going to have a quiet night in, unless you want us to tag along to the undertakers?"

"No, we'll be fine, you two enjoy your quiet night because you both deserve it."

"OK, thanks, Dad, did you see Julie today?"

"No, she was having a nap when I arrived."

"I managed to speak to her earlier today, she was sounding good, she thanked Jason and I for arranging the funeral, but it was a team effort."

"No, Son, not at all, you guys have done us all proud, and I'm sure when Doug gets back, he'll say so too."

"Well, thanks, Dad, but we're only trying to help as much as we can, for everyone's sake."

"OK, I'll let you get back to work, I'm going to have a shower, then have something to eat before we head out again, I'm sure I'll enjoy my bed tonight," he rang off.

He headed upstairs and had a shower, when he came back down the stairs, Mary was just putting their dinner onto the plates. She'd made them macaroni and cheese, with a garlic baguette, for them to share, it tasted great. She told him that Julie had read Mr Mullen's sermon and it had brought tears to her eyes.

"She is happy for it to go as it is, no changes are necessary," Mary told him.

"That's good, something less for us to worry about."

When they were finished with their dinner, Mary headed upstairs for a shower whilst Robert washed and dried the dishes.

Chapter 24

It was ten past six when the left their house and they arrived to collect Dot and Julie. At six thirty on the dot, Robert tooted his horn and out they came, Julie first followed by Dot. She locked her door before getting into Robert's car, both sat in the back seats. Robert turned to Julie and asked her if she was feeling up to this visit.

"Yes, Dad, I need to do this."

"OK, then, let's go."

The journey only took then about twenty minutes. When they arrived, it was drizzling with rain so Robert double-parked right outside the door of the undertakers to allow the women to get out the car and into the undertakers before they got too wet. He drove around the corner and managed to find a space, just big enough for him to squeeze the car in. He limped towards the undertakers as quick as he could, but he was soaking wet when he got into the place.

He joined the ladies, they were sitting waiting on Brendan who was coming out to see them. They spoke with an elderly man when they got in and he asked them to take a seat and Brendan would see them soon. They were nearly ten minutes early. A couple of minutes to seven, Brendan's office door opened, and out came two women, around forty years old, they looked very similar to each other.

"They must be sisters," said Mary, in a hushed voice.

"Yes," Robert and Dot agreed. Julie was very silent. Brendan led the two women out, and then turned to greet them all.

"Hello, Mr and Mrs Clement, how are you this evening? You must be Julie and Dot?" He shook hands with them all, "I'm very sorry for your loss," he said to Dot and Julie. Robert was very impressed, as were, Mary and Dot. Andrew must have given Brendan their names earlier. He asked if they were ready to see Grace. They were. He showed them into the same room as the previous time.

The little casket was sitting on top of a lovely floral blanket, it covered the whole table. Little Grace looked like she was asleep, Julie rushed over and kissed her dead, young baby's forehead, a river of tears running down her face. This set Mary and Dot off too. Robert and Brendan were saying all the right comforting things, but they were not sure their words were enough. Eventually, Mary and Dot managed to get their composures back a little.

"Grace looks lovely and peaceful," cried Julie, "it's like she is just sleeping. Can it be that she's not dead?"

"No, love," said Dot. Julie was in pieces now, crying uncontrollably. Mary and Dot hugged their bereaved young daughter and managed to get her settled down. Brendan and Robert left the room, after getting a signal from Mary to leave the three of them for a bit.

There were four chairs in the room, Mary and Dot managed to get Julie seated in one of the chairs with each of them at either side of her. They spoke for about ten minutes, them both assuring Julie that little Grace was at peace in heaven now. This seemed to calm Julie down a good bit. Outside the room, Robert again said to Brendan that he had done a marvellous job with Grace and he was sure his missing son, Doug, would be very happy with the arrangements.

"It was a nice touch greeting Dot and Julie by their names too."

"Yes, I always try to give a personal service, Andrew had kindly given me Dot and Julie's names earlier."

"I suspected as much," Robert nodded.

"We undertakers know this is a difficult time for families, and sometimes, it's the little thing than can make all the difference. I'm fortunate that I have a good memory for names, that always helps, I suppose. I've spoken with Mr Mullen, he says Andrew has told him he's ninety percent OK with the sermon, he just needs to run it by Julie."

"That's been done, sorry it never occurred to me to get Andrew to confirm it has all been approved. Julie had a look at it earlier today and has no objections to it at all."

"That's great, I will be speaking to him tonight and I'll let him know he's fine to go with it. The two woman you saw leaving my office, whilst you were waiting, were twin sisters. They'd just lost their older brother, to cancer, he died this morning, and they are looking for a celebrant too. I will ask Mr Mullen to give them a call."

"Do you pass many clients onto him?"

"Yes, quite a few, he's very good."

"I can agree with you on that, we've certainly been impressed by him. When we saw his piece for Grace, it read as if he'd known Grace, and our family well."

"He's very gifted. He picks up on everything, and somehow manages to convey it all in his wonderful sermons."

"As they were finishing their conversation, the viewing room door opened and the three women came out. Julie was a bit more composed.

"I would like to thank you, Brendan, Grace looks so peaceful and serene, and how did you manage to make her look so peaceful? It's a miracle."

"Thanks, Julie, we do our best, she was a beautiful baby."

"Can we come back again tomorrow?" she asked.

"Yes, of course, you can, just call ahead to allow us to have Grace ready for you."

"Thanks again," said Robert. Brendan shook hands with Robert and gave the three woman a small cuddle and expressed his condolences, again to them all.

Robert looked outside and the rain had now stopped. As the car was only parked around the corner, he'd decided they would all walk to it rather than him going and bringing it out front. When they got into the car, Julie asked Robert how he had got on earlier today. As he'd not seen her earlier, he hadn't told her his story from this morning.

Robert told her of his visits to the gyms, and of the missing posters. He wasn't sure if Dot had mentioned them to her. She hadn't got around to it yet.

"Do you think anyone will see Doug and let us know of his whereabouts?"

"We can only hope so."

"Have you heard that Jason's dad's got in touch with him and wants to get to know his son again? And it seems he has now finally accepted Jason for who he is."

"That's great, what made him come to his senses now? It must be years and years ago when he threw Jason out."

"Yes, just short of ten years, it seems Jason's mum Sheila, told him about Doug being missing and poor little Grace's passing."

If this upset Julie further, she hid it well.

"Has he met Andrew yet?" asked Dot.

"Yes, when he came to see Jason, at the house, Andrew was there too. They both visited Jason's parents last night, it seems Sheila's delighted she's got her family back."

This set Julie off. "Well, it's good someone's got their family, shame it's not us," she blurted out, and started sobbing.

"I'm so sorry, Julie, that was very insensitive of me, saying that, I wasn't thinking."

"Don't worry, Dad, it's not your fault." Mary had now given her a tissue. "It's just the way I'm feeling. I was sure I was ready to see Grace tonight, but I don't think I'd prepared myself for the sight of her in her burial basket. She did look lovely; can we go home now please? I think I need to take a tablet and get some rest, it's been a rather stressful night."

"Yes, love," said Mary, "it has been for us all."

Robert dropped them off about twenty minutes later. He noticed that Mary and Dot were now scanning everyone they passed, it must be rubbing off on them, him doing it. Mary had decided on route, that rather than go inside for a cuppa, they should let Dot get Julie in the house and settled. They kissed and cuddled before they left. Robert waited until they were inside before driving off.

Mary turned to her husband and said she thought tonight went as well as could be expected. Robert nodded, it was difficult enough for them all seeing Grace lying dead in a crib. They could only surmise what it must have been like for her mum to see her like that.

"Where the devil is Doug? He's always been mister reliable," she said.

"You know Doug would be here if he could be."

"I know that, but where can he be, it's like he's disappeared off the face of the earth."

"If only I knew, I'd go straight to where he was and grab him and bring him home."

They were home twenty minutes later, it was now quarter past nine. Robert asked Mary if she preferred a tea or a glass of wine.

"After the day and night we've had, we deserve a glass of wine."

"OK, wine it is." He went into the kitchen to pour a couple of glasses of wine. Mary lifted the cordless phone and punched in her youngest sons' number in and called him.

"Hi, Son."

"Hello, Mum, how did tonight go?"

"It went fairly well, I was just speaking to your dad. Julie's going through hell right now, but all things considered, she did OK. The initial shock of seeing Grace in her burial dress and basket sent her momentarily over the edge, but that was to be expected, other than that she was fine. How was your quiet night in?"

"It's been good, we watched a film earlier and we've spent the last hour talking about the funeral, where Doug could be and we even discussed the merits of us hiring a private investigator, but as Doug's never had a social media presence, he's not even got a Facebook account. Even you, Mum, have one of those."

"Yes, I know I do, but I don't post much on it."

"Well, we spoke about that anyway, and we think it would be a waste of time and money. We reckon what Dad's doing is best, we really believe someone, somewhere will see the missing poster, and get in touch with Dad."

"Do you really think so?"

"Yes, Mum, we do."

"Here's your dad now," she said, swapping the phone with Robert for a glass of white wine.

"Hello, Dad, I was just telling Mum that Jason and I have been racking our brains trying to think outside the box, so to speak, if there is something else we can be doing to find Doug, but other than hiring a private investigator, we are doing everything we can."

"Great minds must think alike, I was thinking about that this morning but to be honest, I've dismissed the idea. What more could an investigator do that we're not already doing?"

"That's exactly what I said to Mum."

"That's settled then, no investigator, well not yet anyway. How is Jason doing? Has he spoken with his dad today?"

"He's doing great. He's not spoken with Gary today. He did speak with Sheila though, and she says it's as if someone has kidnapped the old Gary and replaced him with a new one. She's very happy her son and husband are back speaking again."

Robert told his son what he said in the car about Jason and his parents, and it upset Julie.

"I'm sorry to hear that, Dad."

I did apologise to her. She'll be fine, it's the only nice thing we've had to discuss for a good while. I could have framed it a bit better, with hindsight."

"Don't beat yourself up about it, Dad. She'll be happy for Jason, soon enough. I spoke with her earlier today and she seemed to be a lot better, I know if things were different for her now, she would be thrilled for Jason, and Sheila, for that matter, that his dad had come back into his life."

"Yes, I agree, hopefully, when we get the funeral over with, she'll start to put her life back together. I know Doug coming back will be a huge factor in that."

"How do you think he'll deal with his daughter being born, then dying, and then to crush him even more, him missing her funeral?"

"God only knows, the answer to those questions, Andrew, but what I do know is we will all be here for him to lean on, and together, we'll get him through it. But let's not be too pessimistic, we've still got time to find him before Friday."

"OK, on that optimistic note, Dad, I'll say goodnight, say goodnight to Mum for me."

"OK, Son, goodnight." Robert pressed the end call button and put the phone back into its cradle. He picked up his glass of wine from the table and sat on the settee next to Mary. They clinked glasses and drank their wine.

"Tomorrow I'm going to visit the police again, you never know, if I keep some pressure on them, they might even look for Doug."

They finished their first glass, and as the previous night, they had decided on another. He went into the kitchen and took the bottle from the fridge and poured them. There was just enough left in the bottle, for two more. He opened the back door, and placed the empty bottle into the recycle bin, it was located just outside the door. He noticed it was turning cold again. He closed and locked the door.

When he returned with the wine, Mary had switched the television on, she had the sound muted and had it on the local news channel. Looking at the ticker tape running at the bottom of the screen, there was nothing too exiting happening, so she switched the television off again. She took the glass of wine from her husband, and they spoke about Jason's dad Gary again. Robert told her about Sheila saying she felt like she had a new man.

"Gary was a completely different person. I really hope it's not just an act. If he hurts Jason again, he will have more than just Sheila to deal with."

"I'm sure he's genuine," she replied.

"Andrew, certainly thinks so. Let's give him the benefit of the doubt."

They spoke about having Andrew and Jason chaperoning Julie on Friday. Mary agreed, they just had to ask them if they would be agreeable. He was sure they would be, but he'd rather give them their place and ask them. They finished their wine, Mary headed upstairs first, Robert washed the glasses and locked up, unlike last night, he was out like a light when his head hit the pillow.

Chapter 25

The next morning, Mary got up and discovered that Robert was already in the shower. She went down stairs and put the kettle on, she looked at the wall clock it was half past eight. She had decided to make scrambled eggs and toast for breakfast. When he came down, the kettle had not long boiled.

"Just waiting on the eggs," said Mary, "I hope you're hungry? I'm making scrambled eggs on toast."

"I sure am."

"Good," she said.

A couple of minutes later, they were tucking into their breakfast. Just as they were about finished, the phone rang. Mary answered it, it was Dot, and she said that Julie had had a good night, and she was up and showered. They were going to go out for a bit of shopping.

"That's great to hear, I will pass this onto Robert and the boys."

Mary had decided she was going to clean the house today, whilst Robert was out. He left at ten-thirty AM he went back to the police station he'd visited. He approached the reception and he asked for DCI Craig.

"Can I have your name, sir?" the young woman behind the counter asked.

"My name's Robert Clement, it's about my son, Doug."

"Please take a seat, and I'll see if he's available."

Less than ten minutes had passed when DCI Craig arrived at the reception, "Hello, Mr Clement, sorry to keep you waiting."

"It's no bother."

"Come with me and I'll get us a quiet room."

They ended up in an interview room, it was very basic.

"Have you any word on my son, Doug?"

"Unfortunately, not yet, but I have given his description to some colleagues, and I've notified the other stations around London. Like I told you the last time we spoke, as your son hasn't committed any crime, there's not much we can do. I understand this isn't what you want to hear, but I would rather be honest with you than give you false hope."

"I do appreciate your honesty, and can I be honest with you? I'm desperate to find him. His daughter's funeral is tomorrow."

"OK, leave it with me. I'll put in call this morning to those colleagues again."

"That's all I ask, DCI Craig."

"You can call me Scott," replied the DCI.

"OK, thanks again, Scott, I will leave you in peace now."

They shook hands and he left the police station, and headed home. He phoned Mary when he was back in the car. She asked him to pop into Asda and get some fresh bread, milk, a bag of baby potatoes, and some roast beef from the meat counter. He arrived home at twelve fifteen. Mary made them roast beef sandwiches. When they'd finished eating, Mary watched some TV.

Robert went upstairs for a lie down. He'd told Mary he'd be back down at around four PM. He took some paracetamol tablets. His bad leg was hurting, it must be all the walking he'd done those past few weeks. He needed all his strength and energy for tonight as he was going to visit Semple's gym. The one he tried to visit yesterday but it was only open in the evenings. He told her that he'd head over there at seven o'clock, he didn't want to be out too late as the funeral was tomorrow.

Robert got up at four thirty. They had their supper at five PM. Mary had made them stewed sausages with boiled potatoes and some green beans.

"It was delicious," he said.

"I enjoyed it too," she replied. They washed and dried and put away the dishes, together, Mary washing and him drying. They discussed the arrangements for tomorrow again. Jason had already agreed that he was going to be the designated driver, he and Andrew were going to collect Dot and Julie at one thirty. John Smith had kindly agreed to come and collect them at one PM, and take them to the undertakers. They wanted to be there waiting on Julie, they didn't want her arriving and getting herself all worked up. This was the last thing she needed. The tablets she was on were taking the edge of Grace's death, but they weren't doing much more.

Dot had confided in them that she'd asked the doctor to up her dosage, but the doctor had refused. He'd said doing that, would leave Julie a bit more comatose and less responsive and he had decided to leave the dosage unaltered.

It was now time for Robert to head out, Andrew had called earlier, and he asked his dad if he wanted him to go with him.

"Yes, please, Son, that would be great if you came along," he'd said. So, he was heading over to collect him at quarter to seven. Andrew was ready and waiting, he came out as Robert was parking outside the house. He jumped into the passenger front seat. And off they went. Andrew asked his dad if they were all set for tomorrow.

"As set as we can be. I've a small favour to ask of you, and Jason. I know you've both went above and beyond in arranging Grace's funeral, but your mother and I have been talking and we feel Julie is in a very fragile state at the moment. I know she's been better the last few days but we're hoping you and Jason will stick to her like glue tomorrow. She's going to need every ounce of courage she has tomorrow and it will be a very emotional day, more so for her especially."

"Yes, Dad, that's no problem, Jason and I will do that for her."

"Your brother will thank you for it."

"I know, Dad, but let's hope we find out some information at this gym. What's it called again?"

"Semple's."

"That's a very unusual name for a gym."

"Yes, I thought that too, it's named after the man that owns it."

They arrived at the gym at ten past seven. There was a light on so at least there's someone in.

Robert parked the car and they both got out. The gym door was unlocked, Andrew pulled it open. It led to a steep flight of stairs, Andrew climbed them without too much difficulty. Robert was limping more acutely. When they got to the top,

Robert was slightly out of breath. He assured himself it will be much easier going down them. They heard a couple of voices, a man in a tracksuit acknowledged them and made his way over.

Eddie thought he recognised the younger man, and was about to shout to him, but as he got closer, he saw it wasn't Doug at all. It was a guy only slightly smaller but very similar facially.

"What can I do for you, gents? Are you looking for somewhere to train?" asked Eddie.

"No, we're here on a bit of family business. My name's Robert Clement, and this is my son, Andrew." They shook hands.

"I'm Eddie Semple," he was wondering where this was going.

"We're looking for my older son, Doug, Andrews's brother." He pulled the missing poster from his coat pocket and showed it to Eddie. He thought he saw a flicker of recognition, Eddie had noticed Robert looking at him so tried to cover himself.

"He looks the spit of you," he said pointing at Andrew, "and I thought this was you in the photo."

"Yes, we do look a bit similar, but Doug's a bit taller and a he has a lot bigger build than I have."

"Is he a boxer then, your son," he said looking at Robert.

"Yes, he's had a few amateur fights, have you seen him around?"

"We get all sorts in here, my friend. Why are you looking for him?"

"He was involved in an accident a few months back, and he's lost his memory. We've been trying to find him, he disappeared a week or so ago."

"I can't say I've seen him around this place, but I only come in a couple of days a week," he lied. If the gym was open, he was here. He wouldn't trust anyone else to do it. "I'll tell you what, you leave this photo with me and I'll ask around the regulars. This place doesn't get busy until about half past eight. You're welcome to stick around if you like," he said, hoping they couldn't tell he was lying, and he was trying to get them the fuck out of here before Doug and Johnny turned up later.

"It's vital Doug gets in touch as soon as possible." Robert never mentioned anything about Julie or Grace, he was getting a negative vibe about this guy. They shook hands again, then Robert eased himself back down the stairs with Andrew right behind. They got to the bottom of the stairs and were about to push the door open, but it was being pulled open by someone coming in.

A big guy was just about to enter, as the stairs very narrow, and there wasn't enough room to pass on them, he stopped at the door and let them get out. Andrew thanked him as he got out.

"You're welcome, mate," the stranger replied.

When they got back into the car, Robert said, "Did you get the same feeling as I did, this Eddie guy knows something. He recognised Doug, from the picture, and then tried to bluff us."

"I thought so too, what do we do now?"

"Do you think Doug goes into that gym?"

"I'm not too sure. Do you think we should stay around here, just in case Doug shows up tonight?" asked Andrew.

"If it wasn't Grace's funeral tomorrow, I'd be very tempted to come back here later tonight, but it could be a wild goose chase, let's get home and collect our thoughts."

Andrew agreed.

Chapter 26

Doug and Johnny arrived at the gym at ten past eight, this would be his last session before tomorrow night's fight with Cranston. The other guys were already there. They said hello to Eddie, Brian. Syd and his mate, Andre, were already in the ring warming up. They saw Doug and Johnny come in, they stopped sparring and climbed out of the ring.

"Hi, guys, this is my mate, Andre," he said, introducing them, "this is Doug, the guy I was telling you about." They shook hands, "And this is his mate, Johnny." Andre shook Johnny's hand too. "Doug's fighting Cranston tomorrow night."

"Lucky him," said Andre. Doug went to get changed, Syd and Andre climbed back into the ring, Brian was ringside, he would keep time and Syd would referee tonight. Eddie seized his chance as soon as Doug disappeared.

"Hey, Johnny, we need a quick word."

"What's up, pal?"

"I had a couple of visitors in here earlier tonight, in fact just about an hour ago."

"Who were they?"

"Two guys, one of them told me he was Doug's dad and the other was his kid brother, they were here looking for him."

"For fuck's sake, you didn't tell them anything, did you?"

"Give me some fucking credit, of course, I didn't tell them anything. I told them I'd never seen or heard of him."

"How do you know if they're legitimate?"

"They said so and the brother's practically his double although slightly smaller."

"How do they know he came in here?"

"They don't, it was just in a process of elimination, his old man's called Robert, and he's been visiting all the gyms within a ten-mile radius. He showed me a picture of Doug, it looks like it was taken pretty recently too. What's his story?" then asked Eddie.

"Doug told me he was in a car crash, and he ended up in a coma and when he awoke, these strange people were trying to pull a flanker on him. He said he didn't recognise any of them, there was a woman there too, and she had a baby with her. She said it was Doug's kid, but he told me he'd never seen any of them before."

"Well, these guys tonight definitely seemed to be credible enough to me, and get this, Johnny, they said Doug was an amateur boxer. I fucking knew he'd been in the ring before, he's a natural," said Eddie. Doug came out the changing rooms, he climbed into the ring with Syd, and Andre. Syd's mate was, indeed, a big lump of a guy, and he'd had a few decent victories under his belt, as an amateur. They discussed what they wanted to accomplish tonight, between Syd, Brian and Andre, they had seen a few of Cranston's fights so it was decided, Andre should try and fight the way they thought Cranston would.

Johnny asked Brian to do the honours with tonight's sparring session, he said he and Eddie were going into the office to talk some business. Johnny led Eddie to the office out of earshot of the others.

"What else did these guys say?"

"They more or less confirmed what Doug told you, with the exception of them trying to pull a flanker. His dad said it was very important he gets Doug back home, as soon as possible."

"What about the others, did they speak to these two guys?"

"No, Syd and Andre hadn't arrived yet and Brian was coming in just as they were leaving. He asked me who they were, I told him they were just checking the gym out, looking for somewhere to train."

"Do you think he believed you?"

"Yes, but I'm not so sure the old guy believed me. When I told him I'd never seen their boy in their photo before, I tried to look as neutral as I could, but it was a bit of a shock seeing your mate, Doug, in the photo. I could see the way he was looking at me, he was maybe not convinced."

"Do you think they'll be coming back again?"

"I'm not sure. Should we tell Doug?"

"No, definitely not, he's got more than enough on his plate with the Cranston fight looming on the horizon."

"What about after the fight?"

"We'll wait and see, I've got a right few quid to put on Doug and at four to one. When are we going to get a better chance of putting one over on that crook Cassidy? So, let's just keep it between you and me, for the time being anyway."

"OK," agreed Eddie.

They walked back toward the ring, and saw Andre going straight at Doug, and he almost caught him with a big left. Doug managed to move his head out of the way of it, just in time. He turned slightly as the punch flew past his left ear, and he caught big Andre, in his mid-riff, with a right-hander. If this hurt Andre, he managed to conceal it. He came at Doug again, this time trying an upper cut, but Doug saw this a mile away and blocked it easily. They then went toe to toe, until the end of this first round.

The second round started much the same as the first, Andre coming forward from the bell, he was throwing lots of punches, but Doug was well-guarded and didn't get touched with anything resembling a decent hit. Doug thought Andre was trying a lot harder than him. Round three was, again, similar to the previous two rounds. Andre was certainly a harder target to hit than his two pals were. Doug was pleased that Andre hadn't managed to land any telling blows on him.

In round four, Doug decided to open up a bit, and see just how resilient Andre was. He managed to land a couple of good solid jabs on the new guy's chin, the last one definitely gave him something to think about. Doug thought this is an even fight going into the last round. Maybe it's time to test Andre's defences to the full.

Round five started and his opponent wasn't as quick to attack as he'd been the first four rounds, the big digs into his lower body had slowed him down a bit. *Let's change tactics*, thought Doug. Instead of sitting back, and letting Andre come onto him, he went looking for Andre. In this final round, the hunted became the hunter, and about a minute in, Doug landed a big, thundering body shot into Andres left hand side, and Andre dropped his hands. Doug seized his chance and smashed a big right-hander into his face, it rocked his head back and his gum shield came spewing out, he landed hard on the deck, game over for Andre.

Brian and Syd jumped into the round, checking the see if the big man was all right. He was helped to his feet, he was a bit groggy, but it appeared he was OK. *Thank God,* thought Doug, Syd and Brian, helped their big pal out the ring and sat him down in a chair. Eddie removed his gloves and gave him a drink of water. He was going to be fine.

"What the hell was that you hit me with?" he asked.

"Just a lucky punch, mate."

"No way was that lucky, I'm definitely going to put a bet on you. Cranston's in for a big shock if he thinks you're a pushover."

"Thanks," said Doug. "I hope you're right."

"Well, I can tell you something, if you can land that punch on him, he's going down big-time."

"Yes," they all agreed it was a knockout punch.

"OK, Doug," said Eddie, "let's get you to work on the heavy bag, try and sweat a bit, then you can do some skipping, that will build a bit of stamina, but nothing too strenuous as there is no point in punching yourself out, there will be plenty time for that tomorrow night."

Doug worked on the big bag that hung on a chain from the roof, it was quite old but seemed to be still in good shape. Andre was now fully recovered and was working with him.

"OK, you two, hit the showers."

As Doug and Andre were getting showered, and changed, Johnny discussed the night's performance with Eddie, Brian and Syd.

"How's he fairing?"

"I think after tonight's heavy sparring, he's good to go. Do you know where he learned to fight like that?" asked Syd.

"I don't know, he was in a car accident, and he had a severe bump to his head and he's not sure about his past. He thinks it will all come back to him, but he must have some boxing training."

"Did you see the way he moves around the ring, you don't get that kind of craft overnight," claimed Brian. "I've seen lots and lots of decent fighters come through this gym, but this guy's exceptional, he can duck and weave, he can block, and did you see the way he delivered that knockout punch on Andre?"

"Yes, I saw it, and Andre was giving as good as he was getting up until Doug landed that blow."

"I'm not so sure he was," said Eddie, "I think Doug could have done that in the first round."

"Do you think he really is that good?"

"Yes, I do," replied Eddie. Doug and Andre came out of the changing rooms, Andre didn't seem to be too affected from his earlier knockdown.

"Eddie, tell Doug how sure you are, that he's got what it takes to beat Cranston," said Johnny.

"Listen to me, Doug, I'm seriously convinced you will win that fight tomorrow, that I'm putting a grand on you Brian, Syd and Andre are also putting a few quid on you, right guys?" he looked to them. They all nodded.

"Dead right, mate, we sure are, we've all been in the ring with you, and I would rather fight Cranston than fight you, and Andre," Johnny turned to his big pal, "if that's not a resounding endorsement, I don't know what is."

Eddie turned to Doug and said, "If you keep your head protected, you will win absolutely, no doubt. Cranston's not a boxer, he's a fighter, he won't be hard to hit but you must be. He won't be expecting you to be a boxer, and from what I've seen from you so far, you know how to box all right. Keep it tight for a couple of rounds, if he can't hit you, he'll get frustrated and then he will go all guns blazing. He's expected to beat you without breaking sweat, this will make him very dangerous, but it will also make him easier to hit and hurt. Keep your cool, and watch out for his head, he will try anything, and don't expect any help from the referee either."

"Yes, I know, Johnny has already warned me about that."

When you see a chance, land that big right-hander straight on his nose, trust me, Doug, he will go down, but he's a hard bastard, he will get back up again. So, make sure you go for the kill if he gets you in trouble, he won't hang back, he's a fucking animal. Just make sure you knock him out, that's the only way to beat him," said Eddie.

"That's my plan, I don't intend being in there any longer than I have to," said Doug, "how will the crowd react if I beat the guy they have all bet on?"

"Don't worry about that, Doug, the only people that will be betting big on Cranston are Big Jim's crew and Cranston's pals, most guys don't bet until the night and when they see the size of you I can assure you there will be plenty of money on you especially at 4/1. They might even push your odds out to capture some more money, these arseholes think Cranston's a sure thing, they won't be expecting anything other than a win for him."

"I wish I was as confident as you lot," said Doug.

"Our confidence is well-merited," replied Eddie. "You'll win if you take what you've shown here into that ring tomorrow night, you'll be the victor and to the victor goes the spoils."

Andre and Syd decided it was time for them to head off, they shook hands with everybody and agreed to meet up at the fight the next night. When they were gone, Eddie asked Doug how he felt it went.

"Well, Andre was a lot harder to hit for a round or two, but I quickly had his measure."

"Do you think you could have finished him earlier?"

"Without a doubt," said Doug.

"That's what I thought," nodded Eddie.

"The reason I didn't end him earlier was purely for practice, he never managed to hit me with any shots that were worrying."

"I've seen some very good fighters through the years, and you're up there with the best of them, how is it I've never come across you before?" asked Brian.

"I don't fucking know," snapped Doug, standing up, now shouting, and filled with rage, he sent the table they were sitting at flying across the floor, "but I'm getting fucking pissed off that you fuckers keep asking me where I learned to fight. The truth is, I don't fucking know. So, can you just leave it at that?"

Brian stood up and put his hand out to shake Doug's. "I'm sorry, mate, yes, we'll just leave it at that, if that's what you want."

"Calm down, Doug," pleaded Johnny.

"I'll calm down when people stop asking me stupid fucking questions."

A couple of guys that were now sparring in the ring stopped and looked over to where the commotion was.

"What are you two fucking pricks looking at?" barked Doug, the guys looked warily at him, they held up their gloved hands in concession and went back to their sparring.

"OK, Doug, time for us to hit the road," said Johnny and with that, they left the gym. Brian looked relieved. "You looked special tonight, Doug," said Johnny leading him down the stairs. "Cranston's in for a big surprise on tomorrow night, he will already think he's won," said Johnny, trying to sound neutral, his heart was racing, he'd not seen Doug riled up like that before. "I think I will put my big wedge on you, odds of 4/1, that's a steal."

"Only if I take the fucking fight," growled Doug.

Johnny decided he would keep quiet the rest of the journey see if Doug, could calm himself down. It worked a treat, the big man's anger had abated now, and he was back to normal. *Thank God,* thought Johnny. They decided to get a carry out Chinese again, for their supper, Johnny ordered a chicken curry with fried rice, Doug thought that sounded OK, but he decided to try boiled rice instead.

Once home, Johnny put the curries onto plates. He had a cold beer, whilst Doug had a can of diet Pepsi. He was even more determined to win now that Johnny had convinced him everyone would be betting against him. No way was he going to let them have a big win, at his expense. They ate their supper and finished their drinks. Doug asked Johnny, what type of people would likely be there at the fight.

"It'll only be guys that can be trusted to keep their mouths shut, if word got out, especially to the police, there would be a raid, and the type of folks that like a good bet and a drink too, I reckon, as there's always a betting stall and a bar selling alcohol. Cassidy likes to put on a show, there's usually some serious money changing hands at these events. I've noticed a few Italians dudes have been at the last couple of fights, I don't know what their deal is with Cassidy, but he's looking right up their arses for something."

"Will it just be me and Cranston fighting?"

"No, mate, there are sometimes four or five fights. You and Cranston will be the main event, that's where all the big bets will be. Cassidy will have informed his pals that he's got a late replacement to fight Cranston, and as nobody will have heard of you, and most of the punters will have probably won on Cranston before, that's where their money will go again, ha-ha, poor losers."

"You really think I'm going to win, don't you?"

"Not even the slightest doubt in my mind, you'll fucking knock him out. I've seen you with my own eyes, tonight, you were holding Andre up for five rounds. Promise me you won't do that with Cranston. If you can take him out in round one, then do it. It's not your job to put on a show, only when you've knocked him out will you have won. I've seen him nearly beaten before, only to come back the following round. This might sound stupid, mate, but you only win when he's out cold, never assume you've won until then. These, ain't no marquis of fucking Queensberry rules fights, Doug, it's a fucking dogfight, you win when the opponent can't continue. None of this counting to ten bullshit."

"OK," said Doug, "I will do my best then."

It was now bedtime for Doug, as he was intending to go for a six AM leisurely run in the morning. Johnny stayed up and watched a film on television, he was having a long lie in as they were now off work for a couple of days. He often wondered how his sons were getting on but he daren't phone his ex-wife. Every time he spoke with her, it always ended up in a shouting match that he never won. He watched the news, and then a talk show. He went to bed a couple of hours after Doug. He thought if Doug was concerned about tomorrow's date with Cranston, he was hiding it well, he knew if it was him fighting tomorrow, he'd be shitting himself.

Chapter 27

It was now the big day for Doug, he'd decided he would run a bit further from the house. It was starting to annoy him that he couldn't remember anything beyond his time in hospital. He couldn't remember the woman with the baby that always seemed to be crying. She'd claimed to be his wife, or the older man and woman that thought they were his mum and dad. And what was it with the gay guy claiming to be his brother, no way would he have a poof for a brother, or was he going mad? Or was this all some sort of scam? Surely, he would remember if he was married, and had a baby? He just didn't know.

He knew how to fight, the gay guy had mentioned to him he was a boxer, strange that he couldn't remember that, but it felt natural to him when he was in the ring sparring. He knew his name, but couldn't remember if this was because they told him it was Doug, he was very puzzled.

What he did know was that he shouldn't have flown into a rage last night, and had a go at Johnny, when he was getting quizzed by the guys at the gym. He would try to remember to say sorry to Johnny when he got home. *He's been good to me and it's not his fault I can't fucking remember my past,* Doug told himself. Maybe a good long leisurely run will jog some memories, off he went. He ran for about an hour, through streets he had never been on before. Nothing he saw brought back any memories. He turned around, and jogged back home, he had a shower. Johnny was still asleep.

Doug put on some clean underwear; he was now down to his last clean pair. He noticed a self-service launderette nearby on his way home. It opened at eight-thirty, it was a quarter past now, he bundled up all his dirty clothes, and put them into a bin bag he found under one of the kitchen cabinets. He left Johnny a note telling him where he'd gone, and that he would be back as soon as possible.

He didn't know how long a laundry would take. He bought a newspaper, a couple of breakfast bars, and a bottle of Lucozade from a small Tesco express shop on route to the launderette. The old guy that served him put them into blue plastic carrier bag for him.

When he got to the laundrette, it had only just opened and there was a young girl sitting behind a counter. She was on her mobile phone and didn't even look up at him when he reached the counter. He coughed to get her attention, only then did she look up from her phone. He asked how much it would cost to wash and dry his clothes.

"Four pounds for a wash, and four pounds for a dryer. The machines only take pound coins," replied the girl

He asked her for some change and he bought a small box of soap powder from her. He handed her a ten-pound note, she gave him back eight-pound coins, and a fifty pence piece. He had just been charged one pound fifty for the smallest box of soap powder he'd ever seen. *It was around the same size as a cigarette pack, fucking robbing bastard,* he thought.

He tipped all his dirty clothes into one of the machines, then he poured all the powder in too, and he put four of the coins into the slots and pushed it in, and hey, presto, the washing machine kicked into life. He looked at the signage, above the machines, it informed him the wash cycle would be forty-five minutes, and the drier would take the same. He sat in one of the eight empty white plastic chairs and took the newspaper out of the carrier bag. He opened one of the breakfast bars, and hungrily ate it. He opened and ate the other one too, and then he drank about half of the energy drink. He noticed there was a glossy supplement magazine inside the newspaper, he'd read that too, if he had time.

Doug was nearly finished with the paper, he'd read it from cover to cover, when he heard the washing machine beeping, it was telling him his wash was done. He got up and went over to it. He transferred the wet clothes into the drier right next to it and fed the other four coins into the slots and pushed the lever in, this started the drier up. He looked over to the young girl, she was still engrossed in her phone. He sat back down to finish reading his newspaper, he heard the door opening, and he looked up to see an older woman about sixtyish enter the launderette. She was pulling a shopping trolley, she said good morning to him, he replied the same greeting.

The woman went straight to the same washing machine that he'd just emptied and pulled some clothes from her trolley and put them into it. She put her hand in her pocket and out it came with the correct amount of coins and put them into the slots. She pulled out a big box of soap power and a small plastic scoop and put some into her washing machine, and she closed the lid and pushed the slide in. Instead of taking a seat as Doug had done, she left the launderette, saying she was going to get some groceries, and would be back before her wash was done. She was obviously a regular and had used this laundrette many times. She'd had no interaction at all with the young ignorant young girl behind the counter.

Doug sat back down, and read the last few pages of the newspaper, he folded it, and left it on the seat next to him, and then he opened the magazine and started on it. There was a story about a premier league football player that had been caught having an affair behind his equally famous wife's back. She'd divorced him, and took his kids abroad. *Poor guy,* he thought, *but then again, if you're married and got everything in life that money can buy, you should be happy with your lot. Guys like me have to work shitty jobs to make ends meet,* he thought.

He then read a story about foxes in the English countryside, their numbers were on the increase again due to a hunting ban, he could just about imagine that. The privileged few that thought they were hard done too because they couldn't hunt foxes any more, oh poor them, my heart fucking bleeds for them. Apparently, farmers are not too happy about the ban either, as foxes are killing their livestock. There was a picture of a hunt in progress about twenty landed gentry on horseback being flanked by about thirty dogs, chasing a poor little fox. He could just picture all these horses and dogs ploughing through fence after fence and wrecking the farmers' fields, and all he was concerned about was losing a couple of chickens to the fox.

Doug laughed to himself, then he read some more showbiz stories about pampered celebrities and had was about to ask the rude girl behind the counter for a pen, he was going to attempt the crossword puzzle. But before he could get off his seat, the drier was making a beeping sound. His clothes were now dry, he put them back into the empty bin bag, and they were still warm. He looked over to the girl with the phone, but she was still zoned out of civilisation. She never even lifted her eyes off the screen as he opened and closed the door on his way out.

Just as he got outside, the old woman from earlier was hurrying down the street to the launderette, he could just about hear her washing machine beeping. She was a real professional, spot on timing, he wondered how often she did this.

He headed back home. Johnny was now up and was in the shower. He emptied his clothes from the bin bag, he put his now clean underwear into the top drawer of the cabinet in his room. He folded his two pairs of denims that he'd bought from the clothes department at the big local supermarket and put them into the second top drawer, they didn't need ironing, *that was a bonus,* he thought. He put his six T-shirts in the bottom drawer, he would get away without ironing them too.

When he was finished, Johnny was out the shower and asked Doug what he'd been up to. Doug told him about his visit to the launderette, he'd obviously not seen the note he'd left for him in the kitchen.

"Is that wee rabbit faced young lassie still there? She never even looks at me when I go there. I was there about two weeks ago, and she never even lifted her eyes off her phone to give me change for the machines."

"Yes, she was there, and she gave me much the same treatment, ignorant little cow."

"That's exactly what she is, its guys like us that pay her fucking wages. Never mind her, did you get your washing done?"

"Yes, all done and put away in the drawers, what about you?"

"I'll have to go in a couple of days, I've enough to do just now."

"What's the plan for this afternoon?"

"I think you should just relax, we'll have a decent sized lunch, then maybe you should go far a nap about three PM for a couple of hours, then we'll have a light supper at about six PM, then we'll head over to Benny's around nine o'clock, that will give you a chance to drink in the atmosphere. It'll be a bit surreal. Like I said earlier, there will be a couple of fights, as a warm up for the punters, before you and Cranston get it on, you and he, are the main event. There should be a decent crowd in tonight."

"How many do you reckon will be there?"

"If Cassidy's put the word out to all his cronies, and they've told their pals and so on, there could be close to three or four hundred in tonight, all looking for a blood bath. But don't worry, mate, there are always plenty of security on hand to make sure there's no trouble. Cassidy always hires top-drawer security, the last thing he wants is the cops, turning up, and closing him down. Everyone will be well warned to be on their best behaviour."

"OK, sounds good to me."

"I'm going to nip out and buy some steak and potatoes for lunch," said Johnny. When he was back, about three quarters of an hour later, Doug said he was going to have to go out too. He needed to get some gear for the fight.

"What kind of gear?" asked Johnny.

"If I'm to impress all my fans, I'll need some new boxing boots and a pair of shorts."

"Good idea, I'll drive you to a decent sport shop I know of, but let me put the steaks on first, and then we can head out."

They went to the shop Johnny knew of and were back home within the hour. Doug had picked a pair of black shorts and black boots. He also bought, a new gel type gum shield. He didn't want to lose any teeth tonight. He'd gotten away with not having one, so far, but he was sure he'd need one tonight, and it was only a tenner.

Johnny put the potatoes on and just less than an hour later, they sat down to a lunch fit for a king. They watched the news for a while then they watched a re-run of a show called myth busters, it was quite interesting too. It was these two guys that perform experiments. They were trying to disprove stories of urban legend. They re-enacted stories and movie stunts to see if they could, in fact, be true.

In this episode, they were trying to find out if a fire extinguisher could hold off a flamethrower. It got busted, as it couldn't, and if a car could create enough dust to blind a surveillance camera, as based in the film Body of Lies, again, it was just special effects, as it couldn't beat the camera. It passed an hour or so when Doug went for his nap.

Johnny had popped back out again, he went to the bookies and put twenty-two pounds on a four horse Yankee bet that was six doubles, four trebles and an accumulator, eleven bets at two pounds. It was for the four televised races. When he returned, he washed and cleared away the dishes. He then settled down in front of the TV to eagerly watch his selections. The first two won, at odds of, 4/1 and 7/2, the third was second and the last one romped home at 9/4, winning by about ten lengths. His luck was changing, he could feel it. He'd just won two hundred and fifty-three pounds and he knew exactly where it was going, straight onto Doug tonight.

When he went to collect his winnings, he met a couple of his old pals, Walter and Chris, in the bookies. He told them about the big fight tonight, they were regulars at these fights, and they already knew about it, and they were going to be there. They were betting on Cranston.

"We've been told he's fighting a no hoper."

"Is that so?" laughed Johnny. "Well, as you two guys are mates, I'm going to put you right, this no hoper is my big, work mate, Doug. I'll let you into a secret, you know Cassidy's two big goons, Frankie and JoJo?"

"Yes, we know who you mean, that JoJo's a scary looking big prick."

"Well, my big mate knocked them both out."

"Are you fucking serious?" asked Walter.

"Yes, mate, deadly serious, and I will tell you this for nothing, he's going to fucking knock Cranston into next week. He's 4/1 your dough, trust me guys, all my money's going on him. I know my lucks been pretty shite lately, but it's changed, my mate will win, no problem, but keep it to yourselves. I don't want that crook Cranston screwing us on the odds."

"OK, Johnny, it's worth us having a think about it." He said cheerio to them.

"I'll maybe, see you both tonight then?" Johnny left his two old pals, and headed home, he went via the supermarket where he bought two pasta ready meals. It was now nearly four PM when he got back home. He had decided he, too, was going for a nap, for an hour or so, it was going to be a long night. He set his phone alarm for six PM. When it went off, he got up, had a quick wash, put the pasta in the microwave oven, and gave Doug a shout to get him up, he too had a wash. When he went into the kitchen, Johnny had put their dinner on the table, Doug quickly ate it, saying it was quite good.

"Yes," agreed Johnny after eating his, "not too shabby."

He told his mate about his little win on the horses. Doug had asked him how much money he was going to put on him to win.

"I have about three hundred and fifty pounds saved now, including my little win this afternoon, and I'm going to put the lot on you."

"Are you sure you want to bet that much?"

"I've never been surer of anything in my life, mate. I know you can and will win. I've seen enough of you in the ring these last few days to know for sure that you're no flash in the pan. After seeing you sparring with Andre and Syd, I'm even more convinced it wasn't luck, the way you took care of those two of big Jim's goons. If you can keep yourself focused when Cranston comes at you on, and he will come at you, from the first bell for sure, then I truly believe you'll win. As I said before, he thinks he's turning up tonight for an easy payday, but what he doesn't know is you're no mug. Cassidy won't have told him that you took out Frankie and JoJo, they're mates with Cranston, and they won't want to look weak by telling Cranston you beat them up either, but even if they did, they're a couple of arseholes, especially JoJo."

If you're going to bet that amount of money on me, I better fucking win or we'll be sleeping in the street. How about I give you five hundred pounds to put on me too?"

"OK, big fella, no problem."

"How much will I get back if I win?"

"Not if you win, mate, when you win, you'll get back two thousand five hundred pounds."

Chapter 28

It was seven AM on the day of baby Grace's funeral, and Robert and Mary were already up and sitting, eating breakfast of tea and toast for Mary, coffee and scrambled eggs for Robert.

"At least it looks like it's going to stay dry today," she said. They both knew this wasn't going to be a good day. "Let's hope we can get it over with, without too much of a strain on poor Julie, and then hopefully, the healing process will start for her," she added, "she's had far too much to cope with this past few months but given time, she'll be a stronger person for this and will soon be back on an even keel."

"Yes, agreed," said her husband, "it will be a dreadful day for her, I just wished we could've found Doug in time for her. She really needed her husband with her today of all days, but sadly, we've tried everything in our power to find him, without success. I really thought we would find him."

They finished their breakfast, Mary was heading upstairs for a shower, and Robert had decided he was going to make a call to check on Andrew and Jason, just to make sure they were all set for the most distressing day of their young lives.

Andrew answered the phone, "Hi, Dad, how are you today?"

"As well as can be expected, Son, neither your mum nor I, had much sleep last night."

"We're both in the same boat, Dad, and we're not looking forward to today at all, but for the sake of Julie, we're going to have to put on brave faces."

"Good lads."

"Jason's mum and dad have confirmed they are coming."

"Good, it will give us a chance to meet his dad. John and Ricky Smith are coming too," Robert added.

"There's something I would like to run by you, if that's all right, Dad?"

"Yes, of course, Son, what is it?"

"Jason and I were talking last night about little Grace's casket, we would rather she was carried into the crematorium by a member of her family, and I think, in Doug's absence, I should carry her in."

"Are you sure you're up to doing this, Andrew?"

"Yes, Dad, I'm sure I am. If Doug were here, he'd be doing it."

"Well, there will be no objections from anyone, I think your brother will be very grateful to you when he returns. I'm sure he will be. I'm going to ring off now, we're going to have some breakfast then Jason and I are going over to see his parents."

"Right, Son, I will see you both at the undertakers." He hung up the phone, he made himself another coffee, whilst waiting on Mary finishing her shower. He'd just drained his cup when she came down stairs. He told her of Andrews's decision to carry Grace into the crematorium.

"That's a lovely gesture," she had to stop tears from falling. "Do you think he will be OK doing this?"

"He'll be fine, and I believe he'll handle himself with great dignity."

Robert's mobile phone was ringing, he saw it was his friend, John.

"Hi, mate, are you all set for collection at twelve thirty?"

"Yes, we'll be ready, I assume there is still no word from Doug?"

"No, unfortunately none."

"I was praying for him to make a last-minute appearance."

"No such luck, John."

"There's still time, miracles can happen you know. I would settle for a little bit of good fortune, it seems any luck we've had lately has been bad luck. The good luck we once had seems to have deserted us big style."

"Yes, my friend, it can sometimes seem that way, but when your back is against the wall and you're feeling at rock bottom, the only way is up. Let's hope, after today, your luck changes, and Doug will come home, and you can all rebuild your lives."

"Yes, let's hope so," he told his friend about Andrew's decision to carry Grace into the crematorium.

"I have to say, Robert; you and Mary have done a wonderful job in bringing your two boys up. You must be as proud as punch with Andrew."

"You've no idea how proud we are of both our sons, but since Doug's been missing, Andrew has been a revelation, I think, when Julie sees Andrew carrying her daughter into the crematorium, it will ease her pain, ever so slightly."

"Yes, let's hope so, I suppose it's better her own kin, rather than a stranger taking her to the final resting place."

"OK, mate, I'll let you crack on before I start bubbling, Ricky is going to come with me to collect you guys, we'll see you both soon."

Robert went upstairs to have a shave, and a shower. When he was finished, he went back down stairs. Mary was on the phone with Dot to find out how Julie was this morning, she was just saying goodbye, and telling Dot she would see her later and she'd just put the phone down when he entered the room.

"I was speaking with Dot, whilst you were upstairs, she said Julie didn't have a good night's sleep either."

"It seems none of us did. Andrew was telling me earlier, neither he nor Jason slept much last night, they were both restless. That's a shame for Julie, in particular though, she could really have done with a good night's sleep, to help her through the day."

"Her ordeal will soon be over," they both hoped.

"She also said Julie's been crying all night. She'd heard her through the wall, and she's not been much better today."

"Has she been taking her medication?"

"Dot says she has been keeping an eye on her and that she's taking her tablets when they're due."

They had another cuppa, and soon, it was time to get dressed, Robert put on a new black suit and shoes that Mary bought him for his birthday a few months back. He'd not worn them yet, he also put on a white shirt and black necktie. Mary was wearing a new black dress suit that Doug and Julie had bought for her at Christmas, she also wore a white blouse, and a pair of black two-inch-high heel shoes. They both scrubbed up well.

John and his brother, Ricky, arrived at twelve mid-day to collect them, they were early, and had time for a quick coffee before setting off to the undertakers. Robert called Andrew, he and Jason, were just about to leave to go and collect Julie and Dot.

"OK, Son, we'll see you all very soon." Robert hung up the phone.

It was time to leave, the four of them headed out the front door. Robert locked up, he and Mary sat in the rear seats with John driving. Ricky was in the front passenger seat, directly in front of Robert. The car was a brand-new, BMW five series, it was dark blue, Mary complemented him on his choice of car, it was beautiful, and the seats were black leather.

Fifteen minutes later, they'd arrived at the undertakers. Brendan was waiting near the front reception, he opened the door when he saw them approaching, he shook hands with Robert and gave Mary a small kiss on the cheek.

"This is my good friend, John, and his brother, Ricky, who's coincidentally my son, Doug's boss," he said to Brendan, introducing them,

"Pleased to meet you," said Brendan. "It's good to put a face to the name," he said to Ricky.

"It's a pity it's not in better circumstances," replied Ricky.

"Yes, indeed," agreed Brendan. Robert and Mary were both slightly confused by that statement from Brendan, but neither said anything.

"Can we see Grace before we go?" asked Mary.

"Yes, of course, you can, please follow me."

The four of them followed Brendan into a different room than before. Baby Grace was in the same little lovely basket as before, but she was now surrounded by four of the most beautiful flower arrangements they had ever seen, and they were all accompanied with little cards. One was from Robert and Mary, one was from Andrew and Jason, one was from Doug and Julie, but the biggest bunch was from John and Ricky Smith, and all at Smith contracts. That solved the mystery statement from Brendan.

"I hope you don't mind?" asked Ricky, "but all my staff wanted to chip in and get these flowers."

"No, we don't mind at all," said Mary, big tears were now streaming down her cheeks, "these are beautiful, please thank them from us."

"I will do that," he assured her.

A few minutes later, Andrew, Jason, Dot and Julie arrived, they too wanted to see Grace before they set off, and Julie was as white as a sheet. Andrew and Jason were supporting her as she was very unsteady on her feet, which was understandable.

After a good five minutes, it was now time for them to head to the crematorium. It was decided Robert, Mary, Dot, Julie and Andrew would travel together in the funeral car with baby Grace resting on Andrew's knees. Jason, and the Smith brothers would travel behind, in their own cars. Jason's mum and dad were going straight to the crematorium.

Mr Mullen was now in attendance, he'd somehow managed to slip in unnoticed, he whispered a few words of condolences to Julie, as Brendan and his fellow undertakers helped them all get into the lead car. Brendan handed the basket, containing baby Grace's remains to Andrew once he was seated.

The journey from the undertakers to the crematorium took no more that fifteen minutes, but for some strange reason, it seemed an awful lot longer. Julie cried loudly the whole journey. Jason and the Smith brothers had managed to get parked OK. Sheila and Gary, had already arrived. Jason introduced his parents to the brothers, John as Robert's old friend and Ricky as his partner's brother, Doug's boss, and warm handshakes were exchanged between them all.

The main car had parked right out front of the crematorium chapel. Brendan helped them back out of the car, they all exited the car with the exception of Andrew, he was asked to stay in the car with Grace until all the others were in the chapel and seated. Once this was done, Brendan instructed Andrew to come out of the car. Andrew handed over baby Grace to Brendan until he was safely out of the car, Brendan then handed the basket back to him. He carried Grace, arms out stretched, he had tears running down his cheeks now, he couldn't help himself and once he got to the front door, he heard the song *Over the Rainbow* playing.

Brendan asked him to stop, he was given some more instructions, he was asked to walk slowly down the centre aisle, and place the basket onto the altar, which was in the centre, right at the front. As he walked slowly down the aisle, he heard Julie sobbing. He looked over and saw that his mother and Dot were also crying, his dad and Jason were doing their utmost to refrain from crying, his legs were shaking like mad, but somehow, he managed to get baby Grace onto the alter without incident, he was relieved.

He then took his place to the left-hand side of Julie, Jason was to her right, and she was in a right state. Mr Mullen took his place in the pulpit and read with great feeling.

He started with saying, "Grace was a beautiful baby and she squealed instead of talked. Today she found out what it's like to hear the angels sing, she didn't live long enough, to meet her daddy, but that didn't mean he didn't love her. Today, God came down and took little Grace by the hand and led her to heaven, it's very cruel that little Grace has been snatched from her devoted family by SIDS, and how she was cherished and much loved and would be missed greatly by her parents, grandparents and uncles."

He told the congregation how her dad, Doug, had suffered an unfortunate accident and couldn't be at the funeral, and how sad an occasion it was, to be here today, committing such a young soul into heaven. He continued his kind words to say that, although Grace was only here on earth a short time, she would leave a lasting impression on all who came into contact with her.

He went on to say that Graces' mother, Julie, was having to deal with a double tragedy, her loving husband's accident has left him with no recollection of his family and had inexplicably disappeared and that he was now tragically absent from his daughter's funeral. Mr Mullen said he was assured, from speaking with Doug's parents and brother, that he's a good man and a kind soul, and that he will be heart broken when his memory returns, and he discovers he's missed this solemn occasion.

At the mention of her husband, Julie was now sobbing more loudly and more uncontrollably than before. Mr Mullen, hearing this, momentarily paused his speech, he then continued when Julie had quietened a little, saying that Doug will be even more distressed that he couldn't be here today to share the burden of grief and to support his darling wife, Julie, through this desperate time.

Julie had only just managed to get herself in check, but this started her off, again. Mr Mullen said no parent should ever have to deal with the loss of a child. He looked straight at Julie as he said this, and he promised her that baby Grace will be welcomed into heaven.

"I'm also sure your family will all gather around you and help you to come to terms with this great tragedy that has befallen you. Please be standing and let us say a prayer now." He led them through the Lord's prayer. Once that was finished, he said, "Let us now commit grace into heaven."

Just then the curtains electronically closed around the basket. There wasn't a dry eye in the place, Julie had to be held up now by Andrew and Jason, there was another piece of music playing, it was *Tears in Heaven* by Eric Clapton, this was written after the death of his own, young son. As it finished, Mr Mullen led them out of the chapel.

Once they were all outside, Julie was a little bit calmer, she thanked Andrew for lifting Grace into the chapel.

Andrew hugged his sister-in-law, "I did it for you, Julie, I thought it would be better than her getting lifted in by a stranger."

"Yes, it was." They embraced again, they were both sobbing now. "Where's that brother of yours?" pleaded Julie, "I need him back now."

"I know, I wish I knew where he was, I'd go and get him right now and bring him to you."

They separated, and Andrew looked over and saw Sheila and Gary being introduced to his parents by his partner. He didn't want to leave Julies side just now.

Dot came over, along with Mr Mullen. "That was a lovely service," said Andrew.

"Thanks, you did well too, your brother will be so proud of you."

"Yes, if only he were here."

"I'm sure he'll show up soon enough."

"I hope you're right."

The car was ready to take the family to the local social club where Jason and Andrew had arranged for them to go to have a drink and some food. Julie was not too keen but after some persuasion from Andrew and her mum, she had agreed to go for an hour, but no more. She'd wanted to go straight home, she went into the car with her mum, Robert and Mary, and the others followed in their own cars.

When they arrived, there had been four tables set aside for them. Jason's mum and dad had come along, as well as the Smiths, and Mr Mullen, they all had a few drinks. The drivers among them had soft drinks. It was still quite sombre. Julie was still very upset and couldn't stop crying, and approaching the hour mark, she'd decided she wanted to go home. Her mum agreed to go with her, Robert called a cab for them, and he slipped Dot twenty pounds for the cab ride. She tried protesting, but he insisted, she reluctantly put it in her pocket. They all hugged and kissed goodbye. Mary promised to visit them tomorrow. Robert went over to have a chat with Sheila and Gary.

"You've a fine, Son," he said to Gary.

"Yes, I know, I'd like to take the opportunity to tell you, I know that I've not been the best dad to Jason, but I'm going to try my best to make it up to him and

Andrew, if they'll let me. I've seen the errors of my way, and my behaviour has been totally unacceptable. It's taken a horrible event, the loss of your grandchild, to make me pluck up the courage and admit to myself that I've been nothing short of an embarrassment to my family." He had tears in his eyes as he said these harsh words about himself.

"Well if you're serious about accepting our sons for the men they are, then you will have all the respect, and support from Andrew, myself and Mary. I don't think I'll need to remind you if you revert back to your old ways, you won't get a third chance."

Gary assured him, he knew full well he was on his final chance, and he wouldn't screw it up. "I'm so sorry to hear that your other son, Doug, has gone missing. I really hope you're all reunited soon, you have my full sympathy for that, it's slightly different reasons in my case, but I can imagine the hell you're all going through, missing your son is not easy."

"Yes, it's not been easy at all, thanks for your words, hopefully, he'll turn up any time soon. As you've seen today, his wife, Julie's, not taking it well at all."

They all stayed for another hour or so. Ricky had called his wife, Angela to collect him. Gary, Sheila, and Andrew went with Jason, he dropped his parents on route to their house.

John dropped Robert and Mary home, she invited him in for a coffee. He gladly accepted. Mary put the kettle on, John and Robert sat in the sitting room, she came in with coffees for the guys and a tea for herself.

"You both handled today magnificently, and that minister guy was good."

"He wasn't a minister," replied Mary, "he was a celebrant."

"He was good though," agreed Robert.

"I know it couldn't have been easy for you both today."

"No, it wasn't easy at all, mate," Replied Robert.

"You'll both need to keep a very good eye on Julie, she was a complete wreck today."

"We will," Mary assured him.

They finished their brew, John hugged Mary and Robert and he headed off home. It was now nearly ten PM, where had the day gone, he asked.

"I'm not sure, but I'm glad it's nearly over," answered Robert

They were now alone. When John had left, Robert opened a bottle of wine and they toasted Grace again, and they both spoke again about how Doug would react to the news about his daughter's death.

"Probably not too well," Robert said. "It's not a conversation I'm looking forward to having with him."

They finished their first glass of wine. Mary poured them another, they discussed how great Andrew and Jason had been today.

"They were both fantastic, especially Andrew, Doug will be so proud of him."

"Yes, Mary, he will be, I'm not sure we could have expected anymore from them, they were truly magnificent."

"I saw you speaking with Jason's dad, what was he saying?" asked Mary.

"He said he'd been a terrible dad, and he was looking to make amends and win back his son's love and respect, our son's too. I told him if he was serious then we'd support him one hundred percent. He knows he's in the last chance saloon, and if he messes up, Jason will probably never speak to him again. He also said he was sorry to hear about Doug's situation."

"Do you think he's genuine?"

"Who knows? I think he certainly deserves a second chance, but only time will tell."

They went to bed exhausted. The next morning, Mary was up first, she was showered and downstairs finishing her second cup of tea when Robert appeared in the kitchen, still in his pyjamas. Mary asked him if he wanted breakfast.

"Just coffee and toast will be fine please."

Chapter 29

Doug and Johnny left for the fight venue at about eight thirty, when they arrived at Benny's, Johnny pointed to the four doormen guarding the door.

"See I told you, mate, there won't be any trouble in here tonight, look at the size of those four gorillas. Who's going to want to fuck with them?"

Luckily, Johnny was a regular, they nodded to him, and moved aside to let them enter. Just before going inside, Johnny told them he was expecting three or four mates arriving later, he gave them their names. Once inside, they found the place was buzzing already, there was a fight in progress. Two guys, about mid-thirties, one of them was about a foot taller than the other, were going at each other hammer and tongs.

Johnny asked one of the punters, what round they were on. The fight was only on round three, he said. Both fighters had visible cuts on their faces. The guy told him they had clashed heads in round one, and each of them was looking for a quick knockout. This fight would never have been allowed to continue, if it had been a regulated fight, but as it wasn't, so they battled on. It lasted another three rounds before the smaller of the two managed to land a screamer of a left-hander and knocked his foe on his back. He tried to get up, his brain was willing, but his legs over ruled it. He nearly managed it though before collapsing back onto the blood-covered canvas, his night was over. There were loud cheers from the rampant crowd.

It looked to Doug that winner was carrying the majority of their money, as there was a mad rush to a makeshift counter over by toilets.

Johnny told his mate, "That's the bookie's desk, they're all rushing to get paid out, or put their winnings on Cranston. I've bet that wee prick that just won before, he never fucking won for me."

This was definitely a popular win as there were more people waiting in line than there were not. There would be about a fifteen-minute break before the next two fighters would enter the ring. Doug saw Cassidy talking to a big guy, they were deep in conversation and they seemed to be laughing about something.

Doug turned to Johnny, "Who's that your big pal's talking with?"

"That's Cranston."

"Fuck me, Johnny, he looks a bit bigger than you described him."

"Yes, but think how much easier he'll be for you to hit," laughed Johnny nervously. Cassidy and Cranston seemed at ease in each other's company.

Doug looked over to the left and saw JoJo handing over a fist full of notes to a small thin man behind the counter in exchange for a bit of paper, *Most likely a betting slip,* he thought. There was still a long queue behind him, apparently all waiting in line, as Johnny had suggested to do the same thing.

JoJo noticed him looking his way and he went over to his pal Cranston and pointed him out, he laughed and moved his finger under his chin, in a cut-throat motion, mouthing the words, 'you're fucking dead, man'.

Doug smiled back at him and blew him a kiss. This seemed to unnerve him, but not the big guy standing next to him. Johnny noticed this exchange between them and told Doug to ignore him.

"Do your talking in the ring," Johnny said.

"Sounds good to me."

"Let's mingle a bit," he said to his big mate, as he saw his two pals from the bookie's shop earlier. He introduced Doug to them, "This is Walter and Chris."

"Good to meet you, Doug," they said in unison. He gave them both a firm handshake.

"Do you think you can knock out Cranston?" Walter asked him.

"I'm not here to fucking dance with him, if that's what you think," he growled back at him.

"Well, you certainly look as if you can handle yourself," said Chris.

Johnny said to Doug, "I'm going to check the odds and get our money on." Walter and Chris followed Johnny, Doug wasn't left alone for long.

Cassidy saddled up next to him, "You're looking fit, Son," he said. "I think I'll put a small wager on you to last six or seven rounds with Cranny."

"But not to win?" asked Doug.

"Do you reckon you can beat him?"

"If I had a tenner for every time somebody asked me that, since I agreed to take this fight, I wouldn't need to fight him. So, here's a little bit of advice for you, don't put too much of your money on him because not only can I beat him, I will beat him." Even he didn't know if this was bravado or not, but he couldn't back down now, even if he wanted to, which he didn't.

"We'll see, may the best man win," Cassidy said, and shook his hand.

Johnny had just returned as Cassidy left. "What was that prick saying?"

"He was just wishing me luck for tonight," winked Doug.

"Really?"

"Don't be so fucking soft, of course not, he was just telling me how his pal's going to knock the fuck out of me. He was also trying to patronise me, telling me I'm in good shape. I am coming around to your way of thinking, as you have said to me countless times, these pricks think I'm here to put on a show for them. Well, do you know what I'm going to give them a fucking show all right, just not the one they're expecting. I'm going knock this big, ugly bastard Cranston out."

"Good man, Doug, that's the spirit," smiled Johnny. "I just got us 5/1. They've put it about you're just a big useless fanny and Cranston's going to out use you as a punch bag for five or six rounds before he knocks you out. Apparently, they've already lined up his next fight against some Russian cunt."

The expression on Doug's face changed instantly. "Is that fucking right?" He was raging now. This had the desired effect Johnny was hoping for. *Get the big guy mad and riled up, light the blue touch paper and stand well back,* he thought.

There was a big cheer in the hall as the next two fighters entered the ring. When the first guy, Archie Withers, was introduced, there was a massive explosion of noise, it filled the place. Then Jock McDonald was introduced, the place erupted again but not with cheers, this time it was boo's and jeers. This unsettled Doug momentarily.

Johnny saw this and said to his mate, "Don't worry about that, big man, they always boo the Scottish fighters."

"Do you think they'll be cheering me on?" Doug asked, his composure regained.

"Not a fucking chance, pal."

"I thought not."

They watched the fight, these two guys were fairly evenly matched, in height anyway, the Englishman looked about a stone and half heavier, but not fat they both started off cautiously for the first couple of minutes. Doug thought this could maybe last a good few rounds, then out of nowhere, the Scotsman caught Archie on the left-hand side of his head with what looked to Doug like a pretty hard right-hander, and Archie was hurt, and he started to stagger a bit.

Jock, sensing his chance, went in like a man possessed and swung punches all over the shop. He was throwing everything but the kitchen sink at his opponent, but sadly for him, most of his punches were missing their target, hitting Archie's gloves. The rest were hitting nothing but fresh air. There were gasps and groans from the animated crowd, luckily for Archie, the bell sounded to end round one, and saved Archie from a first-round defeat. Doug wondered if that bell wasn't a shade early.

There were loud cheers as Archie managed to find his way back to his stool. It didn't take a brain surgeon to work out who the partisan crowd's money was on in this fight. The second round started, Archie looked like he was still a bit unsteady on his feet, not fully recovered yet from that big hit in round one. He was now keeping his defences tight, he now knew his opponent had a decent punch that could hurt him, he just had to make sure he wasn't caught again so easily. He needed to find out if the Scotsman could take a punch. No doubt about it, he'd underestimated Jock.

It was time to slowly try and get the upper hand, he stayed behind his jab and caught Jock with a couple of solid right handers of his own, only getting hit with a couple of soft jabs in return. This went on like cat and mouse for the next two rounds. Round five started evenly, then Jock, sensing Archie was getting on top, decided to go for another big punch, but what he didn't expect was that Archie had anticipated this, and was ready for him. As he swung his arm to launch an attack, Archie ducked under it and punched him right on the temple, down Jock went.

The referee went through the motions of counting him out, but there was no returning from that direct hit. The crowd was cheering crazily, another big favourite for the punters to collect on. After about a minute or so, the Scotsman was helped to his feet and was booed out of the ring. It had been an even fight until the knock out. The Scotsman would rue the chance he had in the first round, if only he had been more clinical he may have taken the spoils.

The announcer climbed into the ring and declared there will be a half hour recess until the main attraction of the evening. "Tam Cranston," the loudest cheer of the night erupted, "will be beating," the crowd laughed and cheered some more, "I mean fighting, Doug Clement."

Doug looked around the room and he was fuming that the announcer had pulled that stunt. Johnny just thought to himself, *That's fucking priceless, Doug will be fuming and even more determined to knock Cranston out.*

"Right, let's get you in and get you changed and sorted." He led Doug through the crowd, there must be nearly three hundred and fifty people in here tonight. As they were pushing their way through them to get to the changing room, Johnny stopped in front of him to speak with a guy he knew.

Whilst they were stopped, Doug overheard few people talking about him. One guy in particular was saying to his mates that guy Doug doesn't look like the mug they say he is.

"I saw his mate in front of me in the queue putting a right few quid on him."

"What price is he?"

"He got him at 5/1 about half an hour ago."

"I think we should put a small saver on him, just in case, Cranston's not fought anybody as big as that guy for many a year. He usually fights guys a lot smaller than himself and I can't see this guy letting Cranston push him around, can you?"

"Not at all, this new guy might just win."

This cheered Doug up a bit, a few of them in tonight thought he had a chance. Johnny definitely thinks I can win, so do I, the more people that bet on me the better, and when I win, they will all collect, and Cassidy and his motley crew will all lose. That'll fucking teach them for trying make me look stupid.

They were on the move again, when they got to the changing area Archie was getting dressed, his opponent was already away. *He must have gone sharpish, probably away to the hospital to get checked over,* thought Doug.

"Good win there, Archie," said Johnny, he had bet on Archie before and knew him well. "This is Doug," he said as he introduced them, they shook hands.

"Watch out for Cranston's head, I've seen him try it on before, I think I'll put a small wager from my winnings on you, good luck," winked Archie. They shook hands again.

"Not too small," winked Doug back at him.

"Good for you, I like a guy with confidence," with that Archie was off, out the changing rooms and away to get paid by Cassidy.

"Where's Cranston?" asked Doug.

"He's too good to get changed with the riff raff, he gets changed in Cassidy's office, he's even got his own shower in there too."

"That's grand," said Doug sarcastically. They sat down, Doug was getting changed when the door opened and in walked Eddie, Brian, Syd and Andre.

"How's it going?" asked Eddie.

"I'm feeling good and confident."

"That's excellent."

"I see you lot got in OK," said Johnny.

"Yes, I told the bouncers on the door we're pals of yours, I don't think they believed you've got any pals though." They all laughed.

"Well, Doug, between the four of us, we've got two thousand quid on you."

"Did you get 5/1?" asked Johnny.

"Did we, fuck, we only got 7/2?"

"That's crazy, I got 5/1 about an hour ago."

"You know why that's happened? There's a fair few guys out there who have seen the size of you and like the look of you, so they've put their money on you."

"Yes," piped up Syd, "most of the punters in front of us at the betting desk, were all betting on you too, Doug. The bookie will've had to reduce your odds."

Eddie sat next to him and gave him a run down again of how he thought Cranston would fight tonight. "Just make sure you're ready as soon as that bell goes. I've been asking around about this geezer, and he will try every trick in the book and even some that aren't and make sure you watch out for his head."

"Another fighter warned me about that earlier."

"Well, it was good advice, he'll come in with his head down as a soon as you're near enough and he'll try and jolt it upward onto your chin or better still, your nose to try and blind you. Make sure you don't fall into that trap."

"OK, anything else?"

"Yes, look out for him trying to bite you, he's a dirty bastard of a fighter an animal, make sure you keep him at arm's length at all times."

"Thanks for the warnings, is it too late to concede?" Doug asked and Johnny looked concerned by this.

"Only joking," smiled Doug.

Johnny relaxed a bit, "Don't fucking say shit like that, Doug, you'll give me a heart attack."

"Don't you need a heart to have one of those?" laughed Eddie.

Chapter 30

Doug was now ready and waiting for the call to head to the ring for his long-awaited fight with Cranston. Johnny kept reminding him that Cassidy and his co-horts thought he was just cannon fodder and they'd bet all their money on him losing and that he was just the entertainment for them.

"They're only here to see you getting your face punched the fuck out of," Johnny said.

Eddie was nipping his ears too, reminding him to keep a watch for Cranston's head.

Doug was getting a bit angry with them all now, "I know what I need to do, stop bending my fucking ears."

Johnny gave Eddie a sly nod. It was working, they were both trying to get him angry just before he entered the ring. In came a small fat guy to the changing room.

He said to Johnny, "Your man's up now, Doug got up and all five guys wished him good luck."

Johnny led the way for Doug and Eddie, they were going to be in the corner with him, the others went to find a good vantage point to watch. As soon as they left the changing rooms and entered the main hall, the noise was deafening, there must have been over five hundred people in now. There were boos and jeers as Doug made his way into the ring, they saw Frankie first.

He never made eye contact, there was something not quite right about him, thought Doug, then he spotted JoJo, he was laughing and mouthing off, but he was far enough away from him that they couldn't hear what he was saying, but he could guess what it was.

Eddie told him to ignore the boos and concentrate on the job in hand, the noise seemed to crank up a couple of notches as he saw Cassidy's office door open and out came Cranston. He was followed by the guy that was in the ring earlier announcing the fighters. There were cheers and whoops, and tribal chants.

One guy shouted, "Come on, big Tam, knock this arsehole out in the first round." Cranston seemed to be ignoring the crowd.

The announcer climbed into the ring first, followed by Cranston and Doug.

He picked up a mic and announced to the crowd, "This is the main event we have been waiting for, in the blue corner we have the unbeaten Tam Cranston." As soon his name was mentioned, there was an almighty cheer.

Doug thought the roof could cave in, he'd never heard anything remotely close to this noise before.

"And in the red corner, the challenger, Doug Clement."

There was a ringing of boos around the place. If this was designed to put Doug off, it had the opposite effect. He was as pumped up as he'd ever been. The referee had somehow managed to slip into the ring un-noticed by Doug.

"Right, guys," he summoned them both to the centre of the ring, "I want a good clean fight no biting and no headbutts," he said looking directly at Doug, "no kicking but everything else goes."

Cranston was staring at Doug trying to psych him out. Doug stared back. "OK, back to your corners, when the bell rings for round one, come out fighting."

Doug sat in the small stool in his corner. Johnny and Eddie were waiting for him. Johnny asked Doug to look casually over to big Cassidy's office. The window had been slid open and he had a bird's eye view of the ring, he was seated at a table, around the table were three other guys, all smartly dressed in suits.

"Who are they?" asked Doug.

"I think they're the Italians I was telling you about and they're associates of his. I think they're into all sorts of no good things, including drugs, prostitution and definitely protection. They own a construction business too, I've seen them at fights before. I'm sure they bet big money too. They've probably put a big amount on Cranston, he's supposed to be fighting one of their guys next."

"Well, we'll just have wait and see if he's still able to after tonight." Johnny thought he now has the big man as riled up as needs to be.

"Doug, most of these guys in here have their money on Cranston, but remember, mate, every single penny we have is on you so, don't let us down."

The bell rang to start round one, just as Doug was just getting to his feet Cranston was half way across the ring, he was coming full steam toward him. Doug just about managed to get off the stool in time and duck to the left out of the way of a big right-hander.

Fuck, thought Doug*, this guy's keen.* He spun around just in time to see Cranston lining up another, he couldn't quite get out its way but did manage to absorb the punch with his forearms. This guy means business, he's trying to get me out of here sharpish. The crowd sensed this fight could be all over in the first round. They were chanting, "Cranny, Cranny, Cranny."

Doug stood up straight and started moving about a bit, trying to make himself harder to hit. Cranston was relentless, he kept coming forward, forcing him onto his back foot. Doug was using his feet well and managed to avoid any serious blows, Cranston came at him again, but missed wide left. Doug managed to catch him on the top of his shoulder with a left-hander, it had no effect but at least it let Cranston know this guy could also throw punches. They squared off in the centre of the ring; Doug spent the remainder of round one avoiding the erratic punching of Cranston.

He tried throwing some jabs of his own to keep him at bay, but credit to Cranston, he was not as easy to hit as his sparring partners had been. Cranston did manage to glance past his head with a big left-hander, but it only just skimmed by the side of Doug's head. The crowd erupted thinking their guy had landed a telling blow, it may have looked to them like he had, but both he and Cranston knew better, the bell sounded to end round one.

Doug returned to his corner, Eddie had the stool waiting and as he sat down on it.

Johnny asked him, "Did he catch you there?"

"No, calm down, it just missed by a whisker, no damage done."

"Thank fuck, Doug, this is harder to watch than any of the other fight I've bet on."

"Feel free to swap places if you want," snarled Doug.

"No, you're all right I'll stay this side of the ropes."

The bell sounded for round two and Doug was up like a flash, he wasn't getting caught out again. He was up and ready this time as Cranston came looking again, he was testing Doug's defences, he was probing with a right jab. Doug kept his hands up and was protecting his head he wasn't quite sure why he knew this, but he was aware he had to protect his head especially against a guy with the power Cranston had. Although he hadn't managed to hurt Doug yet, he could sense the power behind the punches. He was now trying his luck downstairs, attempting to hit Doug with body shots to make Doug lower his gloved hands from protecting his head and face, but Doug kept solid.

Toward the end of this round, Doug noticed that when Cranston going full pelt at his body his head was left slightly unprotected. The bell sounded and there was another massive cheer from the crowd. Cranston had easily won the first two rounds and the crowd were even more so expecting an easy victory for their man, they thought it was only a matter of time.

The third round, again, had the same pattern, Cranston throwing about three times as many punches as Doug. He caught Doug with solid punch on the nose right at the end of this round, some blood was now running down the sides of his mouth. Doug had committed the cardinal sin and left his head exposed for a split second and he'd paid the price. The bell rang to end round three and the crowd were even more animated now that they'd seen blood. They were chanting Cranston's name again, "Cranny, Cranny, Cranny." He was definitely their man, as if he'd been in any doubt.

Eddie managed to stop the nosebleed pretty easily, it was nothing that was going to stop the fight. Round four started and again Cranston doing all the chasing. He hit Doug with some good solid body shots making him drop his arms down a bit to protect his ribs. They were now nose to nose and then, just as Eddie had predicted, Cranston tried to stick his head on him, but he'd been expecting him to try that and he moved his head backwards managing to avoid full contact, and as a result, Cranston's head just glanced off the side of Doug's cheek.

Doug looked over to the referee, but he was non-committal. If he wasn't sure before the fight started, he now knew for certain that he was on his own in here. He landed a couple of jabs and then he threw a big left hander at Cranston, straight on the money, but his hands were up, and his gloves took most of the sting out of the punch, but he did manage to hit him on the forehead with the follow through. If nothing else, it at least backed him off a little. The bell rang and round four ended.

Maybe that round was a draw, thought Doug, but the crowd didn't think so. They were still cheering Cranston on, Doug was sitting on the seat getting a wipe down from Eddie when Johnny told him he saw one of Russians handing over another bundle of cash.

"They think he's got your measure. I'm just sussing him out, I think I've spotted a weakness and I'm about to see if I'm right."

Round five started and Cranston was not rushing over to Doug's corner this round, he must have felt something in that punch Doug threw at him, that caused him to be a bit more cautious and he was going to play it a bit safer. He was now beckoning Doug onto him, he was either getting a bit cockier or he was changing tack. Doug moved toward him, and started throwing some punches of his own, and he had some success too, he landed a couple of solid jabs. One even managed to find its way onto Cranston's nose, it was his turn for a bloody nose.

The crowd gasped, but Cranston never showed any concern, the rest of this round was eachy peachy. They both threw the odd big punch but neither troubled their opponent, the bell rang to end round five. When Doug was seated, Johnny asked him about the weakness he thought he'd found.

"Not yet, he's changed tact. I think he knows I can hurt him so he not so gung hoe now, but I'm getting the feel of this. I bloodied his nose in that round."

"Yes, I saw that, I hope it doesn't make him angry." Doug and Eddie gave him a funny look.

"He's already fucking angry," snapped Doug. Round six started and Cranston was back to his old trick of coming straight at Doug from the off. Doug was up and ready, Cranston was going for the body again, trying to get Doug to drop his hands and around a minute into the round, Doug saw his opportunity. Cranston was too busy trying to hit Doug with body shots to make him drop his arms and allow him to get a good head shot onto him.

Doug hoped, as before, he'd leave his head exposed, and as expected it, he did. He went to hit Doug hard on the left side at his ribs. Doug feigned that he was getting hurt. The crowd were going crazy, thinking this is it, their man's going to knock Doug out now. Cranston was going full tilt into Doug's mid-riff, and in a split second, Doug turned slightly to the left and back a little, then he wrapped his left arm around Cranston and turned him and at the same time, thundered the biggest right-hander of the night right onto Cranston's temple.

He staggered a little and was completely stunned, but Doug, unlike Raymond, in the earlier fight, he'd watched, wasn't taking any prisoners. He seized his chance and threw three big punches in succession. Cranston was done, he collapsed to his left and somehow managed to fall out of the ring between the first and second ropes, hitting his head as he landed on the concrete floor. There was an eerie silence, except for a few cheers from the sensible in the crowd who had bet the underdog. The referee didn't know where to look as he was as stunned as the punters, he looked up to Cassidy's office for advice, but the fight was won.

Chapter 31

JoJo looked distraught. Doug went back to his corner and looked over to big Jim's office and he saw one of the three suited geezers giving big Jim some grief. They all stormed out.

Johnny jumped in the ring and slapped Doug on the back. "I never doubted you for a second, buddy."

Frankie and JoJo and some others were trying to revive Cranston, he was just about coming around. Doug climbed out of the ring and headed toward the changing rooms.

Cassidy met him half-way, "It seems we under estimated you, Doug, come into my office when you're changed and I'll square you up."

Brian, Syd and Andre and came in to the changing rooms whilst Doug was in the shower.

"Any problems getting paid out?" asked Johnny.

"No, not a problem. I think the bookie made a killing, nearly everybody had bet against Doug, except us, any others only had small wagers on Doug as a saver. All the real money was on Cranston."

"Good, I'm going to collect our share." Johnny disappeared outside and caught the bookie who paid him the money owed.

The bookie congratulated him on the win, "Not too many big bets on your man apart from you and your four mates, a tidy profit tonight."

"I don't think big Jim will see it that way."

"Don't kid yourself, Johnny, did you no see those guys with suits in his office. They all had big bets on Cranston, Cassidy never knew they were coming, and he never had time to lay the bets. I told him I couldn't cover them, far too much dough for me. If Cranston had won, he'd have had to pay them an absolute fortune. Your man done him a right favour in the ring tonight."

This displeased Johnny, *But so fuck, we won, he won, I'll just have to live with it*, he thought to himself.

Johnny returned to the changing room just as Doug was finished getting changed. "Right, let's go and see what Cassidy's got to say for himself."

"We're all heading off," said Eddie, "thanks again for your efforts, Doug, this is a great windfall, it's always good taking money off these crooks." They all shook hands and the four of them left.

Johnny and Doug headed up to big Jim's office. JoJo was coming down the stairs carrying Cranston's clothes and shoes, they stopped at the bottom to let him pass. He was about to say something to Doug but decided wisely not to and carried on out. When he was gone, Johnny led the way up the stairs, big Jim was sitting alone in his office. He got up and shook Doug's hand and gave him an envelope.

"It seems there's a new champ on the block and his names Doug Clement," said big Jim, pouring three glasses of whiskey and handed one the each of them. "That's you owing me three and a half now, Son," he said to Johnny.

Doug counted out three thousand five hundred pounds from the money in the envelope and threw it onto big Jim's desk. "He's all square now."

"OK, if that's what you want then fine." He put the money into a drawer in his desk and locked it. "Have a seat, that was a good performance, I thought Tam had you a couple of times tonight in there," he said pointing to the ring.

"I'm sure he did too, but I never had a doubt I would win, your man's biggest problem was he thought he just had to show up to win. I knew I had to fight to win, that's the difference. I'm sure if he had the fight again he would do it differently."

"Is that you angling for a re-match?"

"No, not at all, I'm just saying that's the way it is."

"How do you feel about another fight, this time against somebody with a bit more class than Cranston?"

"Who do you have in mind?" asked Johnny with more confidence that he'd ever had with Cassidy before.

"Who the fuck do you think you are son, his fairy godmother?"

Doug glared at Cassidy, and said, "He's my fucking pal and he can ask questions if he wants, so who's it going to fucking be?" growled Doug.

Big Jim relaxed a bit, he didn't want them thinking they had got the better of him, but he stored this outburst in his head for future reference. *This cheek will come back to haunt the little bastard of a Scotsman,* thought big Jim.

"Did you see my guests in here earlier?" big Jim asked.

"Yes, I noticed you had some suits in," said Doug.

"These guys are fellow businessmen, only not as legitimate as me, if you understand my meaning, and they have got a couple of fighters of their own. They're running out of decent opponents for their best fighter. They thought Cranston might give a good account of himself, they've seen his last two fights. Tonight was his last audition, but you put paid to that."

"Well, my heart bleeds for him," said Doug.

"I think these guys liked the look of you tonight, even though you cost them a right bundle of cash. They were so sure Cranny would take care of you tonight."

"It's just my luck I've got Johnny here to look out for me, or the whole world will be against me," smiled Doug.

"How's Cranston?" asked Doug.

"He's away to hospital, JoJo thinks you broke his jaw, and he hit his head pretty badly when he fell out the ring, possibly concussed too."

"I hope JoJo and Frankie didn't lose all their pocket money on their big pal?"

"I'm sure they did."

"What about you? Did you lose a packet tonight too?" Doug asked him.

"Oh, quite the contrary, I never lost a penny on Cranston, those guys you saw in here earlier covered any losses I may have had on him. They thought he was a sure thing."

"I wonder where they got that information from," smiled Doug.

"I noticed you two weren't alone tonight either," said big Jim, "I saw you with four other guys, quite the entourage. I recognised one of them, he fought Cranston a while back, I don't remember his name, nobody remembers the losers. I can't place the other three."

"They're just guys I've been sparring with to get me into shape, you didn't think I was daft enough to just turn up and fight your best fighter without some sparring, did you?"

"I certainly don't think your daft at all, Doug, and for your information, Cranston was, maybe, once upon a time one of my better fighters, but now he's not even close to be my best fighter. That could be you now, but he was a good earner for me, I'll not deny that. I just hope you can be too. I am thinking of putting you up against Jake Crawford, do you remember him?" he asked Johnny.

"Is he the big cropped, blond-haired guy with all the tattoos on his back and on his Popeye like arms?"

"Yes, that's right, that's him. What do you think, Doug, your fairy godmother here can fill you in on him. I'm sure you could certainly give him a run for his money."

"Nothing would surprise me when it comes to Doug," replied Johnny.

"My Italian friends are looking for a big fight night, and they've asked me to put up a man to take on one of their guys. It would be like a final eliminator, you or Crawford against their man. It would be a very big payday for the winner. Well, how about it, big man, do you want the fight?"

"How much, it'll need to be a handsome offer, you've just talked this Crawford guy as a much harder proposition than Cranston, so you'll need to up the ante," Doug replied

"OK," said big Jim, "I'll give you six thousand pounds to fight him, and I'll give you another six if you win."

"What do you think, Johnny?" Doug asked his pal.

"For fuck's sake, Doug, is he your manager?" spat out big Jim.

"Calm yourself down, big man," urged Doug. "I value his opinion; I don't know this guy." He looked at Johnny as he spoke.

Johnny nodded, "I think you can beat Crawford."

"OK, that's settled, I'll take the fight." Doug and big Jim shook hands. "When will this happen?"

"How about a week today, in here next Friday?"

"Sounds good to me."

With that exchange over, Doug and Johnny left the office and were just coming out the front doors when they saw the three suited Italians getting out of a big fancy black car and seemed to be heading back inside. The main guy was carrying a leather case, he looked Doug up and down and spoke to the others in a whisper. They all nodded and went inside.

"What do you think they were saying?" asked Doug.

"Fuck knows."

"I wonder what they want to see big Jim about now, they just left about half an hour ago."

"None of our business anyway," added Johnny, but it's certainly not to collect their fucking winnings, that's for sure," laughed Johnny. "I feel fantastic, Doug and it's all thanks to you. I don't owe fuck face in there a penny now, and we made a right few pounds into the bargain, 5/1, we'll not get those odds again."

"No, probably not," agreed Doug, who was still not fully understanding how betting worked.

Chapter 32

Mary called Dot to see what kind of night Julie had. Dot answered the phone after two rings, "Hi, Mary," she said.

"Hi, Dot, how is Julie this morning?"

"She's still in bed, she went straight there when we got home yesterday. I'll give her another half hour then I'll knock her door and get her up. The quicker we can get her into a routine, the easier it will be for her to get her life back on track, sometimes you've got to be cruel to be kind."

"OK, let me know how she is. Is it all right if I come over around lunch time?"

"Yes, Mary, that will be fine."

"Good, I'll see you soon then," she rung off.

"How is she?" asked Robert.

"Dot said she went straight to bed as soon as they got home yesterday, and she's still in bed now. Dot said she was giving her another half hour before waking her, maybe she needed a good night's sleep. After all, yesterday was a complete nightmare for her, more so than for us."

Robert finished his coffee and toast then he headed upstairs for a shower. He was just finished getting dressed, when he heard the house phone ringing.

"Oh my God," he heard Mary shriek, his first thought was something dreadful had happened to Doug. He was rushing down the stairs as quick as his bad leg would allow him. Mary was running up, tears streaming down her cheeks.

"What's up, is it Doug?" Robert asked.

"No, it's Julie, she's taken an overdose."

"Oh, my goodness, is she all right?"

"I'm not sure, Dot's just called an ambulance, she went into her room and found her unconscious. She said she couldn't get her to wake up, she thinks Julie might be dead."

"Oh, no, what has she took?"

"It looks like she's taken all the tablets she got from the hospital, and some other unknown ones too all at once. Dot's in a right state."

Just as Mary was telling him the story, Dot called back from her mobile phone now, "The ambulance has arrived." Mary could hear the paramedics in the background. "Julie's alive only barely though, and they're taking us to the Victoria Hospital."

"OK, Dot, hang in there, we're on our way." Dot ended the call. "We'd better head over to the hospital at once," said Mary. "Dot's sounds like she's in a right state."

They both grabbed their jackets and headed out the house to their car. Mary called Andrew, from her mobile phone, on route to the hospital.

"My God," exclaimed Andrew, "I'll call Jason and we'll meet you guys at the hospital as quickly as we can, he went into work this morning to catch up on some paperwork. Which hospital has she been taken to?"

"Victoria Hospital," replied his mum.

As soon as he got off the phone with his mum, he called Jason. He relayed the newest tragedy to befall them. "Our luck would make a saint swear," Jason said.

Andrew agreed. He told his soon to be husband, he'd collect him in twenty minutes.

Robert and Mary arrived at the hospital, it felt weirdly familiar as this was the same hospital Doug had been in. They managed to find Dot, they all hugged.

"Dear me," exclaimed Dot, "is this never going to end?"

"It's terrible run of luck we're having to be certain," agreed Robert, "but by the laws of average, our lucks due to turn."

"Have the doctors told you anything yet?" asked Mary.

"All they've told me so far is that Julie is very lucky to be alive, and that she's in a coma."

"That sounds ominous," said Robert.

"Will she be OK?" asked Mary.

"Who knows?" cried Dot, "I've been asked to wait here until they've had a chance to fully assess her."

Robert went to get them a hot drink. When he returned, Andrew and Jason had arrived. He asked if they wanted a coffee too. They both said they were fine for the moment. They had been waiting nearly two hours before a doctor came and spoke with them. He was a young Asian doctor. He told them, unfortunately, Julie had taken an awful lot of pills the paramedics had managed to scoop all the empty bottles and pill packages that'd contained the pills she'd swallowed. She's been put on a ventilator to keep her alive until they can dilute the pills she's taken and attempt to pump her stomach.

Dot sobbed when she heard those terrible words, no parent wants to hear their child is on a life support machine.

"Will she make a full recovery?" she pleaded.

"We just don't know that yet, but I can tell you this, if you hadn't found her when you did, she wouldn't have survived. Do you have any idea why she would attempt to take her own life?"

"Where would you like me to start?" exclaimed her mum. When she'd finished telling the doctor about the woes the family have had to contend with recently, he was very sympathetic.

"Did Julie leave a note?"

Dot looked quizzically at the doctor. "What kind of note?" She had just gotten the words out when it dawned on her and the colour drained from her face, he'd just asked her if her daughter had written a suicide note. "I'm not sure," she blubbered and burst out crying again. The tears were blinding her now. Mary quickly hugged her. "I called the ambulance right away," she whispered, "I'm sorry, I didn't think to look for a suicide note."

"Don't be sorry, I'm the one that should be sorry," replied the young doctor, "it was insensitive of me asking you about a note at this time, please forgive me. It's not the first thing you would be expected to look for."

Andrew volunteered he and Jason to go back to Dot's house to have a look.

Two police officers arrived to speak to them. They'd been called by the hospital staff. It was protocol when someone attempted suicide, the doctor assured them. The officers were very polite and arranged with the doctor to allow them the use of a private room to discuss Julie. He also kindly organised some tea and coffee for them all. The senior officer, McCann, asked some questions about Julie, between them all, they filled in the blanks for the officers about Julie's husband Doug's accident and subsequent disappearance, about her baby daughter, Grace's death and that her funeral was only yesterday.

"It sounds like you lot have had a terrible time of it lately, you have my sincere condolences for the loss of the little one, and your missing relative, Doug."

After they were finished, it was agreed the police officers would accompany Andrew and Jason back to the Dot's house. Robert, Mary and Dot would stay at the hospital and hopefully, get a chance to see Julie. Dot gave them the layout of the bedrooms, then she handed Andrew her house keys. He assured her he would bring them straight back to her. The two officers, Andrew and Jason left the hospital together, but they travelled to Dot's house in their separate vehicles.

They arrived at the house around twenty minutes later. As Andrew stepped out of the car, he was approached by Dot's next-door neighbour. She introduced herself as Sue and asked about Julie's condition.

"She's in a serious condition in the hospital but unfortunately that's all I honestly know," replied Andrew.

"Please let Dot know we're all praying for her, Julie and Doug's safe return."

"I will tell her, and thanks so much for your concern. I'm Doug's brother, Andrew."

He opened the door with the keys that Dot had given him, and the four of them went inside. The officers went into Julie's bedroom, they found it easily from the layout described by Dot. Officer McCann saw an envelope on top of the bedside cabinet with the word 'Mum' written in black ink. He slid the single page note out and read it.

Mum

My life has become too hard for me to live anymore. I'm sure it's my fault that Doug didn't want to stay. I should have tried harder, I didn't allow him the time he needed to adjust. It was all a shock to him that horrible accident wasn't his doing. It was my fault that Grace died too, I must be a terrible mum. I'm just so shattered and defeated. How can I go on living without Doug and Grace? It will be better for everyone when I'm gone. I feel too much sadness and pain and guilt to carry on. Please, Mum, find it in your heart to forgive me for taking the easy way out. I wish I could have been as good a mum as you.

Love, Julie

The officer handed the note to Andrew, and as he read the short note, he had a huge lump in his throat and he had big tears gushing from his eyes. He took a tissue from his pocket and dried them. He passed the note to Jason, he read it and he, too, couldn't prevent tears from falling.

"Poor Julie, what torment she must be feeling to try to take her own life?"

"What happens now?" asked Andrew.

"I'm not sure, if I'm honest," replied officer McCann, "as Julie has not committed any crime, I think the note should stay with you for now at least. Let me make a call to my desk sergeant at my station to confirm this. Do you mind if I take a picture of the note on my phone? Just for our records, should we need it."

"No, I don't mind, I don't have any problem with that at all."

The officer took a photo of the note with the camera on his phone, he said to them not to be in any rush to let Julie's mum read this, not just yet anyway, she's got enough to deal with at the minute.

"OK," agreed Andrew, "we'll keep it from her, for now."

Officer McCann called his station and when he came off the call, he'd had it confirmed, "It was as I'd thought," and the note could stay with them.

Chapter 33

Andrew and Jason led the police officers out of Dot's house. Andrew locked the door again, and they bid the officers' goodbye and watched them drive away.

"What now?" asked Jason.

"God only knows what to do for the best, let's go a get a coffee and have a brainstorming session and see if we can come up with some options."

They both got into the car, Andrew drove to a coffee place he'd been to before with Julie. Andrew ordered a latte, and Jason a cappuccino without the sprinkles of chocolate. They sat near to the back, where there were a few empty tables. This afforded them some privacy.

"Let me see the letter again please?" Jason asked.

Andrew handed him the envelope and he removed the folded piece of paper and re-read it, he put it back into the envelope and gave slid it back across the table.

"What shall we tell the others? I'm seriously thinking we don't tell Dot, or my mum that we found this at all. I think it'll be all right keeping my dad in the loop though, he won't let on about this," Andrew said, looking at the envelope. He carefully put it back in his inside suit jacket pocket.

"Not that I disagree with you but explain your motives," Jason asked

"Let's try and look at this from Julie's perspective, she was obviously in a terrible state of mind when she wrote it, and I'm pretty sure she will be mortified that we've seen and read it."

"I agree, let's pray she survives and makes a full recovery, don't you think it will be easier for her to recover if she knows her mum and my mum haven't seen the content of the letter?"

"I see where you're heading, so option one is what? We keep the letter and when we feel the time is right, we discretely return it to Julie?"

"Yes."

"OK, let's call that option one, what's the next option?"

"We tell Dot but not my parents, that way she and Julie can discuss it between them when the time is right. I'm not sure that's as good as option one."

"I totally agree with you on that, but let's leave it on the table."

"Option three, we tell my parents and Dot, and Julie will have to try and explain her decision to everyone."

"I'm still leaning towards option one," said Jason.

"Me too. There's one more option, I think."

"OK, tell me what that is?" quizzed Jason.

"When we find Doug, we give him the letter."

"Good option, if we really think your brother will show up very soon. We are not considering the real possibility that Julie doesn't pull through this and all the options become moot."

"I know, but I was trying to avoid that scenario but if the worst happens and she dies then it doesn't really matter who sees the letter."

"I suppose not, let's go for option one for the time being, then if Julies pulls through and Doug returns, we roll one and four together."

"OK."

It was settled, they keep the letter a secret from the mums for the time being. They finished their coffees and headed back to the hospital.

Chapter 34

Saturday morning, after the fight and Johnny noticed his mobile phone was off, damn battery had died. He plugged in into its charger and switched it on. Two minutes later it rung, it was big Jim.

"What the fuck's the score, Son, I've been trying to get hold of you since last night."

"Sorry, my battery must have died. We were having a drink to celebrate Doug's win last night."

"There's been a change of plans, Son, that Italian crew that dropped a few bucks on Cranston want your big pal to fight one of their guys, no eliminator needed against Crawford."

"Is it the one they had lined up to face Cranston?"

"No, it's a different geezer and they are demanding it happens on Monday night."

"I don't know if he will want to fight again so soon."

"Listen to me, Son," big Jim barked down the phone, "this isn't a fucking request. These guys are heavy duty and they don't take no for an answer, if your pal doesn't fight, we'll all be in shit trouble, Son, and by that, I do mean all of us. These guys dropped over one hundred and fifty thousand pounds on Cranston to another family and it turns out, it wasn't their money, it was their boss's money from the collections they were doing. They barged in here last night and put another hundred grand on their man with me. They demanded even money, I tried to knock them down to four to six, but they weren't in the mood to deal. So, if your big pal doesn't win against their geezer, I'm down a hundred grand. That's an awful lot of money I'll have to pay out if your mate loses and the odds are definitely stacked against him this time."

"What price is Doug?" asked Johnny.

"I'll get you three to one and tell him he fights for me now."

"I don't think you understand, mate, Doug is his own man and you've seen what he did to Cranston, JoJo and Frankie. Are you seriously telling me you think you can threaten him into doing your bidding, he's an independent kind of guy."

"You're very cock sure, Son, have you been taking brave pills? These Italian fuckers make Cranston, Frankie and JoJo look like bouncers for Mothercare, and I'm not your fucking mate," roared big Jim. Johnny wondered to himself if he'd pushed Cassidy too far this time. Then he softened a little, "Tell Doug I'll sweeten the pot by giving him an extra ten grand if he wins."

"OK, I will speak with him and get back to you."

"Make sure you get back to me within the hour, Son."

Big Jim hung up, Frankie and JoJo were standing in his office, listening to the conversation albeit only their bosses end. "That prick's gotten ideas well above his station. After this fight, when his big pal's no longer a threat, I want you two to take him on a one-way trip to the Thames."

"Sure thing, boss," said JoJo, "it'll be our pleasure. What about his big mate?" he asked.

"We'll see about him, he could still be useful, depending on how things pan out. I will need you two to get out and about this afternoon and put the word out there's a big fight on Monday night. Doug whatever the fuck his second name is against one of the Italians, and make it sound as if he's a shoe in. I need to take as much money off all those losers as possible, understand, boys?" They both said, yes boss and nodded together. *They're definitely a double act*, big Jim thought, he just couldn't fathom which of the two was the brains of the operation. He sent Frankie out to get them all a coffee from the local Starbucks.

Around thirty minutes after Johnny had spoken with Big Jim, Doug surfaced from his room.

"Good morning, champ," Johnny had the kettle boiled and was awaiting Doug getting up. Johnny made him a cup of tea and when they were seated at the table, Johnny relayed the call from Cassidy.

"Is he serious, he actually wants me to fight again on Monday night?"

"It didn't sound like he had any choice, those guys we saw going back into the gym last night are a lot heavier duty than he is. It sounded like to me on the phone to him that he's scared of them. I've never known him to be like that, it's usually him doing the scaring. There's always a bigger fish somewhere, I suppose as the saying goes, and it seems Cassidy's trying to swim with the sharks."

"What do you know about the guy they want me to fight?"

"To be honest with you, mate I know fuck all about him, not even his name but if what Cassidy is saying is true, we don't have much of a choice. Unless you want him and those dodgy Italians on our backs, we'd always be looking over our shoulders."

"I don't know about you, Johnny, but I run from no cunt. Call him back and say it's a goer but try and find out as much as he knows about this Italian dude. It's just lucky Cranston hardly laid a glove on me or I wouldn't be in any shape to fight on Monday."

"We both know that wasn't luck, you out classed him in every department." Johnny called Cassidy's mobile phone, he answered right away. "OK, he'll take the fight, and do you know anything about the guy he's fighting?"

"No, not much other than he's supposed to be good, a big hitter but seemingly not their best. Lucky for us, their best fighter had to go home to Italy, his mother died and he's away to bury her. I'll ask around and get some background. Get Doug to come in tonight and I'll arrange some sparring partners for him."

"No need, Son, we've got that covered," and Johnny hung up before Cassidy could react.

"Fucking cheeky horrible little Jock bastard," said big Jim as he bounced his mobile phone off the table in his office, it broke into about five or six pieces. Frankie and JoJo were stunned by this unusual out burst from their boss. "He's fucking lucky I don't get him fitted for concrete welly's tonight. That little prick has defied me for the last time."

JoJo was on his hands and knees picking up the remnants of big Jim's mobile, it was wrecked.

"Just get me the fucking SIM card and battery," barked big Jim. He then went into one of the drawers in his desk and pulled out an identical, brand-new, boxed mobile phone. He grabbed the phone from the box and fitted the retrieved SIM card and battery from JoJo into the new phone carcass. He switched it on and within thirty seconds, it started to ring. He saw it was Carlo, the leader of the three Italians. He answered the call but asked Carlo to give him a minute, he covered the mouthpiece of his phone with his hand and told the boys to head out as discussed earlier and put the word out about the fight on Monday night.

Off they went, like the dutiful fools they were. Cassidy closed his office door and walked round his desk and sat in his seat.

"How are you doing, my good friend?" he asked Carlo.

"Is it all set for Monday night?"

"Yes, all set my end, my guy's ready for action." Carlo knew already the man fighting Salvatore was not one of Cassidy's guys, but he never mentioned it. Carlo didn't like or trust this fool Cassidy, and he may not live long enough to become his friend either. Carlo suspected Cassidy had paid his man Cranston to throw the fight against the big newcomer to swindle him and his associates out of their money. He was not going to let that go without retribution, it was not the Italian way.

Chapter 35

Andrew and Jason arrived back at the hospital within half an hour of leaving the coffee shop. It took them another twenty minutes to find a parking space. When they finally got to the waiting room, Robert got up to meet them.

"How did you get on?"

"OK, Dad," replied Andrew. "How's Julie, have there been any updates? Is she still in a coma?" Robert ushered them outside the waiting room for fear of starting the woman off crying again. It had taken him nearly an hour to get them calmed down. "The doctor came out to see us about an hour ago, Julie's still very gravely ill, at this point it's touch or go if she pulls through or not. On a plus note, they've taken her off the ventilator as she's now breathing on her own again."

"Why don't you grab a seat," Andrew said to his partner, "Dad and I will go and get us a brew."

"OK, that sounds like a plan. What should I tell your mum and Dot if they ask about the note?"

"Tell them we looked around with the police officers, but there was no sign of a note and it could just be an accidental overdose, hopefully they will think this is possible."

"It's probably better if they think that than an attempted suicide," said Robert.

Jason asked him if he needed some money for the drinks.

"No, but thanks for the offer, Son." That was a pleasant surprise to Jason as Robert had never called him son before. He went back into the waiting room, and Andrew and his dad went to get the brews. Once they were away from the waiting room, he told his dad all about the note. He removed it from his pocket and handed it to him. He read it in silence, he could see it was as upsetting to his dad as it'd been for them, although his dad was trying to conceal it. His dad folded the note and placed it back into its envelope.

"I know that that was a difficult read, Dad."

"Yes, it was, it's something we can all do without, we've got enough to deal with."

"Yes, I know, Dad but poor Julie, what must be going through her mind to think the best solution is to take your own life?"

"It's very difficult to understand why anyone would do that, Son. Your mum and I have a missing son, you've got a missing brother. Julie has a dead daughter and she thinks Doug's gone for good. That puts things into a very different perspective for her. I just wish I would have seen the signs. I feel so guilty; I should have insisted she came back home with us yesterday after the funeral."

"You can't beat yourself up over this, we all could've seen the signs, but you read that note, she was in a very dark place and I think, if she had it in her mind to do what she did, then there's every chance she would have done it at your house anyway. Just think how that would have made you feel."

"I suppose you're right," Robert read the note again, then folded it and gave it back to his son.

"Jason and I discussed not telling the women about this over a coffee after leaving the police. I take it you agree it's the best thing if we don't reveal its existence to Dot, or Mum."

"It's hard to argue with your logic, I agree, I think they've got far too much to deal with already. I know I'm just about coping, but if I'm honest, I've not had the time, nor the capacity to deal with Grace's death. Let alone Julie's over-dose. If only your brother was here, just maybe this wouldn't have happened."

"No, Dad, even if Doug was here, what happened to little Grace couldn't have been prevented, you heard what the doctor said, SIDS is a terrible occurrence. I concur, if Doug were here maybe he could've helped Julie cope a bit better." Robert nodded and conceded his son was talking more sense than him just now.

"I sometimes forget just how switched on you are, Andrew."

"Thanks, Dad, I know it's a very trying time for you especially just now, with all that's going on let's get the teas and coffees before they send out a search party looking for us."

The cafeteria was down two floors, they ordered two teas and three coffees, they also bought some doughnuts and a couple of packets of crisps, it could be a long wait. Robert paid the woman in the cafeteria, he got one pound ten pence change from twenty-five pounds. *Ouch,* he thought. They somehow managed, between them, to carry the five brews and sustenance back up the lift and into the waiting room.

It looked like Jason was glad to see them back, he must have been getting the third degree from Mary and Dot. Robert gave the women their teas, and Andrew gave his partner his coffee. Robert offered Mary and Dot a doughnut each with their tea but neither wanted to eat one, but after some gentle coaxing from Robert and Andrew, telling them it could be a good few hours before they find out any news, or get anything to eat, they both took one. Robert also had one. Jason and Andrew shared a packet of crisps. Around about an hour later, another doctor came out and gave them an update on Julie, it was much the same as it was about three hours ago. She was still in a coma and unresponsive.

They were informed that the next twenty-four hours were crucial. The doctor suggested they all go home and try to get some sleep; they'd be called if anything changed. They all had a discussion and it was decided that at least one of them would stay at the hospital, no matter what, until Julie comes out of the coma. Andrew and Jason agreed to take the first shift, neither of them were working tomorrow with it being a Sunday.

Robert asked the doctor if they could go and see Julie before they left. The doctor agreed, as long as no more than two people were at the bed at one time. Mary and Dot went in first, they spent a good half hour at Julie's bedside, talking gently to her, saying she needed to come out of this coma to allow them to help her get over her difficulties. They both told her how much they loved her.

When they came out, Andrew and Robert went in next. They spent ten minutes telling Julie none of this was her fault, they hoped she could hear them. Robert pleaded with her to pull through and let them help her get her life back on track, he assured her Doug would be back soon. They came out and Jason was going in next, Dot, asked him if she could go back in with him.

"Yes, of course you can," he replied. "Do you want to be alone with her?"

"Yes, for five minutes, if that's OK?"

"It sure is, Dot."

They all sat back in the waiting room, about ten minutes later, Dot, reappeared. "Thanks, Jason," she said. "I needed that."

Jason said he'd go into see her with Andrew a bit later to let her have some peace for a while. Robert, Mary and Dot all hugged Andrew and Jason, Robert said he and Mary would come in and relieve them in six- or seven-hours' time. This would give them a chance drop off Dot, get some food and have around four hours sleep. Dot agreed to take over from Robert and Mary at eight o'clock tomorrow morning, and that she would get a taxi in, she insisted. Although Robert did offer to collect her.

"You're doing enough as it is," she said.

"OK, if you're sure."

"I am," she countered.

They said goodbye to Andrew and Jason who assured them if there's any changes, they would be in touch right away. When the others were gone, they went into see Julie. Jason thought she looked so peaceful. They spoke to her, and discussed Doug coming back as soon as possible, and her getting out of hospital. They sat at either side of her bed and they each held a hand. The monitors were bleeping away in the background. Every fifteen minutes or, so a nurse would come in and check all the readings on the monitors.

Around two hours into their watch, they informed the nurse they were going to the cafeteria to get some food, they would be back in half an hour, Andrew gave her his mobile phone number and asked her to call him if there were any changes. The nurse agreed she'd call him. She wondered if they were brothers or friends. *Andrew was quite good looking,* she thought.

When they arrived at the cafeteria, it wasn't too busy, it didn't have a big extensive menu. They both decided to have the fish and chips, it was self-service, Andrew had a coke and Jason had a sprite. They found an empty table next to the window. They weren't expecting the food to be Michelin star quality, but for a hospital cafeteria at seven thirty on a Saturday night, it wasn't too bad.

They were in the waiting room forty-five minutes after leaving it, they'd made another stop on route back. They called into the hospital shop and bought a couple of magazines and a puzzle book to help relieve the boredom. They were the only two people left in the waiting room, they sat side by side. When the nurse walked past, she noticed they were holding hands. That cleared the mystery of them being brothers or friends.

It's a pity, she thought to herself, *all the good-looking ones are taken.* She approached them and said that if they were quiet, they could sit in the room by Julie's bedside. They thanked her and Andrew assured her they would be as quiet as little mice.

That made her smile, "OK, in you go then," she said.

Chapter 36

Johnny called Eddie and told him about the call from Cassidy.

"Why would he arrange a fight just three days after Doug's just fought Cranston?" asked Eddie.

"I don't think it was his choice, it seems to me that Cassidy has gotten himself into bed with the Italians, and it looks like they're calling all the shots. We found out last night that Cranston's next fight after Doug was with one of the Italians, apparently Doug knocking him out scuppered all their plans. It appears they lost a right few quid betting on him too. By all accounts, they expect their guy to beat Doug and they're demanding Cassidy sets this up for Monday, he's offered Doug six grand to agree to the fight, and another ten grand if he can win. I'm looking to see if you can get a hold of the guys again to see if they're up to some sparring to-night and tomorrow. I appreciate it's the weekend, but we can pay them a couple of hundred quid each for the two nights."

"Leave it with me, Johnny, I'll call them and ask the question."

"You're a real pal, Eddie, thanks a lot."

"OK, I'll call you back soon." Johnny told Doug Eddie was going to try and line up Syd and Brian and Andre for some sparring, but nothing too strenuous.

"We don't need you punched out before Monday night. How are you feeling after last night's exertions?"

Doug said he was feeling OK, and he was going out for a little jog round the park to clear his head after last night's booze.

"That's a good idea, I'll go to the supermarket and get us something nice to eat. How about some pasta? Speaking about those Italians has put me in the mood for something Italian? How does spaghetti and sardines sound to you?"

"It sounds fucking great, but can you make it?"

"You'll see soon enough, big man," chortled Johnny. Doug left for his jog and Johnny jumped into his car, he was probably still over the drink drive limit from last night's festivities and he hoped he never got pulled over by the coppers. He was lucky he never encountered a single police car the both trips to and from the local Asda store where he bought a pack of Spaghetti, two cans of skinless and boneless sardines in a tomato sauce, a can of chopped tomatoes, a couple of cloves of garlic and two baguettes of garlic bread.

His ex-wife, Betty, used to make this for him and the kids quite often as it was one of his favourite dinners of all time. He used to watch her cook all the time, he missed her, and his boys more than he would like to admit. The meal was very easy to make, well Betty always made it look so easy. Johnny had been back for about an hour, Doug had not returned from his jog yet, but Johnny thought he would re-turn imminently, so he started making the dinner.

It was too late for lunch and too early for supper, it was mid-afternoon. If they were hungry again later on after the visit to the gym, they could always grab something from a chip shop or a burger from McDonalds or even a KFC. Half way through Johnny's culinary excursion into the kitchen, Doug arrived home.

"Have I got time for a shower?"

"Yes, if you're quick."

"OK, I thought I'd come into the wrong house as there's a delicious smell coming from the kitchen, I hope it tastes as good as it smells?"

"It will, ya cheeky bastard," assured Johnny, "if I learned anything whilst I was married, it's was how to make Spaghetti and Sardines."

Doug had his shower and had changed clothes now, he went into the kitchen just as Johnny was putting their meal out, it looked fantastic. They both tucked in and Doug complemented Johnny on his excellent cooking skills, it was every bit as good as he'd said it would be, even better.

"You'll make somebody a good little housewife," teased Doug.

"Fuck you," laughed Johnny, "you're on the dishes for that smart-arse remark." Now they both laughed. Just as Doug was finishing putting the plates away, Johnny's mobile rang, he thought it might be Eddie, but it was Cassidy. Johnny answered it.

Cassidy cut to the chase, "Listen, Son," Cassidy used this term often with Johnny, but it was not out of endearment, "I've asked around, and the guy your big pal's fighting on Monday night is called Salvatore. I don't know his second name, he's not that well-known, I've discovered that he's had five fights we know of, and he's won four of them in the first round, and the other in the second round. Apparently, he's a very big hitter, the first guy he knocked out is still eating through a straw. He's known as the Italian Tyson, around his gaff, so tell your man as long as he gets by the third round, his opponent will be in unchartered waters."

"Are you trying to scare us?"

"No, I'm not trying to fucking scare you, Son," growled Cassidy. "I just fucking need your pal to win. Understand this, Son, losing isn't an option or I'm getting taken to the fucking cleaners by these Italian bastards, so you just make sure he wins, OK. Because I'm holding you personally responsible if he fucking loses."

Johnny tried protesting. "How's it my fault if he loses?" but he was talking to himself, Cassidy had already hung up. "What a prick," Johnny said to Doug, telling him what Cassidy said, both about his opponent for Monday night, and about losing not being an option.

"Maybe you should call him back and tell him to fight the fucking guy," Doug replied.

Ten minutes later, Johnny's phone rang again. This time it was Eddie.

"How'd you get on with the guys? Are they up for it tonight?" asked Johnny.

"I managed to get a hold of Syd, but not Brian, his phone went straight to voice mail. Syd said he will come in tonight and he'll get a hold of Andre and bring him along too. He said as long as it's just gentle sparring, and some tactical moving around the ring. I don't think he's up for Doug slamming anymore sledgehammer punches into him."

"That's brilliant, I'm sure the big man will take it easy on them, after all he won't want to tire himself out. The guy he's fighting on Monday is an Italia named Salvatore, we couldn't get a surname, but surely there's not too many of them kicking around the fight game. Can you ask around and see if you can get info on him? He's supposed to be a bit of a hitter or so that prick Cassidy informed me. He threatened with all sorts if Doug loses."

They got to the gym about half past seven, Eddie was already there, "Sometimes, it feels like I never leave this place," Eddie stressed to Johnny. A couple of minutes later, Syd and Andre arrived. Up close, these two were big strapping lads.

"Do they stand these guys in grow bags when they're young?"

"Your guess is as good as mine," replied Eddie, "I'll say this though, Johnny, I've come across some seriously big dudes in this boxing game."

The three boxers were in getting changed. Johnny asked Eddie if he'd managed to find out anything about this Salvatore guy.

"Not a peep yet, mate," he said, "but I've put some feelers out there, so hopefully someone will get back with the SP on him."

"Fair enough," said Johnny. "I get the impression he's new in the country, he must be if he's only had the five fights."

The guys were out the changing room and had climbed into the ring. Eddie and Johnny went over to ring side. "Right, Doug, from the limited information we have on this guy you're fighting on Monday night, here's what we know, he's got a big punch, and he's never been beyond two rounds."

"That's not a lot to go on," said Johnny.

"Oh, on the contrary," said Eddie, "that's plenty. Here, what I want you guys to do tonight, it's called the rope a dope technique. Doug, don't you throw any punches. I need you just blocking tonight, use the ropes to try and absorb the impact of the punches, the most important thing is to use the whole ring and keep moving. Syd, you go first, in round one, try punching Doug in the head only, no body shots at all, and no stopping for rests. I need you to keep going forward. Doug, your job in this round is to make yourself hard to hit, you need to move around the ring as much as possible. If you can last the first round against Syd without a major hit then great."

They started, Doug used the full size of the ring and kept his hands and arms up protecting his head. He was bouncing into the ropes, it was working. Syd was throwing big punches, he wasn't holding back. The big man had succeeded in the first round as planned. The second round was the same, only now he was facing Andre, again without too much hassle, he managed to remain relatively unscathed. Using the full square of the ring, Andre chasing him and trying to land a decent punch, he was as unsuccessful as Syd.

Round three and four were much the same, again with Syd and Andre only managing to hit Doug's forearms or gloves, with no damage done to Doug. He was bouncing on the ropes and it was doing exactly as Eddie said it would, taking all the sting out of the punches.

"OK, that was brilliant, Doug, you move around the ring like you belong in there. Well done, guys, that was excellent work. Did you see what we were trying to achieve in there?"

"I think I understand what you were aiming for, if I can make myself difficult to hit then there's less chance he can knock me out."

"Yes, perfect and if you can last for a good few rounds, we can get this geezer out of his comfort zone and the better chance you have of winning. Syd, Andre, how do you feel?"

They both said they felt knackered.

"Exactly," said Eddie, "when you're doing all the running and all the punching, it takes its toll, and the longer you go on without any success, it sucks your energy. This is what you will need to do on Monday night, Doug. Right, let's get you three out of there and Doug's turn to throw some punches into the heavy bag."

They all climbed out the ring and headed to the hanging bag. Doug set about the bag as Syd and Andre took it in turns holding it to give it more resistance. Eddie and Johnny headed into the office, once the door was closed, Eddie turned to Johnny.

"Did you see the way he moved in there? This guy could've been a professional, he has it all. If I'd had him in my gym ten years ago, he could have been a champion."

"Yes," Jonny agreed. "He really looked good."

"Have you thought any more about telling Doug about his dad and brother coming here looking for him?"

"I was going to break that news gently to him today, but events with Cassidy have overtaken me. I think I should wait until Monday's fights over with and then I'll tell him."

"Do you promise me you will, Johnny? I think he deserves to know."

"Yes, mate, I promise, but I don't think it will make any difference to him, he's the one who bolted from them. If he wanted them to know where he is, he'd tell them."

"Fair enough, but let's shake on it then," said Eddie, they did. They could hear the big heavy bag taking a pounding from Doug. "We'd better get out there and get Doug to slow down a bit, the last thing he needs is to get in the ring on Monday and have used all his strength punching that bag," said Eddie.

They left the office but were surprised to see it was Andre punching the fuck out the bag now, not Doug. Eddie said to Doug, "We were just coming to tell you to lay off for a bit, but I see you have already."

"Yes, I want to save some for the Italian geezer on Monday night." Eddie looked at Doug, and asked him if he'd had his office bugged because that's exactly what he had just said to Johnny.

"Great minds think alike," Doug replied and winked at him. They were all smiling.

"OK, guys, hit the showers."

The three boxers all trudged off into the changing rooms. "What did I tell you, that guy's got some smarts when it comes to boxing," said Eddie.

"But where's it coming from? He told me he can't remember anything prior to his accident. Do you think Doug's legitimate?"

"What do you mean by that?" asked Johnny, without any malice.

"Do you think his accident was for real? Or could it just be an excuse to get away for a situation he didn't want to be in?"

"What kind of situation?"

"You said he mentioned a woman with a kid."

"No chance, Eddie, I'm sure it's real, we were talking about my family the other night and he was racking his brains, and he couldn't come up with anything since the accident. I'm positive it wasn't an act."

"OK," replied Eddie, "we'll leave it at that for now. How are your family?"

159

"Now you come to mention them, same old same old, not much contact with them at all nowadays."

"That's a shame."

The three guys came out the changing rooms, Johnny walked towards them and pulled out a bundle of notes he was peeling off some twenty-pound notes, asking Syd and Andre how much he owed them for coming in to the gym on a Saturday.

"You owe us nothing, Johnny," protested Syd, "we both made a few quid betting on Doug last night, and if I can help get him to beat this Italian geezer, I'll be putting some more dosh on him, so we're square."

"Me too," said Andre, "I wasn't doing anything exciting tonight anyway, and I'll be betting more money on him too."

"Well, that's kind of you two. How about you, Eddie? Do I need to give you something for your troubles?"

"Forget it, Johnny, you know fine well, I did OK last night too, and the way the big man shaped up tonight, there's more to come on Monday night."

They all agreed to meet at the gym again tomorrow night at seven thirty for some more training. They all shook hands and headed for the door. It was nearly ten o'clock. Johnny and Doug climbed into the car and it started after a few attempts.

"This fucking car is going to give up the ghost one of these days," Johnny said.

On the journey home, Doug said he was feeling strong and he was sure he'd give the Italian Tyson a run for his money.

"Good, maybe when you win, I'll have enough for a decent car, this one's headed for the scrapper." Johnny told Doug that Eddie was going to put out some more feelers to see if anyone had heard of this Italian. "The more we know about him, the better we can prepare. Someone somewhere must have info on him."

They got home, and Johnny asked Doug if he was hungry. "Yes, I'm a bit peckish," replied Doug.

"How about I make us some beans and toast? It's a bit late for too much more than that."

"Beans and toast sounds good," replied Doug.

When they finished their snack, Doug went to bed, he was getting up at six thirty to go for a run. Johnny, as usual, stayed up a while longer.

Chapter 37

Robert and Mary had just gotten home after dropping Dot off at her house, it was just gone seven o'clock. Mary had not been for her weekly grocery shop. She didn't want to start cooking at this late hour so they decided they were going to have an Indian carry out.

"What do you fancy?" she asked Robert. "I think I will have some samosas, and for mains, I will have Tandoori chicken."

"That sounds smashing, I'll have that too, and we can get a naan bread and a portion of rice as well," suggested Robert.

"I'm famished."

"OK, I'll go and get it."

"I'll get the plates ready and we've got a nice bottle of wine in the cupboard."

"I'll just have a soft drink; remember we've got to relieve the boys at three AM."

"OK, sorry, my minds gone haywire, I'll just have some tea instead."

Off Robert went. He was back around thirty minutes later with their supper. It was delicious as it always was from their local Indian take away. When they'd finished, Robert helped Mary clear away the food cartons, he put them into the bin outside, he didn't want the smell to linger. Mary washed and put away the dishes. They went upstairs to try and get a few hours' sleep, and Robert set the alarm on his phone for two AM.

Mary wasn't sure she would manage to get any sleep at all, but she did. As soon as her head hit the pillow, she was out like a light, Robert, on the other hand, didn't fall asleep for at least an hour. He was wondering if there was anything he hadn't tried in order to find his son. He couldn't think of one more single thing he could do. His mind kept going back to that last gym he visited, he was sure the guy was holding back. Robert had seen a flicker of recognition in his eyes when the guy looked at Doug's picture. He'd now decided if Doug hadn't shown up by the middle of next week, he was going back there to confront the manager. He was sure the guy's name was Eddie.

Chapter 38

Andrew went to get them another coffee, whilst Jason stayed by Julies bedside. They had been speaking to her all the time they'd been there, there was no sign that Julie could hear them. It was now just past midnight, another three hours to go until Andrews's parents got there to let them get home for some sleep.

Andrew had just returned with the coffee when one of the monitors attached to Julie started making a loud beeping noise. A nurse rushed into the room followed by a young doctor. The nurse asked Andrew and Jason to go into the waiting room.

"What's just happened?" asked Andrew.

"Julie's heart just stopped, now please go to the waiting room."

They went there immediately as instructed. They were now terrified that Julie had just died. About twenty minutes later, the nurse came into the waiting room and told a very relieved Andrew and Jason that they'd managed to get Julie back.

"Oh my God, that was the scariest thing that's ever happened to me," said Jason.

"Yes, me too," said Andrew, "my hearts racing now. Let's go outside for a bit of fresh air."

They told the nurse where they were going, and that they would be back in half an hour. They went down the lift and as they walked toward the main doors, they could feel a chill in the air. They walked outside for a bit.

"Do you think Julie will make it?" Andrew asked.

"I thought so before but now, I'm not so sure. The neurologist said earlier that the next twenty-four hours are crucial to her chances and I don't think what happened to her in there just now is part of the process of getting through this," Jason replied.

"Let's try and be positive, they did manage to resuscitate her," said Andrew.

"Yes, but she's still in a coma," replied his partner.

They headed back up to the ward, they went to speak with the nurse. She told them that the doctor has asked to see them when they returned.

"OK, please let him know we're back," replied Andrew.

She went to find the doctor. Andrew said to Jason, "This doesn't sound too promising if the doctors want to see us as soon as we're back."

Two minutes later, she returned with the doctor. They were still the only visitors in this particular waiting room. The doctor asked them to sit, this worried them more so, but then he sat too.

"I'm Doctor Sullivan," the doctor told them.

"I'm Andrew, this is Jason, my partner. Julie's my sister-in-law. Thanks for reviving her earlier," said Andrew.

The doctor looked embarrassed. "Just to let you know, Julie suffered a mild heart attack, but we managed to get her back without too much trouble, but we've had to put her back onto the ventilator. The problem is that as she's in a coma, we don't know how badly this has affected her. Generally, we would expect the patient to come out of their coma within a few days, but it varies."

"Yes, I know," said Andrew, "my brother was in a coma for two months."

"Has he recovered fully?" asked the doctor.

"Well, that depends on your definition of recovered, he's out of the coma, but he can't remember any of his family. That's why Julie's tried to end her own life, she lost her baby daughter, Grace too. Her funeral was yesterday."

"That's awful," replied the doctor, "where's your brother now?"

"We wish we knew," said Jason, "he's been missing for nearly two weeks. He missed his daughter's funeral."

"That's very unfortunate. Let's just hope that she regains consciousness in the next day or two," said Doctor Sullivan.

"Can we see her now?" asked Andrew.

"Yes, I'll take you in, follow me."

They all stood up, crossed the waiting room floor and entered Julie's room.

Chapter 39

Robert awoke when his alarm went off, he got up and had a shower, dried off and put his clothes on. He went down stairs and put the kettle on, he made himself a strong coffee and made Mary a cup of tea He carried them upstairs to their bedroom. He gently shook his wife awake, and gave her her tea.

"Good morning," she said, "have we over slept? What time is it?"

"No, we're fine for time. It's just past two AM."

She sat up and had her tea. "Any news from the hospital?"

"No, none at all, I'm going to call Andrew now," Robert dialled his son's mobile number, he answered right away.

"Hi, Dad, I was going to call you in fifteen minutes if I hadn't heard from you."

"What's up?"

"Julie's had a setback."

"What sort, is she OK, is it serious?"

"Yes, she flat-lined, but the doctor managed to revive her pretty quickly, they've put her back on a ventilator."

"My goodness, I'll tell your mum, we'll be there in about forty minutes or so."

"OK, Dad, we'll see you when you get here."

Robert hung up and told Mary what their son had just told him. "That's not good is it?" she asked her husband.

"Probably not the best thing that could have happened, that's for sure."

She finished her tea and went into the shower. Twenty-five minutes later, they were in the car heading back to the hospital. The traffic was practically non-existent at this time in the morning. They pulled into the hospital car park and got a space quite near to the entrance. As they walked towards the main doors, there were a couple of people smoking cigarettes just outside the entrance. Once inside, they got the lift to the ward. They opened Julie's door, Andrew and Jason got off their chairs and they both hugged Mary. She then sat in one of the chairs and held Julies hand, she was telling Julie everything would be all right. Although she knew about the ventilator, she was still quite shocked to see it. Robert and two guys went out to the waiting room. Andrew told his dad exactly what had happened.

"You two must have got the shock of your lives," Robert said.

"Honestly, Dad, we thought Julie was gone for good, but the quick action of the nurses and doctors saved her. The doctor spoke with us and said the ventilator should only be temporary until her body recovers enough strength to breathe on her own again. We'll go back in and say a quick goodbye to Mum and Julie then we're heading home. We're shattered."

"Yes, you must be, and thanks again for being here for Julie."

"That's OK, Dad, we're glad to help," said Jason, hoping for no reaction to him calling Robert dad, not even a flicker of awkwardness in Roberts face.

"You two are saints, I swear it," Robert told them.

They went back into Julie's room and they both said goodbye to Julie and Mary they both kissed Julie's cheek and they hugged Mary again.

Robert walked them out the room and he shook both their hands and thanked them again.

"We'll be back in tonight, if there's no changes. I'll call you around six PM tonight, Dad."

"OK, drive safely and I'll see you both soon."

With that, off they went home. Robert headed back into Julie's room, he sat on the opposite side of the bed from his wife.

"Do you think I should I call Dot and let her know about the ventilator?" he asked Mary. "That's a difficult decision," she replied. "What if that were Doug lying here, would you want to know if he'd been put on a ventilator?"

"Yes, I would."

"Well, I think we should tell her but not until later on this morning, there's no point in calling her now. She should be sleeping," said Mary.

"Yes, you're right again."

"Andrew and Jason must have gotten a right old fright," she said.

"They did, they told me so."

Mary said to Julie, "Listen, love, we don't need any frights at our age, so please get better soon and come out this damn coma and let us help you get back on your feet."

Robert decided he was going to get them a brew, a coffee for himself and a tea for Mary. He went down to the cafeteria, Faye's, it's called, it was open twenty-four hours. He ordered one coffee and one tea and two caramel wafer biscuits, he was charged eight pounds twenty pence. He thought this was excessive, *but I suppose the coffee was quite superb,* he said to himself.

Chapter 40

Doug was up at six-thirty AM, he'd over slept. He was meaning to be up at four-thirty AM, he must have needed the extra two hours. He went for a run, it was cool and damp outside, he'd decided he was going to do an eight-mile run this morning. The streets were fairly empty, it was, after all, a Sunday. He felt really good, all the hard work he'd been doing in the gym and his morning running was helping him build up a bit of stamina.

How hard will it be to stay out of reach of this big puncher he was facing tomorrow night? As Eddie had said, let him do all the chasing, and soak up his punches but he thought, *if I get a chance to punch his fucking head off, I'm taking it. No point in prolonging the fight, this geezer maybe unbeaten but he's not fought me.*

Doug was starting to believe he could win, after all he'd already taken out three big guys, Cranston, and those two arseholes, Frankie and JoJo, as well as all the sparring partners he's faced, and he just knew he could have taken them out in any round. He was thinking back to what the gay guy said to him, about him being a good boxer. He even said he'd been to some fights. *Why the fuck can't I remember? I don't know why but when I'm in the ring, I feel like a king, nobody can beat me,* Doug said to himself.

He was determined to win for all his new buddies' sakes, they were going to make a lot of money. He was not too bothered that Cassidy thought he was fighting for him. He was sure this was going to be the last fight he was going to take for that prick anyway. He ran the last mile a bit harder than the rest. He was back home and, in a shower, just less than an hour and a quarter after he left the house. *Not too bad a time,* he thought.

When he got out of the shower, Johnny was still asleep. He put the kettle on. As it popped off to signal it had boiled, Johnny arose from his sleep.

"Good morning, mate, have you been for your run already?" Johnny asked.

"Yes, not long back from it, I've been up for ages."

"How do you feel?"

"I feel great, bring on this Italian geezer, I'm fucking ready for him right now."

"That's good to hear, I'm going in for a quick shower, then I'll make us some breakfast."

Ten minutes later, Johnny was taking some sausages and eggs from the fridge, he was also making toast. When it was ready, they both tucked into it. Doug was starving, Johnny was hungry too, they finished in no time at all. Johnny's mobile phone was ringing, he noticed it was his boss calling. He wondered what he wanted at nine AM on a Sunday morning. He answered it, his boss, Arthur, was hoping he and Doug would be up for covering a shift today, ten AM till six PM. He'd been let down badly by one guy phoning in sick and another guy chucking it in. He promised them a fifty-pound bonus if they could cover the shift.

"OK, let me ask Doug, I'll call you back in two minutes," he ended the call. He told his mate who was calling. "Arthur wants us to cover a shift today, he's been let down again."

"I'm up for it if you are, we're doing fuck all today anyway. Call him back and tell him we'll do it," Doug replied. Johnny called back and his boss thanked them for bailing him out on short notice.

When they arrived at the site, it was nearly empty. There were only half a dozen contractors vans in the car park, and one car belonging to one of the two Ronnie's. There were rarely less than thirty vans during the week, but not a Sunday. When they went into the security office, they discovered Ronnie Sweeney was not with his usual mate, he was working with a new guy, apparently Ron Baker had phoned in sick. *There's a lot of it about,* thought Johnny.

The new guy was named Bert, he was in his fifties. Sweeney introduced them all, they had nothing to report. "I wasn't expecting you guys, I thought it would be Paddy and another newbie that were on next shift."

"Paddy phoned in sick and the newbie couldn't handle the excitement, so he decided on a new career and fucking chucked it. So, Arthur called the Calvary and here we are."

Ronnie told them the only guys working on the site today were flooring contactors, a Sunday's the only time they could get their flooring done as the rest of the site were off. They were putting down big slate tiles in the two newest building; the decorators were due to start tomorrow. The flooring guys said they'd be done by four PM.

"OK, no problem," said Johnny.

Ronnie and Bert left soon after the handover. "Right, big man, first things first, you put the kettle on. I'll go and make sure the flooring guys are out of here at four." Johnny left the office and went onto site.

Doug filled the kettle and sat down to watch the security monitors until Johnny came back. He returned about fifteen minute later and they had their coffee. The rest of the shift was long, boring and uneventful, and the flooring contractors all left at three thirty.

At a quarter to six, the next shift guys arrived. They were being replaced by Old Jimmy, a fellow Glaswegian and a Polish guy named Filip. Johnny and Jimmy had a good old natter for about ten minutes, neither Doug nor Filip, whose English was spot on, understood too much of it. Doug thought he heard the words Rangers and Celtic, but couldn't swear on it. Once the two weegies were done gossiping, Doug and Johnny left them to it.

As the site was now empty, the new shift was sure to have a quiet time of it. On the way home, Johnny confirmed he and Jimmy were discussing football, there was an upcoming old firm game between Rangers and Celtic. Johnny supported Celtic and Jimmy supported Rangers, they had a tenner bet on which of their teams would win the game.

Once home via the local Asda for some groceries, they had a light snack of a chicken and mushroom pot noodle and a packet of readymade sandwiches. Johnny chose cheese and tomato and Doug had tuna mayonnaise. They would have a fish supper later after the visit to the gym. By the time they had finished, it was nearly half past six. They could relax for about half an hour before they headed to the gym.

Chapter 41

Doug and Johnny left the house at ten past seven. They had to stop off and get diesel for the car, it was running on fumes, said Johnny. They got to the gym at seven thirty-five. Eddie, Syd and Andre were there already as well as four other guys. Syd and Andre were in the ring doing some sparring.

Johnny asked Eddie who the four strangers were. Eddie told him not to worry, they were regulars, just doing a bit of weight training and they wouldn't be using the ring. Doug went into the changing rooms and emerged ten minutes later.

"What delights have you got planned for me tonight?" Doug asked Eddie.

"A bit of the same as last night, but more shadow boxing than actual boxing. I don't want you absorbing too many punches on your arm, I've already discussed it with the guys in the ring," replied Eddie.

Doug climbed into the ring, Eddie and Johnny headed into the office. "I have had some feedback from the feelers I've put out about this Italian geezer. One guy I know very well, Kevin, has told me this Italian is very young, about twenty-one, he's very raw and only knows one way to box and that is an all-out attack. He's watched two of his fights, he thinks they were his last two. He said he does have a great knockout punch, but the guys he was up against didn't look too good," Eddie relayed to Johnny.

"Well, that's a relief. Why do the Italians think he's a shoe in to beat Doug?"

"I've been thinking about that since I spoke with Kevin. He was due to fight Cranston who's about mid-forties, and everyone thought he'd knock Doug out no problem."

"Everyone except us, you mean."

"Yes," they both smiled. "Anyway, maybe they've just assumed Doug will be easy meat for him."

"Doug's right up for this, he was out for a run this morning and when he came back, he told he was feeling great."

"That's good to hear, make sure he doesn't go for a run tomorrow, tell him he'll need all has strength for the fight. I suspect he'll be doing enough running in the ring."

They went outside and watched the three guys in the ring shadow boxing. They were both marvelling the way Doug was taking to it, like a duck to water.

"I'd like to find out his story," said Eddie. "He moves like a champion."

"He does," agreed Johnny.

Eddie called time and told the guys to hit the big bag for twenty minutes. They all climbed out of the ring and worked on the bag as instructed. When they were finished, they went into the changing rooms, and after a shower, they emerged from the changing rooms. Syd and Andre shook Doug's hand and wished him good luck for tomorrow night and assured him they would be there to support him. He thanked them.

Eddie told him he'd done fantastically well the past two nights and that, in his opinion, he was ready for anything this geezer could throw at him. Johnny and Doug thanked Eddie for all his help.

"I'll see you guys tomorrow, if you take what you've learned in here and stick with the plan, let him do all the chasing, he'll tire. And if you can get him beyond round four or five, he'll be knackered then you go after him and hit him with the big right hander you've got, and I promise you, he will go down like a sack of spuds," Eddie said.

"Here's hoping, I feel more confident going in against this guy than I did against Cranston." Doug noticed the four other guys from earlier had disappeared. He asked Eddie, where they went. They left ages ago, they come here about once a month and they only stay for about an hour.

The three of them left together, Eddie locked up, "See you both tomorrow." Then he climbed into his Ford Mondeo and drove off. Johnny and Doug got into Johnny's Focus.

"Whoopee," said Johnny as the car started right away, "our lucks still good," he said.

The stopped off at the Broadway chippy. Johnny had a cod and chips, Doug had the Roe and chips. They ate them when they got home, straight from the newspaper wrappers. Johnny told Doug what Eddie had said about not going for a run in the morning, "Best to keep all your strength for the fight."

"OK, what time do we start work at tomorrow?"

"We're on six AM till two PM, that'll give us plenty of time to get back here and have a bit of lunch. You can grab a few hours' kip, I'll get us something decent for supper around five PM, the fights at ten PM."

Doug went to bed; it was just past ten PM. Johnny said he was hitting the sack too. The next morning when Doug got up at four forty-five AM, Johnny was already up. That was unusual, he was making scrambled eggs with toast, it smelled good. Doug ate his, then went for a shower.

They were at the building site at ten minutes to six. There was only one other car parked there, it was a ford focus a bit like Johnny's but at least six years younger. They signed in, Johnny saw the guy through the office window, he recognised the guy as he'd seen him a couple of times before, but he couldn't remember his name. He casually looked at the sign-in book and saw that his name was Raymond Elliott. It turned out the poor guy had done the shift as a loner; his mate never trapped the previous night.

Raymond was a pleasant type of guy, he was newish, but he seemed to be reliable, that was the only criteria his boss, Arthur, looked for. Raymond told them that he'd been out on patrol during the night when he thought he'd heard something amiss. It turned out it was a fox raiding the bins, he said he was quite nervous being on his own.

"Yes, I feel your pain," said Johnny, "I had to do a lone shift about two weeks ago, and it's no fun."

"Yes, dead right," Raymond nodded in agreement. He signed out and wished the guys a good shift. He left, Doug went and put the kettle on.

170

"You're learning, big man," laughed Johnny. "You've got your priorities in good order."

"Well, it's your turn next time, Son," Doug said in a Cassidy like voice.

"That's fucking scary, you sound just like that prick."

Doug washed a couple of mugs and made them a coffee.

"The site mangers should be getting in shortly, we'd better go for a quick walk around the site after we've finished," said Johnny.

Ten minutes later, a couple of builders arrived, they signed in the contractor's book. Doug opened the gate to allow them to drive their van to their work place to off load their materials. Vans were not allowed onto the site proper, unless they were delivering supplies, which, in this case, they were. Too many vans impeded the big plant equipment from freely moving materials around the site.

Doug reminded the driver that he'd need to drive the van back off site and park it out front. The driver acknowledged this and fifteen minutes later, he tooted his horn for Doug to open the gate to let him back out. The first of the site managers arrived at seven thirty, he said good morning to them as he signed in. He asked them if they had a good weekend.

"No, not really," replied Johnny, "we were working here yesterday."

"Oh, well no luck then, did the flooring contractors turn up?"

"Yes, they were here Saturday and yesterday, although we weren't here on Saturday, they were signed in."

"OK, thanks, I'd better get started," he went to his office.

The remainder of the shift was spent with them walking around the site and he and Johnny gassing to some of the tradesmen. They had lunch at ten AM, Doug bought them a soup and filled sandwich from a take away van parked just outside the site.

The afternoon went by very quickly, they spoke briefly about tonight's fight. Doug wasn't too worried about it, he'd experienced a hostile crowd on Friday, but Johnny said he may be the local favourite with them tonight. The signed out at two PM, two guys Johnny had never met before took over from them. They'd been working this site for a few weeks, Ivor, who was welsh and Gav, he was a scouse from Liverpool.

"Nothing to report, all things quiet on the western front," said Johnny, he and Doug left to go home.

Chapter 42

Robert and Mary had been sitting with Julie for nearly four hours. Fortunately, they'd none of the drama that Andrew and Jason had, the nurse came in every hour or so to check on Julie and take readings from her machines. About two hours into their vigil, Robert had managed to have a word with one of the doctors. He said the longer Julie was on the ventilator, the harder it would be to try and get her out of her coma. He said they were aiming to remove it at eight AM.

It was fast approaching six thirty AM. He'd discussed with his wife that he was going to call Dot at seven AM to try and get her here for eight AM, just in case there were any complications. Dot would never forgive them if anything happened to Julie and she'd not been told about the ventilator. He went outside and decided to call Dot now. She answered right away.

"Sorry, Dot, I didn't wake you, did I?"

"No, Robert, I've been awake for hours, I can't get back to sleep."

He told her about the ventilator, her heart skipped a beat. "They're going to try and take her off the vent at eight. How soon can you be ready? And I'll come and collect you."

"I'll jump into a shower now, and I'll be ready when you get here."

"OK, I'll leave here in five minutes." He went back into Julie's room and told Mary he was going to collect Dot.

"I hope you didn't wake her?"

"No, not at all, she said she's been awake for a few hours, and was about to get up anyway." He kissed Mary and headed to his car. The roads were starting to get busy, it took him forty minutes to get to Dot's. It only took him fifteen minutes on Saturday night. She was waiting by the window watching for him. She came out as soon as she saw him and locked her front door, she climbed into the passenger seat.

"Good morning," she said.

"Good morning," he replied. He gave her a rundown of events as told to him by Andrew and Jason.

"My goodness, they should have called me."

"There was no point in getting you even more upset. They never called us either. I'm sure if they'd not gotten her on the ventilator, they would've called us all."

"Yes, you're right, Robert, I just pray she comes off the ventilator OK and can be breathing on her own."

"The doctor said if she doesn't, they'll quickly put her back on it."

They arrived at the hospital at twenty past eight, traffic was a nightmare, although he did manage to get a parking space easily enough again. When they arrived at the correct floor, they were heading to Julies room and noticed Mary was now sitting in the waiting room. Mary got up, she and Dot hugged. She told them that the doctor and two nurses were in the process of removing the ventilator and they'd asked her to wait here. They all sat down, Mary and Dot were holding hands.

About twenty minutes later, the nurses and the doctor came out of Julie's room, the doctor approached them and sat beside them.

"We've successfully removed Julie's ventilator, and Julie's breathing OK on her own. We'll be keeping a very close eye on her,"

"Has she come out of the coma?" asked Dot.

"Unfortunately, not yet but there's hope we would normally expect a coma of this sort to last only a few days. We'll hope to see some progress in the next day or two, you can go back in and sit with her, but only two at a time," he instructed.

They thanked the doctor. Mary and Dot went into Julie's room. Robert asked them if they wanted a tea. They both declined his offer. He said he was going to get himself a coffee, he said he would sit in the café to give them some time with Julie and off he went.

The cafe was now busy, he waited in line and got himself a café latte, as well as a Mars bar. He was hungry but didn't want anything to heavy, he was going home for breakfast with Mary soon or, so he hoped. He found an empty table; a couple had just vacated it as he was scanning the room. He unwrapped the chocolate bar and bit it in half, he made short work of it. He did the same with the other half, then he drank his latte.

His thoughts were again drifting to his missing son. *What drama will envelope them* next, he wondered. He went back into the lift, and when he arrived outside Julie's door, he knocked on it and entered. It was time for him and Mary to head home for some needed food and rest. Mary kissed Julie on the forehead and hugged Dot, as did he.

"Andrew or Jason will be in around mid-afternoon to take over from you," he assured her. "Give us a call if anything changes."

"OK, I will."

They left Dot and Julie and headed for the lift. They were back in the car and heading home. The journey took them just over half an hour, thank God it was still Sunday. Robert didn't think he could handle a traffic jam today. On the way home, Mary suggested they get some shopping from Asda.

"We've got hardly anything to eat at home," she said.

"Good idea," he agreed, "I fancy a big cooked breakfast this morning, we'll pick up some eggs, bacon and sausages."

"OK," she was now feeling a bit peckish too.

There was a big Asda store a couple of miles from their home, they went there. Forty-five minutes later, they were home. Robert checked the answer phone, whilst Mary put the groceries away. They had no messages. Robert called John Smith, he'd not informed him about Julie yet.

"For Christ sakes, mate, you lot must be going through the mill again?"

"Yes, it feels like it."

"What about Doug, any news?"

"No, nothing new at all."

"If you need me to do anything to help, Robert, you know you just need to ask."

"I know, thanks for that," he hung up and went into the kitchen to see if Mary needed any help, but she'd already put most of the groceries away.

She was now about to make them breakfast. Robert filled the kettle and got a couple of plates and some cutlery, he laid them on the kitchen table.

"When do you think this will end, Robert?" she was now crying inconsolably. *She'd been holding it back for too long,* he thought. He was doing his best to reassure his wife that it will all end soon. He wished it would too, it was taking its toll on every one of them. Once Mary had settled down, he took over at the cooker, he'd managed to persuade her to sit down at the table. They had their breakfast and went to bed for a couple of hours.

Before he knew it, Andrew was calling his mobile phone. Robert answered it after a few rings, he was wiping sleep from his eyes.

"Hi, Andrew."

"Hi, Dad, did I wake you?"

"Yes, but it's no problem. What time is it?"

"It's five to eight, Dad."

"My word, we had breakfast when we got home from the hospital and went to bed to get a couple of hours kip, we've been asleep for nearly nine hours."

"That's great, you must have needed it."

"I'll get your mum up and we'll get to the hospital as soon as we can."

"No hurry, Dad."

"Is Jason with you?"

"Yes, he dropped Dot off home at half past two this afternoon."

"Good, thank him for me."

"I will."

"How's Julie doing?"

"Still no change, she's still in a coma but still breathing without the ventilator."

"Thank goodness no dramas like your last watch."

"Yes, you're right, we've only just recovered from that. I'll let you and Mum get sorted then."

"OK, Son, we'll see you around ten PM, is that OK?"

"Yes, Dad, that'll be fine," he rang off.

Robert turned to Mary, she had been wakened but Robert on the phone. "It's about eight PM," he said to her.

"Are you sure?"

"Yes," he checked the time on his phone, 20:03 it displayed.

"Well, I never thought I would get a sleep but I'm glad I did, I feel a bit better for it."

"I will go and make us a brew, you get showered and then I will go in next," he said.

"OK," she said.

He went downstairs and put the kettle on he made himself some toast too. He would probably need to get something to eat later from the café in the hospital. They had been intending to get up at around five PM and have some dinner before their night vigil. He must've forgotten to set the alarm on his phone, he checked, and he set the time but never saved it.

"Oh well, a sleeps as good as a feed," he thought the saying went, but it must be wrong because he was starving. He'd just finished his coffee and toast when Mary came down the stairs. He asked her if she wanted some toast too.

"Yes, please."

He made her tea and two slices with butter. He set them down at the table for her.

"Thanks," she said.

He went up for a shower, when he'd finished and was back down stairs, Mary had washed the dishes and cups and they were ready to go to the hospital.

He called Andrew to let him know they were on route, they got a parking space no bother again, one of the few benefits of strange hours visiting. They were at the ward and in Julie's room in no time at all, Mary hugged Andrew and Jason.

"It's been an uneventful day for them," said Jason.

"Are you both working tomorrow?" asked Robert.

"Yes, we are," replied Andrew.

"I think I can swing a couple of days off, if needed," said Jason, "Tuesday and Wednesday. I need to go in tomorrow though, we've an audit happening."

"Oh, that's great, I'll see if I can get any days off this week too," said Andrew.

"We'll manage somehow," countered Robert.

"OK, we're going to head off home then," they both hugged Mary again and kissed Julie's forehead. Robert, as before, walked them out and shook them both by the hand.

"Thanks for doing this for Julie."

"Dad, it's no problem, us taking turns to be here, we're all family after all."

"Yes, indeed, Son, we are," he said looking at Jason in particular. This made Jason feel good inside. He was accepted as part of this family, he thought it's a pity his own dad hadn't felt this way about him, but he supposed, he's trying now. He should be thankful for that.

After the boys left, Robert went back into Julie's room, Mary was chatting away to Julie, telling her everything was going to be fine, and that she and Robert had overslept today. He only wished his wife believed her own words. They'd been sitting with Julie for over three hours, they were both famished when the nurse came into check on Julie. Robert told her they were just going to the café to get something to eat, and would be back in about forty-five minutes.

Robert asked her to jot down his mobile number, more for reassuring Mary than anything else. She did and promised Mary she would call if there were any changes. They left the ward and got the lift down to the café. They both had lasagne and chips, and a coca cola, the meal was not too bad. They were back in Julie's room around thirty-five minutes later. It proved to be an uneventful vigil.

Robert called Dot, and she said she would get there at eight AM she was early, arriving at seven forty. Robert and Mary told Dot that there was still no change in her daughters' condition, they would be back this evening to relieve Andrew or Jason, and Dot thanked them.

Julie's condition hadn't improved, but on the plus side, it had not deteriorated either. The family members had managed, between them, to always have at least one of them in attendance, if nothing else, they were a resilient bunch. It was now Monday evening, at six PM. Andrew was the sole visitor on this occasion.

Chapter 43

Fight day two was now upon him and Doug was starting to get butterflies in his stomach. He never had these when he was up against Cranston, at least not until he'd got to the venue. *Was it maybe because he knew a bit more about him, and he knew very little about this Italian geezer, who knows?* thought Doug.

Johnny called Eddie to see if there had been any last-minute news on Doug's opponent. Eddie had only found out one more snippet of information; all the Italians money was on their man and if he won, Cassidy would be broke.

"I'm tempted to tell Doug to lose, just to see that fat prick destitute," Johnny said,

"Yes, mate but that would also see us fail to make any dosh though."

"Yes, very true but it would be worth it, but Doug's not the kind of guy that would deliberately lose so it's a no brainer anyway."

It was three PM, they had been home from work for about half an hour. Johnny made a coffee for himself. Doug didn't want any caffeine in him just now, he was going to grab two hours sleep. Johnny busied himself preparing the potatoes for their dinner at five, his mobile rang. It was Cassidy.

"Whatcha, Son," he said, "how's our boy looking for tonight?"

"He's not your boy and I'm not your son either, Doug's looking good, and feeling confident."

Cassidy let Johnny's insubordination go this time, but he'd get his comeuppance from JoJo soon enough. "That's grand, be here at nine thirty, Son, OK." Cassidy hung up on him again, just before Johnny had the chance to dig himself a bit deeper into Cassidy's bad books. He was determined now Cassidy had no hold on him, and he had Doug on his side. He was not taking any more shit from him or his two fucking book ends.

Johnny wrapped the steaks in bacofoil, and put them in the oven, he peeled the potatoes and put them in a pot of water. He didn't put them on just yet, he watched an episode of the popular game show Countdown hosted by Nick Hewer. That killed another half an hour or so, he put the spuds on now. He checked and turned over the steaks in the oven, he opened a tin of processed peas and put them in a pot and onto the hob. Everything was ready at a quarter past five, he went and knocked on Doug's door.

The big man got up, gave his face a wash and joined Johnny at the table. He was famished now, he complimented Johnny on his cooking skills again, and the dinner was great. He washed his down with a glass of cold milk. Johnny had a beer with his.

"There's a few cold beers left in the fridge for later," he winked at Doug, "but only if you win."

By the time they were finished, and the pots and dishes were washed and put away, it was nearly half past six.

"What time are we leaving?" asked the big man.

"Around nine PM."

They watched some news. Johnny asked him if he was ready to face this Italian dude.

"As ready as I'll ever be, this fucker's not going to knock me out in a couple of rounds, that's for sure."

"Good, that's the spirit."

"Did you speak with Eddie earlier?"

"Yes, but nothing new on your opponent, he told me that all the Italians are into Cassidy for a right few grand. If you lose, he'll be penniless."

"You shouldn't have told me that, I might take a fall in the first round."

"Would you do that?" inquired Johnny.

"Not a fucking chance," growled Doug. "We're betting on me, remember?"

"Yes, mate, I told Eddie you wouldn't throw the fight. I think if Cassidy stands to lose everything on you losing, he'll try and hedge that bet."

"What does that mean?" Doug asked with a curious expression on his face.

"It means Cassidy will try and get as much money as he can onto the Italian geezer, but the odds will be shit, just in case he beats you. Then Cassidy will collect from that bet to pay out the Italians. So, in short, Cassidy is really fucked unless you win. But I don't think he fancies your chances against this Italian. So, by hedging, he'll guarantee he wins, but depending on how much he bets on you versus how much he bets against you, will determine if he makes any profit."

"You've just confused me even fucking more than I was before, this gambling larks not for me. And why the fuck does Cassidy not think I'll beat this Italian prick?"

Johnny was trying successfully to rile Doug up.

"Anyway, it doesn't fucking matter how much he puts on this geezer, he'll fucking lose it because I'll fucking win tonight."

"Oh, I know you will, pal, but all those tossers that will be there tonight, with the exception of us, Eddie and the guys will all be betting against you. So, hopefully we will get great odds."

It was time to go, Doug grabbed his gear and they set off. The car started first turn of the key tonight. "See, big man, what did I tell you earlier, the lucks still with us."

"I don't fucking need luck," barked Doug.

"I know, mate," replied Johnny. Doug was definitely riled up for sure, *Just what the doctor ordered,* thought Johnny.

Chapter 44

There was no need for introductions on the door tonight, the same four bouncers nodded courteously to Doug. They'd remembered him from four days ago. The place was crammed full, there seemed to be even more guys in tonight than there was on Friday. What was even more surprising was there was no other fights scheduled for tonight, neither Johnny nor Doug knew this beforehand. They'd assumed there would more fights on.

They were greeted by Cassidy, "All right, boys?" He was being too friendly for Johnny's liking. "You're looking good, big man, I'm sure you'll do well tonight just remember to keep your chin away from Tyson. Unlike Friday night, you're carrying a few quid of mine tonight."

"Yes, but I bet you fucking hedged some of it," said Doug to a startled Cassidy.

"You're just full of surprises, you are," he said. Then he stormed off toward the wooden steps up to his office.

"Good shout," laughed Johnny.

"He's a real prick, he wasn't too happy with you, was he?"

"I'm not fucking here to make him happy."

Eddie and the guys arrived, they all shook hands, Johnny and Eddie went to put their bets on. Doug was 7/2, between Johnny and Doug, they had three grand on him. That would return them thirteen thousand five hundred pounds. The bookie told Johnny that their bets were the first on Doug tonight, everyone else had bet on the Italian guy.

"Even Cassidy?" Johnny asked.

Eddie now at the counter, "Here's another four grand on big Doug." That would return him eighteen thousand pounds.

"Good luck," the bookie said, "I'll be happy to pay you guys out, it will be more than a tidy profit if your man wins."

Johnny could hardly wait to tell Doug that Cassidy never placed a pound on him to win, that should keep him angry. They went into the changing rooms.

The Italian Tyson, AKA Salvatore, had not yet arrived. "Maybe he would be a no show," said Johnny.

No such luck, as just as he got the words out, in came the Italian and one of his trainers. The geezer must be six foot six and twenty stones of pure muscle. *Thank fuck I'm not getting into the ring with him,* thought Johnny, he looked around at the others, he could see the expressions change to dread on all but Doug.

The Italian never even looked at them, his trainer though, looked Doug up and down and turned to his man and spoke in their native tongue. They were doing a lot on nodding and smiling.

Johnny leaned over to whisper in Doug's ear, "By the way, big man, when we were putting our bets on, Eddie and I discovered that Cassidy hasn't put a bean on you to win, he thinks you're a patsy, and the Italian wanker is going to smash your brains in."

"Is that fucking right? We'll see about that, I had enough of this, lets you and me go right now," he shouted over to the Italian. His trainer was waiving his hands and shouting.

"No, no, we go in ring, we not fight in here, no room, we fight in ring OK," he said to Johnny.

"OK, in the ring it is." He never wanted to get him this anxious, Doug's outburst seemed to unsettle Johnny. Eddie told Doug to calm down and remember the strategy, rope a dope, let him chase you, noise him up and grab hold of him, keep trying to sap his energy, he's a big guy.

"He looks like he's built to punch and punch, make sure every time you break from clinches, you hit him, he'll get mad and make mistakes."

"OK," said Doug, "I'm ready now."

The Italians had went out first and Doug and his entourage followed. Eddie and Johnny were in his corner, the others blended into the baying crowd. Doug and Salvatore climbed into the ring.

The announcer said into the mic, "Gentlemen, let's have some noise." The crowd went mental.

Doug was sure there was twice as many people in tonight as there was on Friday.

"In the blue corner, we have local man, Doug Clement." There was a small ripple of applause, mostly coming from Johnny, Eddie and the three sparring partners. "In the red corner, we have the challenger all the way from Italy, Salvatore Mancini." The crowd were cheering and yelling. They had obviously bet the Italian. *So much for being the local favourite,* thought Doug. Johnny looked at him and he was fuming, just what he was looking for, this would focus him.

The referee called the two boxers into the centre of the ring, "I want a good clean fight, no biting and no kicking, and do you both understand?" Doug nodded, Mancini grunted. "OK, back to your corners, when the bell sounds, come out fighting."

Johnny was standing on the apron of the ring telling Doug to keep to the plan. The bell sounded, and Doug had expected Salvatore to come charging straight at him like Cranston had done, but he was in no hurry. Doug had his hands up high, protecting his head, he stayed in his own corner until his opponent was nearly upon him.

He came at Doug steady and strong, he moved to the left just as Salvatore fired a big right-hander at him. He missed completely but adjusted his direction and smashed a left-hander at him. Doug managed to lean against the ropes just as it hit his forearm, he hardly felt it. He was now on the ropes, beckoning the big Italian onto him, he didn't need to be asked twice. Salvatore was throwing lefts and rights. The crowd were going crazy, thinking these punches were hurting Doug, but they weren't. The ropes and Doug's arms and gloves were taking all the sting out of them. He grabbed hold of his opponent and grappled with him.

The referee was shouting for them to break and as they did, Doug landed a big right of his own. It didn't hurt the Italian, but it let him know Doug was still in the fight. Doug was backing off, the Italian kept coming onto him, Doug would back away, and now, he was on the other side of the ring doing as before. Letting the muscle bound young Italian throw punch after punch after punch, all the power getting absorbed by the ropes.

Doug grabbed him again and was now shouting into the young man's ear, "Is this all you've got? You hit like a woman, you're a fucking pussy."

He wasn't sure his foe could understand English before the fight, but he could tell now from his anger that he did. As they released their clinch, Doug somehow managed to hit him with another solid punch. The Italian shrugged it off and was throwing big bomb punches now, he was trying to end the fight in the first round. Doug had escaped onto the adjacent ropes now, the big chap followed, again most of the steam from the punches was being absorbed by the ropes. The bell sounded for the end of round one.

The crowd were now cheering, they knew their new hero had won round one, but Doug took no notice. This fight wasn't going to be decided on points. Johnny told him he was doing great, just keep him on the run.

"It's easier said than done, he's on me like a fucking rash every time I escape his big punches."

"I hope Eddie is right with this running scared strategy, is he getting tired yet?"

"Does he fucking look tired?" Doug growled

"No, he doesn't."

"Well, then why ask a stupid question?"

"I'm sorry, Doug, I'm just nervous."

"Well, don't be, there's no point in the two of us being nervous, is there?"

"No," gulped Johnny, but Doug winked at him.

Doug had a mouthful of water and spat it into a bucket as the bell sounded for round two. The big Italian was off his stool like a man possessed. He came quickly charging at Doug and he managed to land a solid punch right on the top of Doug's head, it staggered him, the crowd went delirious. Doug managed to find the safety of the ropes as the big Italian threw more big punches his way. The ropes helped Doug absorb them, he took heart from his early success in this round, and he was now throwing nearly twice as many punches than he was in round one.

Thank fuck for the ropes, thought Doug. The heavy punches were starting to have an effect on Doug's arms, they were getting sore, but he soldiered on. It looked like he'd weathered the storm, he definitely didn't want to have to take another blow like that. He managed to grapple and hold and bob and weave around the ropes for the remainder of this round. The bell sounded, another three minutes out of the way.

Eddie was waiting in the corner, "Are you all right, Doug? Did he hurt you?"

"Just a little but nothing to worry about, he's starting to get cocky now, he knows I'm not coming back with any punches." Doug had another slug of water, and again spat it out.

"Look up there," Johnny said to him, and he pointed to Cassidy's office, "he's got his three Italian pals in there and they're all laughing and smiling. You should've seen his face when that big prick landed that punch, he nearly jumped out of his seat."

"Oh, is that fucking right? I think I've had enough of this running away shite. If I get the chance in this round, I'm going for it."

The bell sounded for round three, Doug was up like a flash, Salvatore was now thinking he could finish the fight in this round as he came looking for Doug right from the bell again. Doug managed to get onto the ropes quickly, the Italian was now re-doubling up his punches.

Doug kept on the ropes and then he grabbed Salvatore again and shouted into his ear again, "I told you you're a pussy, I've been hit harder by my granny." He looked like he was ready to explode now, but Doug holding him and wrapped his arms around him to prevent him throwing any punches, he was struggling to get free of Doug, and Eddie said this would sap his energy by doing this to him.

The referee had to come in and break them up, the Italian tried to land a big punch as there were breaking but it missed. Doug winked at him, the big Italian kept coming forward, and he was throwing everything at Doug except the kitchen sink.

Doug kept goading him, "Come on, hit me, hit me."

The big foreigner was getting madder and madder, Doug grabbed him again and managed to get a couple of digs into the Italians ribs. Doug kept holding the crowd were screaming at Salvatore to finish Doug off. They broke and again and Doug caught him with a right-hander on the forehead, not a big punch just a reminder. As the round drew to a close, the big Italian was now sending fewer and fewer punches Doug's way and he could sense his opponent was getting tired. The bell sounded for the end of round three.

"How are you feeling, Doug?" asked a concerned Eddie.

"My arms are killing me but other than that I'm fine. You were right, this big dick is getting tired. I can sense it, his last few punches had nothing on them." He looked up at Cassidy's office and they were all still smiling, looking smug.

Round four now, Doug climbed to his feet. The Italian didn't look as keen to come forward as in the previous rounds, but he had no option. Doug sure as fuck wasn't going to charge forward, he stayed close to the ropes. Eventually, the Italian came at him, the first few punches were solid enough, but between the ropes and his forearms, they had no sting.

Again, Doug grabbed him and goaded him, "You're a big girl, come on try and hurt me."

The Italian was getting red in the face, he was not used to this treatment, he tried to shrug Doug off, but he was struggling to shake him off. This was definitely sapping his strength. When they broke, Doug smashed a solid punch into the big Italians nose, it rocked him. Doug could sense his opponent was getting weaker by the round, just as Eddie had predicted. Half way through this round, the big Italian went for a haymaker punch but, unfortunately for him, he was now too slow and Doug saw it coming. He ducked under it and on his way back up, he thundered an upper cut straight onto the Italians chin.

The Italian was staggering all over the place, the crowd gasped, Doug went in for the kill, he smashed a left, then a right straight onto the big Italians face. The big man was staggering about like a washing in the wind. Doug seized upon him and threw a haymaker of his own straight into the Italians temple. This was not like the movies, you just didn't just get up from a punch like that.

The referee started the count, but he knew it was a formality. After ten, the Italian was still not getting up, his trainer jumped into the ring to help his man up. The crowd fell silent. Doug raised his hands and the crowd grudgingly started to clap him. He looked up to Cassidy's office, what he saw was a man that looked distraught, the Italians were gesticulating at him, he looked a beaten man.

All Doug's entourage were now at ringside, congratulating him. He said most of the credit should go to Eddie, he called the tactics and they were spot on. Eddie was blushing. Johnny gave Eddie his betting ticket to collect for him, he was going to get Doug's dosh from Cassidy while Doug got changed, and Johnny had decided he wanted them off this place ASAP.

Doug climbed out of the ring. Johnny headed toward Cassidy's office, he saw Johnny climb the stairs and enter the office. Doug walked into the changing room, he heard four gunshots, he was about to rush back outside when he saw, out of the corner of his eye, Jim Cranston, but before he could react, Cranston swung the metal baseball bat he was holding and nailed him straight on the bridge of his nose. He went down like a condemned building, his head hitting the concrete floor, he was out cold.

Cranston was about to finish him off, but he heard a police siren getting louder and louder, he'd also heard the four gunshots. He'd decided to scarper out of there as quick as he could. As he was about to run out, he saw the three Italians rushing down the stairs from Cassidy's office, they were carrying two cases. They looked at him and the unconscious Doug lying on the floor, one of them aimed a pistol at him and shot him straight threw the forehead, they were leaving no witnesses. Cranston crumpled like a cheap suit, he fell straight to the floor, lying dead, next to his unresponsive victim.

Chapter 45

It was nine-thirty PM on Monday evening, Robert was at home with Mary and they were about to head over to the hospital to take over from Andrew. Robert's mobile phone started ringing, he answered it. It was Rob Smith, the manager from Doug's gym, calling him.

"Hi, Rob," he said, "what can I do for you?"

"It's about Doug, I've just had a guy call me at the gym, he said he was in here earlier, and he saw the missing person poster of Doug, and says he thought he'd seen the guy in the poster somewhere before, but he couldn't remember where. Now, he's remembered where he saw Doug. It was in a gym called Semple's early last week. He thinks he was training for a fight."

"I was in there only last week with Andrew, we were looking for Doug. I had a suspicion the guy that's owns it was lying to us, he said he'd never seen Doug before."

Rob continued, "He says Doug's an angry man and that he was having a shouting match with two or three other guys. He and a pal were in the ring sparring and they looked over to where the argument was, and he said Doug threatened them and shouted abuses at them both."

"That doesn't sound like Doug."

"That's what I said, but this guy told me he was one hundred percent positive the man he saw is the man in the poster."

"Where is he now?"

"He said Doug's involved in an underground boxing match against a big Italian guy, and it's happening right now. He said the place is packed with spectators."

"Where?"

"He said it's in a building in Hackney, East London, where the old power house night spot used to be."

"Thanks very much for the call, Rob, I'm going to call the police and head over there now."

"Please be very careful, Robert, these events have some very insalubrious characters attend them."

"I will and thanks again, Rob."

Robert quickly told his wife what Rob had just told him. He called the police station and he asked for DCI Craig. He was put through to another detective.

"Hi, I'm sorry, DCI Craig is off duty, I'm detective Paul Dickson, and can I ask who this is?"

"My name is Robert Clement, I was in last week, and spoke to the DCI regarding my son, Doug. He's been missing for a few weeks. I've just been told he's fighting in an unlicensed fight in Hackney and apparently, the place is full of people. I'm going to go there now."

"We've been trying to catch these fights for a while now, usually we get the locations too late, and you say it's happening right now?"

"Yes." Robert gave the detective the address, he ended the call. He asked Mary to call Andrew and tell him about this development. He got into his car and headed to the place, he was sure he knew the building. He certainly knew where the old powerhouse nightspot was.

Robert was nearly at the fight scene when he was overtaken by three police vans, sirens blaring. He had to swerve to avoid being hit by a dark car heading at speed going in the other direction. He arrived a few minutes after the coppers, there were people running in every direction. He stopped his car and got out. A policeman stopped him from entering the building.

Robert asked if Detective Paul Dickson was there.

"What's your name?" the copper asked him.

"Tell him it's Robert Clement."

He was waiting for about two minutes; two ambulances had just pulled up at the scene. A man in a tight fitting, dark blue suit approached him, he'd come out of the building.

"Hello, Mr Clement, I'm Paul Dickson." They shook hands. The detective told him DCI Craig was on route, he also said they'd managed to round up about twenty people they'd caught trying to flee the place.

"Is my son one of them?"

"I'm not sure, but unfortunately, there's five dead bodies in there," he pointed to the building.

Robert's heart sank. "Oh, my goodness, what happened to them?"

"They've all been shot, execution style. There's one guy still alive, but he's unconscious, and he's wearing shorts, possibly one of the fighters. He's lying next to one of the dead guys. It looks like he's been beaten over the head, there's a baseball bat on the floor next to them."

The paramedics rushed in and a couple of minutes later, they came out with an unconscious man on their stretcher. Detective Dickson held up his badge and asked them to stop for a second.

Robert looked at the man on the stretcher, his heart skipped a beat, it was Doug, and he said to the detective, "That's my son, Doug." Robert asked the paramedics which hospital they were taking him to.

"Victoria hospital," he replied, "and can you give as some details about your son?"

"What do you need?"

"His name and date of birth, and if he's got any allergies and blood type, if you know it?"

Robert told them Doug's full name, his date of birth, he had no allergies and his blood type is O positive.

"That's great." They then sped off toward the hospital. Detective Dickson told Robert they would need to speak to Doug as soon as he wakes up, to see if he can shed any light on these murders.

"OK, can I please go now?" Robert asked.

"Yes, you can go and thanks for the tip, Robert."

As soon as he got in his car, he called Mary. He gave her a rundown of events, and he said he would collect her in twenty-five minutes. He next called Andrew.

"Hi, Dad, are you on your way yet?"

"There's been a development. I've found your brother."

"That's great, is he with you now?"

"No, it's complicated. He's on his way to the hospital, in an ambulance. He's been beaten with a baseball bat and he's unconscious. He was involved in an illegal boxing match and the police raided it. I got a call from Rob Smith, he was called by someone who'd recognised Doug from the missing person poster in Rob's gym."

"I told you that would bear fruit."

"Yes, it was fortunate the guy saw it and called Rob. As soon as I got off the phone with him, I called the police and gave them the address. They just managed to get there before me and they arrested a couple of dozen people that were trying to run away. There were only six people left inside the building, five of them are five dead. Doug's the only one still alive."

"Oh my God, is he badly injured?"

"I don't know."

"How did he end up in that situation?"

"Your guess is as good as mine, Son. I'm going to collect your mum and we'll be there in about forty minutes, keep a look out for him."

"OK, Dad, I will, I'm going to call Jason and let him know. Should we tell Dot?"

"No, not yet. Let's find out how he is first and see if he remembers us."

"Fair enough, Dad, I'll see you and Mum soon." He ended the call. Andrew called his partner and told him the story.

"OK, I'm on my way over, I'll see you soon, let's pray it's the old Doug."

Robert and Mary arrived at the hospital around eleven fifty-five. Andrew was waiting for them at the main entrance. They took him into the A&E. First, he was away to get a CT scan. He had a broken nose and possibly a fractured skull, and was still unconscious. They were sitting waiting for about an hour and a half, Jason had arrived by then.

A doctor came out and said they'd had taken Doug to get a CT scan, it showed he hadn't fractured his skull. "We've put him into an observation room to keep a check on his condition," the doctor said,

"Can we see him now?"

"Yes, if you come with me, I will show you where he is."

When they entered the room, Mary collapsed into Roberts's arms, sobbing. Seeing her first born son lying unconscious with a massive bump on the side of his head and a big plaster over the bridge of his nose, and a ventilator tube down his throat, was too much for her to bear.

There were two chairs in the room, Robert guided her to one of them and managed to get her seated on one of them. He sat on the other and promised his wife everything would be OK.

"Listen, love, we've got him back and he's not leaving our sight until he's better."

Andrew said he and Jason would go and see if they could find another couple of chairs. They managed to find two chairs in another room. Andrew asked a nurse if it would be OK to take them. She said they could. Mary had calmed down a bit when they returned to Doug's room. She had moved her chair next to the bed and was now talking to her son.

"Please wake up, Doug, it's your mum. I need you to come back to us, Julie needs you."

Andrew and Jason had lumps in their throats at her desperate pleas. An hour later, they were sitting, talking away, as normal. Mary was asking Doug when he was going to awake, he never stirred. Jason volunteered to go and get them some brews, Andrew agreed to go and help him bring them back.

They were gone for about twenty minutes when Doug opened his eyes. He was looking at his mum as she was talking to him at the time, he was trying to speak, but it was coming out as a grunt. He looked angry, Mary was startled. One of the doctor had seen this happen via a monitor on a desk. He came into the room and asked Robert and Mary to wait outside while he attended to Doug. Andrew and Jason had come back with the brews, Andrew was concerned when they saw his parents outside the door. Mary told the boys, it looked like the new Doug was back again, their hearts sank.

After around fifteen minutes, they were allowed back in. Doug was now sitting up, the ventilator tube had been removed from his mouth. As they walked in, his eyes went straight to Mary. She froze.

"Mum, give your son a hug."

Mary rushed over to her son. "Doug is that really you?"

"Of course, it's me. Who else would it be? I was trying to speak to you earlier, but I couldn't get any words out because I had that tube down my throat."

"Hi, Dad, Andrew, Jason, it's good to see you all. Where's Julie? That was some crash eh, straight into a bus, how's my car? A write off probably, how long have I been in here? It seems like forever, but I bet it's only been a week or so." He looked at his dad for some reassurance, but he wasn't getting any.

"Listen, Son, I am going to sit down. I've got some very upsetting news for you."

"Oh my God, its Julie, isn't it? Is she all right?"

Robert looked at Mary, then Andrew and Jason. "Where do I start?"

"Start at the beginning, Dad, you're starting to scare me, please tell me Julie and the baby are OK."

Mary was now sobbing uncontrollably Doug was cuddling her, trying to console her.

"Mum, calm down, whatever it is, it can't be that bad." He now looked at Andrew, he had tears streaming down his cheek, this started Jason off.

"Andrew, can you and Jason please take your mum out for a bit of fresh air to let me speak to your brother alone," Robert said.

Mary hugged Doug and left with the boys. When they were gone, Robert sat and held his oldest son's hand. "Doug, what I'm about to tell you will cause you great pain and sorrow, for that, I'm truly sorry."

"Dad, please don't tell me Julie's dead."

"No, Son, it's not Julie that's dead, it's your daughter, Grace."

Poor Doug, he now had tears running down his cheeks and it was he, that was now sobbing. Robert handed him a tissue.

"How did she die?" he managed to splutter out.

"She died of sudden infant death syndrome known as SIDS."

"I've heard of that, but how can she have died of SIDS? How long have I been in here?"

"You only came in here tonight."

"Then I don't understand, if my accident was tonight, Julie wasn't due for at least another six weeks, how can that be?"

"Doug, your accident was about three months ago."

"But you said I was only brought in tonight," he sobbed.

"After your accident, you were in a coma for two months, you then had a good few weeks of physical therapy, then you got home."

"I don't remember any of that, how's that even possible, Dad?"

"Apparently, you were in what's called a disassociate fugue state, the impact trauma you suffered from the car crash caused it. It means you had no memory of the time before the accident, you didn't even recognise any of us, or even Julie."

"Oh my God, she must be crushed. Can you please get her to come here to the hospital?"

"That's another piece of bad news. Julie's here in the hospital, but she's now in a coma, she attempted to commit suicide."

Doug was now hyperventilating. "Why, why, how can all these terrible things have happened to me? Can I see Julie? Where's my daughter's body, can I see her too?"

Robert managed to calm him down. "We had her funeral on Friday, Son, we've been looking everywhere for you."

"How did I get here? What happened to me tonight?"

"You were involved in an illegal boxing match."

"I was involved in a what?" said a now astonished Doug.

"An illegal fight down by the old power house nightclub. I got a call from Rob Smith, he'd been called by a guy that recognised you from the missing poster."

"You've lost me again, Dad."

"We had some posters made up to try and find you. I called the police and they raided the place, it was carnage, Doug, there were five dead bodies. You were the only one still alive in there when the police and I arrived. When you came out of the coma after the car crash, you were a completely different guy, you were very aggressive, and you were very rude to everyone, me, your mum and Julie. You were very homophobic towards your brother and Jason."

Doug now looked distraught and ashamed. He tried to apologise to his dad, but he assured his son none of this is his fault.

"I need you to get Mum, Andrew and Jason in here. I can't stand another minute knowing I've hurt them, please, Dad, can you get then in here now, unless there's more bad news?"

"I think we've covered it for now." Robert left Doug alone to go get the others.

He sobbed and sobbed, how could his daughter have died and the woman he loves more than life itself be clinging to life, whilst he was fighting in illegal fights. He looked upwards, "God, please help me, I've never asked you for anything but please help me. I need you to make sure Julie survives, I need her."

Robert returned with Mary, Andrew and Jason, Mary rushed over and hugged her son again. They were both crying a river of tears, they ended their embrace. Doug looked at his little brother and his brother's partner and asked them both for their forgiveness for any hurt he had caused, and they both hugged Doug. They said they forgive him, and don't blame him, it wasn't his fault.

Chapter 46

There was a knock at the door, it was DCI Scott Craig and Detective Paul Dickson.

"Hi, Robert, we need a word with your son. Can I ask you all to wait outside for a few minutes?" said the DCI

"I would like to stay," said Robert, "my son's just been given an emotional rundown of recent events."

"OK, you can stay."

The others left the room.

"Doug, I'm Detective Chief Inspector Craig, this is my colleague, Detective Dickson, we'd like to ask you some questions about the five dead bodies at the fight venue earlier tonight."

Doug looked at his dad. Robert told them he'd just told his son about the five dead souls. "I don't know anything about any of this."

Robert told them about Doug awakening earlier thinking he'd just regained consciousness after the car crash some months ago.

"Really?" asked Detective Dickson. "Do any of these names trigger a memory, Jim Cassidy, Joseph Johnston, Francis Everett, Johnny Wilson, or James Cranston?"

"No, I'm sorry, I don't recognise any of those names, who are they?"

"They're the five people murdered tonight, one of them was an undercover police officer, Detective Sergeant Francis Everett, AKA Frankie. He was in deep with Jim Cassidy's crew. We think there's a strong possibility they didn't shoot you was that they thought you were already dead. Sergeant Everett had been in for nearly two years, we're building a case against an Italian mob, and they're the big fish. They're into prostitution, human trafficking, and selling drugs and counterfeit currency, that's just the things we know about. Jim Cassidy was small fry, but he was involved with the Italians, they were getting closer and closer. We were making inroads, albeit slowly," he said.

Doug told them, the last memory he had before tonight was getting his car rammed into by another car that was speeding, and it pushed him head on, into an oncoming bus. The detectives didn't look too convinced.

Robert said his son was telling them the truth, and suggested they go and speak to Mr Robinson, "He's a top neurological consultant and he'll tell you all about my son's condition."

DCI Craig wrote that name down. "OK, we will," and he handed Doug his card and asked him to call him if he remembered anything. "This is now a serious investigation into the murder of a police officer. We have twenty-six people we've detained from the fight tonight; we'll see if we can get any relevant information from any of them. We'll be back in touch with you soon." They shook hands with Doug and his dad and they left.

Robert quickly told Doug about Julie's suicide note. Doug looked like he was going to cry again, but somehow managed to keep his composure.

"Your mum nor Dot, know about this, they think it may have been an accidental overdose."

"OK, thanks, Dad."

"It's Andrew and Jason you have to thank for that. Andrew has it, he will give you it when he can."

Just then Mary, Andrew and Jason came back into the room. "What did the police want?" Mary asked them.

"They wanted to know about the fight tonight, I couldn't help them, the last thing I remember is the car accident."

The doctor came in and asked the family to leave the room for a few minutes. They had to check Doug's blood pressure and give him another check over. Once this was done, Doug asked the doctor if he could go and see his wife, Julie. She was in the intensive care ward. The doctor said as long as he felt he was up to it; he could go and visit for an hour or so. He asked the doctor when he would be able to go home.

"As you've suffered a serious blow to the head, you'll be kept in overnight and assessed in the morning."

When the doctor left the room, he went outside and told everyone he wanted to go and see Julie. Andrew and Jason both hugged him and told him they were going home, and they would see him tomorrow. Doug said he wanted to walk them out to the lift, leaving his mum and dad in the waiting room.

When they got to the lift, Doug told them that his dad had told him about the note. Andrew took it from his pocket and handed it to his big brother. As Doug read it, tears were streaming down his cheeks, his little brother hugged him tight.

"None of this is your fault, Doug," Andrew said.

"But I feel responsible."

"Why don't you go and see Julie, and try to coax her from that dreadful place she's in."

The brothers released their embrace. He apologised to them again for any heartache he'd caused them and told them both how much he loved them, they were all crying now. They dried their eyes then Doug thanked them both again for their understanding. He waited until they were in the lift, then he turned and headed back to the waiting room. His parents led the way to the room where his wife was in a coma.

As soon as he saw her, he started crying again, she looked lifeless. "Oh my God, Mum, what can I do to get her back?"

"All you can do, Son, is sit with her and talk to her, the doctors think she can hear you."

He sat next to her bed, he held her hand and started by telling his wife how much he loved her, and that he was here, and would she please wake up. He needed her more than he'd ever needed anything before.

After a while, Robert remembered he hadn't called Dot to tell her about Doug, it was nearly seven AM. He stepped outside Julie's room and called her mother. She answered quickly when she saw it was Robert calling.

"Hi, Robert, what's wrong?"

"Hi, Dot, sorry for calling you so early. Nothing's wrong, Doug has returned, he's in with Julie just now."

"He's really back?"

"Yes, it's the old Doug."

"That's great, maybe our luck will turn for the better."

"He's had a terrible beating, the last thing he remembers is the car crash. He was in a terrible state when I told him about Grace and then Julie."

"I can imagine, I'll be over to see Julie about ten AM, hopefully I will get to see Doug too."

"OK, Dot, I'll let you go just now."

"Say hello to him for me."

"I will," Robert said, ending the call. Robert entered the room and heard his son pouring his heart out to his still unconscious wife. *He has an awful lot to deal with,* Robert thought. They sat with their son and daughter-in-law for another half hour, in all the time they were there, he never stopped talking to her the whole time.

Robert and Mary needed to get home and get some rest and a change of clothes. Doug said he would stay with Julie for as long as the doctors would allow. He also said they'd have to drag him out though. As they were about to leave, Doug scooped his mum up and hugged her telling her he was so sorry for all the sorrow and grief he'd caused.

This set Mary and him crying again. "It's great to have you back, Son, just promise me you'll never vanish again."

"I promise, Mum," he said looking straight at her through blinding tears. Robert wasn't an emotional man, but even he was fighting hard to keep his own tears at bay. They left Doug sitting with Julie, Robert told him that Dot would be in around ten AM.

"That's good, I look forward to seeing her."

When his parents had left, Doug was now alone with his wife, he talked and talked, again telling his wife how special she was. He kept telling her how sorry he was, and that what happened to Grace was not her fault, neither was it her fault he disappeared. He bore all the responsibility not her.

Doug had lost track of time and before he knew it, Dot had entered the room. When he saw her and immediately stood up and rushed to her and hugged her.

"I'm so sorry, Dot, you must hate me for what Julie's been through."

"No, never, Doug, how can I hate you? You're the son I never had, we all know none of what happened to you is not your fault. Julie knew that too, I'm sure. You're the best husband a woman could want. That terrible accident robbed you of a chance to meet your daughter." They were both crying.

"What was she like?"

"She was beautiful."

"Just like her mother then?"

"Yes, she was."

They hugged some more then they sat either side of Julie. Both holding a hand and speaking gently to her.

"Your dad told me what happened to you last night."

"Yes, he had to tell me too, I don't remember a thing. Did he tell you about the dead people?"

"No, he never mentioned that."

"They found me unconscious and there were five dead bodies, all murdered by gunshot."

"Oh my God, you're lucky whoever shot those people never shot you too."

"The police think they thought I was already dead, otherwise they would probably have shot me too."

Just then Julie made a moaning sound, Dot rushed to get a doctor. Doug bent over Julie's bed, Julie screamed. The doctor and a nurse came rushing into Julie's room and asked Doug and Dot to wait outside. They did as they were told.

"Did you hear that scream?" said a shocked Doug.

"Yes, I did, she must have gotten a fright when she awoke and saw you, but don't read too much into it, Son." Dot tried to reassure him, "She's not had a good time of it since you went missing. She's been on antidepressant medication since Grace died. I think she took too many pills by mistake and now she's woken up petrified, you're probably the last person she expected to see when she opened her eyes."

"Yes, most likely," he agreed.

Chapter 47

They sat in the waiting room for nearly an hour before the doctors came out of Julie's room.

He sat beside them. "She's asking to see you," he said to Dot. She went into her daughters' room.

"How about me? Doesn't she want to see her husband?" Doug asked the doctor.

"Unfortunately, when someone survives a suicide attempt, they feel guilty and sometimes embarrassed, it will take a little time for your wife to have the courage to see you. It took me a while to convince her to see her mum. She's confused just now, when she saw your face she told me she thought you were both dead. She couldn't believe she'd survived. Like I said it will take time, you have to be patient, Mr Clement."

"Thanks, doctor, you can call me Doug. My dad's Mr Clement."

"OK, Doug, just give her a little space, she'll come around eventually."

He waited outside her door for nearly two hours, Dot came out and told him Julie wanted to see him now. In he went, and he sat next to his wife. She had big tears running down her cheeks, he tried to comfort her, but she shrugged him off.

"Julie, it's me, Doug, my dad told me I was rude and aggressive toward you before but please believe me, Julie. I don't remember any of that. I love you and I'm sorry if I scared you, it wasn't me. I don't understand the situation I find myself in any more than you do, but please, please, give me a chance to prove to you I'm your husband. What happened to Grace isn't your fault either, Andrew found your note. Julie, please forgive me for causing you so much pain that you would consider ending your life. I love you too much to lose you. We've already lost our beautiful daughter." He couldn't stem the flood of tears. "I can't bear to think of life without you, please let me help you. Let me show you we can get over this."

"You don't understand, Doug," she shouted. "I killed our baby." She was in floods of tears and sobbing loudly. "Why should I trust you?"

"Oh, Julie, you didn't kill Grace, she died of a terrible illness. You can't blame yourself for that."

"I'm absolutely hopeless, I can't even kill myself without failing."

"Well, I'm glad you failed, Julie because if I came back and discovered you were dead, I wouldn't want to carry on, I'd kill myself." This seemed to jolt her to her senses. "I love you, Julie, and what happened to our daughter was a tragedy. Together, we can rebuilt our lives, we owe it to our families, we've both been to hell and back. With my love and your commitment, we can rebuild our lives, Julie. I promise," he reached in and hugged his wife, this time she didn't object but she didn't reciprocate his hug. They were crying so much; they were soaking her bed sheets.

"Where have you been, Doug? I've needed you so badly."

"I don't know, the last thing I can remember is it was raining heavily. I was on my way home from the gym, and a car came speeding out of a side street and ploughed right into me. It pushed me into the path of a bus head on, next thing I remember was waking in here late last night."

"You were in a coma for ages, them when you awoke, you were this horrid person, you were rude to everyone."

"I know, my dad told me, I don't know what to say, I don't remember any of that."

"Grace had been born by then, you didn't even acknowledge her."

Doug's tears started running down his face again, "For that, Julie, I will be forever guilty, I can't even remember seeing my baby girl."

"You scared me half to death too, you were swearing at me, telling me I was trying to con you."

"Again, my love, I'm so sorry," he sobbed, "I just don't remember anything from that time, I can only tell you now, Julie, I would never ever hurt you or anyone else for that matter, it's just not me." He tried to hug her again, but she turned away.

"Have you been fighting?" she demanded, "it looks like you have been."

"Yes, the police informed me I've been in an illegal fight, then I was hit by a metal baseball bat. It looks sore, but it's nothing compared to the hurt I've caused you and the others."

"Why were the police involved?" she asked.

"It's a bit of a mystery to me, I don't remember the fight or the baseball bat."

"And how did you get here?"

"Well, it happened like this, a man called my gym manager, Rob Smith. The man recognised me from a missing person's poster that was hanging in my gym. He told Rob I was fighting in a building in Hackney, and he gave Rob the address. Rob called Dad, he in turn called the police. Dad said, he went straight to the place, but on route was overtaken by the police and once he got there, he discovered there were five people inside the building that had been shot dead."

Julie's face was creased with astonishment and worry, and she was crying again. Doug tried to comfort her, she flinched as he touched her, this worried him, but he continued his story.

"Dad said he feared the worst, but I was brought out unconscious and brought here, the police came in and asked me a serious of questions. One of the dead men was an undercover police sergeant, they were trying to catch some Italians that are up to all sorts of illegal activities. The police think the Italians killed all those people."

"Why didn't they shoot you too?"

"The police think they were in a hurry to get away as they must have heard their sirens getting closer, and they think the Italians probably thought I was already dead."

"And you don't remember any of this?"

"No, not a thing."

The doctor came in and told Doug he'd need to go back to his ward to see his own doctor. "He's phoned asking for you to return."

Doug tried to kiss his wife and assure her he would be back as soon as possible. But she turned away from him.

He left Julies room and spoke with Dot before he went to his own ward and he told her that Julie blames herself for Grace's death and him for not being there and for everything else that's gone wrong lately. He told her he'd tried to assure Julie none of this is her fault.

"I need to go to my own ward, but I'll be back over soon. I'll get signed out soon and spend as much time is necessary to win her back."

"OK," said Dot, "I'm going to go back in with her and I'll try my best to help you." She hugged Doug, "Welcome back, Son, it looks like our lucks changing. Julie will come around, don't worry."

"Let's hope so, Dot."

Off he went back to his ward, and when he arrived, he was fully examined by the doctor. He was asked if he was suffering from any headaches or dizziness. His answer to both questions was no. The doctor told him he was very lucky man.

"If you'd had the news I've just received from my family, I'm sure lucky is the last word you'd use to describe me." He asked the doctor if he could give him some advice on how to help his wife as she'd tried to commit suicide.

The doctor asked Doug if he was aware of anything that would cause his wife to take her own life.

"Where should I start?" sighed Doug.

"The beginning is always a good place to start," replied the doctor.

Doug told the doctor everything he'd learnt from his dad and Julie about the past few months.

"My word, I stand corrected and you're right, lucky is not the word to describe you. The first thing to try and understand about your wife is she'll most likely be very reluctant to speak openly about her feelings. She'll need to admit she needs help, it's like the gambler or the drinker until they can admit they've got a problem, only then can they seek help. There are some good grief counselling courses available for her, and I think you could do with some too, losing a child is never easy. More so for you as you'd not met your daughter. I know you'll probably want to try and be strong for everyone around you, but trust me, Doug, if you don't deal with this now, it will haunt you later in life. Your wife will have trust issues, although deep down she'll know what happened to you wasn't your fault. She'll need someone else to blame until she can face up to the facts, and admit it was her own decision. These things will fester inside unless you talk them out. Your wife will feel anger at both herself and you, for her to try and end her life will have been a very traumatic decision for her." The doctor gave Doug some leaflets about grief and depression counselling. He thanked him.

The doctor told him he'd be released mid-afternoon, if he remained as he was. He went for a lie down for an hour or so. At one PM, his mum and dad arrived. They brought him some clean clothes and his shaving kit. He went for a shower and a shave. He returned and looked a lot healthier; he hadn't broken his nose which, according to the doctor was a miracle, but he did have two black eyes. He hugged his mum and told them both of his visit with Julie earlier.

"We've not long heard she's awake and she's still a bit raw and angry with herself. Dot called us about an hour ago. How was she with you?" his mum asked.

"She was very angry and I'm not too sure she's convinced it's me again. She told me how dreadful I'd been to her and that I ignored Grace." He had tears running down his cheeks, he tried to hide them, but she saw them, and she hugged her son again.

"Listen, love, this will all be in the past soon enough."

"Julie doesn't trust me anymore, how can I get her to trust me again?" he asked his dad.

Robert told his son to stop worrying about Julie for a minute, "It's best to get yourself sorted first, then you can tackle Julie. Dot, your mum and I will work on Julie. There's a few things you need to do first. I forgot to tell you about your call to Ricky."

"Oh, my goodness, what did I say to him?"

His dad told him, without the swear words. Doug was cringing with embarrassment.

"Can I borrow your mobile to call him?"

Robert handed his son his phone. He went outside the room and dialled his boss's mobile number from memory. The call was answered within three rings.

"Hi, Robert," Ricky answered, "any news on Doug."

"Hi, Ricky, this is Doug."

Ricky was silent for a second. "Hi, Doug, is that really you?"

"Yes, mate, it's me, I believe I owe you an apology."

"You don't owe me anything, Doug, I'm just relieved you're back safe and sound."

"Thanks, can I come and see you tomorrow?"

"Of course, you can, mate, and don't you be worrying about your job, it's safe here. You've enough to content with at the minute. How's Julie doing?"

"She's awake," he replied.

"Brilliant, things are looking up for the Clements then?"

"So, so," replied Doug. "She's still very angry and guilty."

"It'll all work out, mate. Trust me, Julie and you were meant for each other."

"I wish I had your optimism, Ricky."

"Things will sort themselves, I'm sure of it, onwards and upwards, mate."

"OK, thanks again, Ricky, I will come tomorrow afternoon."

He hit the red button and killed the call. When he went back into the room, his dad asked him how he got on.

"Great, Ricky was fine, my jobs safe. I said I would call over and see him tomorrow. How's my car?" asked Doug.

"It was a write off; the insurance will pay out."

Doug asked them about grace's funeral and what undertakers they'd arranged to carry it out. His dad told him it was Andrew and Jason that arranged the funeral, they'd engaged a celebrant to conduct the service.

"It was beautiful, Doug, Mr Mullen done a marvellous job, everyone that attended said so. Andrew carried little Grace in the chapel." This started Doug and his mums crying again, the comforted each other.

When they'd regained their composure, Doug said he'd need to hire a car tomorrow, and that he'd call his brother to see if he'd accompany him to collect Grace's ashes.

"We'll have a burial service for them when Julie's all better," he stated.

Chapter 48

After several months of counselling for both Doug and Julie, and several bunches of flowers and chocolates from Doug, they'd managed to put most of their heartache behind them and get their lives back on track. Julie was back at work; she had no long-term medical complications from her overdose. Doug was back at work and back training two nights a week. Andrew and Jason had gotten married, Doug and Gary were the best men.

It was a Thursday, fourth of July 2013, one year and one week after Doug's accident, Julie came home and announced that she was six weeks pregnant. Doug was delighted to say the least. For the next seven and a half months, he treated her like she was a Faberge egg. Then on the twenty eighth of February 2014, Adam, their son, was born. This was the final piece of the jigsaw puzzle that had been their life for near on two years.

Six days later, Julie and baby Adam were at home asleep, it was the middle of the night. Doug sat bolt upright in bed awoken from his sleep by a baby crying. He got up and went to Adams crib, but he was sound asleep. He saw baby Grace in his mind's eye, he remembered seeing her and all the horrible things he'd said to Julie, Andrew and his parents, but most of all, he remembered hearing the four gunshots coming from Cassidy's office, and seeing Cranston too late to avoid his baseball bat. The Italians had murdered them all including poor Johnny…

The End